the FOREST of GHOSTS and BONES

LISA LUEDDECKE

SCHOLASTIC

Published in the UK by Scholastic Children's Books, 2020
Euston House, 24 Eversholt Street, London, NW1 1DB, UK
A division of Scholastic Limited.

London – New York – Toronto – Sydney – Auckland
Mexico City – New Delhi – Hong Kong

ISBN 978 1407 19554 4

A CIP catalogue record for this book
is available from the British Library.

Printed by CPI Group (UK) Ltd, Croydon, CR0 4YY
Papers used by Scholastic Children's Books are made
from wood grown in sustainable forests.

1 3 5 7 9 10 8 6 4 2

www.scholastic.co.uk

For Tom and Atlas, my everything.
And, of course, for my Szilvási grandparents.

SÓAR

ANASTADT

WÖERNZ PAS

SAVENČE

SEA OF SENŽA

N

Please note that I have taken some liberties with how things are pronounced in the world of *The Forest of Ghosts and Bones*.

QUICK GUIDE:

zs - the zh of measure	ţ - the zz of pizza	žs - the sh of ship
sz - the s of sad	cs - the ch of change	č - the ch of change
ş - the sh of ship	ž - the zh of measure	

Benedek Csekeny	BEN-uh-deck check-EN-ee
Liljana Vahani	lil-YAWN-uh va-HAHN-ee
Béata Rovedosi	bay-AH-ta rove-eh-DOSE-ee
Marcosza	mar-CO-sa
Zírany	zeer-AHN-ee
Dungléd	DUN-glade
Izsak	EE-zhak
Miha	MEE-ha
Szaliri House	sa-LEER-ee House
Roşesti	roh-SHEST-ee
Tăru	ta-RU
Miloš	ME-losh
Morós	more-OHSS (rhymes with gross)
Zalya	ZAHL-ya
Tabíta	tab-EE-ta
Sóar	so-ARE
Iulia	YOO-lee-uh
Morţa	MORT-za
Senža	SEN-zha
Csáno	CHAIN-oh
Sovažska	so-VASH-ka
Savenče	sa-VENCH-ee
Anastadt	ANN-uh-stot
Wöernz Pass	WOORNZ Pass
Vyesta	vee-EST-uh
Alíz	uh-LEEZ

Hell is empty and all the devils are here.

WILLIAM SHAKESPEARE, *The Tempest*

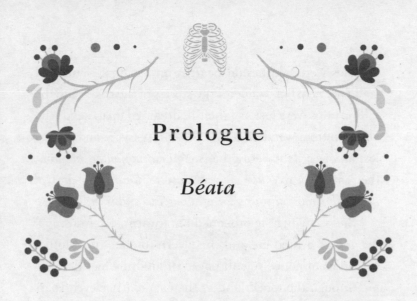

Prologue

Béata

My mother said the deadly rains over the castle wept for the fallen king and queen. They never abated, for their sorrow was unending. *Stay far away from that place*, she said. *Do not let the magic draw you in. Do not get close enough to tempt it. You are too young now, but one day you will know why.* Her words invited a chill into the room where candlelight sent wild shadows dancing along the walls. The warning felt like a breath close by my ear, raising hairs along my neck.

And for a time, I heeded those words. For a time, the whispers and shudders when people mentioned the castle kept my feet close to home. But as the days wore on, seasons melting together, snows and winds rushing in the warmth of spring, time put a distance between me and those fears.

As tales were told beside hearths on autumn evenings, I could not help but wonder if the stories of the castle and the killing rains were just as fanciful, dreamed up to keep wild children from wandering into the empty castle and getting lost amongst its towering halls. *You cannot enter the rains*, they said. *Not you, nor me, nor anyone, for a single drop of the castle's rain on your skin is enough to end your life.*

But as twilight approached on a warm, clear evening, my chores behind me and the tavern too busy for Mother or Father to notice my absence, I found my feet drawing me through the forest lane to the castle. My eleven years should have been enough to warn me away – I was far from the child I'd once been, and grown enough to fancy myself an adult. But the allure of the cursed castle was too much to bear, so at last, I'd given in.

I slipped along the lane beside the rushing river with the careful footsteps of a child playing hide-and-seek, glancing about for whatever prying eyes might be watching. But only the silent, vast forest stared back. The trees soon yielded to the mighty, baleful Castle Vyesta. The reddish-grey stone of the keep rose up overhead, elevated to the sky by the low hill on which the castle made its home. Arrow slits glared down, the narrowed eyes of a cat that dared me closer. They seemed to flash red suddenly, as if the rumours had grown flesh and become real. I shuddered and took a step further away from the small river that wound past the castle and off into the great forest.

Ancient trees dotted the grounds, their gnarled branches growing at the odd angles of broken limbs. Here and there, across the river that ran in a circle around the castle – part of which broke off and flowed directly through the castle itself – bones bleached by the poisonous rain lay stark white against the ground, and in a few places, so did bodies that were somewhere between flesh and bones. I knew I should look away, save myself from the nightmares that would no doubt haunt my dreams tonight, but I stared instead. I'd never seen death so bare and real, the bodies of what had once been people like me. I ran a hand along my arms, imagining the bones lurking beneath my skin, just like the bones littering the grass.

Malevolence thickened the air. *It's just rain*, I thought, staring up at the droplets that made a wall around the castle grounds. It looked like rain. Smelled like rain. Sent mist along the ground the way summer rains always did.

But it wasn't just rain.

Whatever wickedness filled each droplet had managed to kill everyone lying here on the castle grounds.

My mother's voice somewhere in the back of my mind ordered me home with stern words, but I pressed forward. In the tavern, not long ago, I'd heard a boy tell his sister in a whisper that that there were some who could survive. That there were some, though few, who could step into the deadly shower and live to tell the tale. I'd never met anyone

3

who had claimed to have done so themselves, but I wanted it to be true. I wanted there to be a way in.

"Father said they're angels," the boy had whispered. "Mother thinks they're demons."

Go home, my heart whispered. *Go home*.

But an invisible rope seemed to be thrust suddenly from the castle, and my feet began to move. *Home is the other way*, I thought, but in that moment, I was powerless.

Taking slow but deliberate steps across the bridge, I made my way on to the castle grounds and into the deadly rains.

Droplets kissed my skin, as gentle as a passing storm on a summer's day. Where was the pain? Where was death? I waited and waited, then smoothed down my white dress with shaking hands. I edged closer to one of the bodies lying slumped in the grass. His hands were red and peeling, a harsh stench rising up even despite the downpour.

"I'm sorry you died," I said softly, because speaking seemed like the only way to calm the fear clawing away at me. "You don't deserve to lie here like this." Whoever this man was, he deserved a ritual. A grave. Somewhere his family could visit. But I was just a girl, skulking about a murderous castle, too weak to lift a body on my own. "Maybe one day I'll give you a proper burial."

The castle glowered down, something in the air around me whispering its displeasure at my intrusion. "I'll find out what happened in there, you know," I said quietly, staring

4

into two arrow-slit windows. "And you won't like it when I do."

Standing, I looked back out to where the forest waited, not another soul in sight. No one came here, if they could help it. Not unless they were foolhardy enough to fancy they could make their way in to save us all, or were caught up by its deadly draw when night fell. The Round Road that came close to the castle had all but been abandoned, leaving travellers to journey further afield to skirt this cursed place.

The rain hadn't killed me. I did not know why, or how, or what that meant. All around me were the bodies of those who'd died before me, those the rain had murdered for reasons no one seemed to know.

But I was alive.

My head pounded a bit, my heart racing at all the dreadful possibilities, but I would have days enough to worry later. So, in the freedom of isolation, I raised my arms to the rain and spun in a slow circle. The raindrops ran down my face, tickling my neck, soaking my dress. I spun again and again, ignited by the sense of wrongdoing, knowing I should never have come here. But the day was warm and muggy, the air almost too thick to breathe. The glorious chill of the rain on my skin was as welcome as a glass of fresh water.

I swayed and swirled about, palms to the sky, water flying from the hem of my dress at every turn. I had already shattered the rules beyond recognition; a brief frolic in the rains would do no further harm. So twirl I did – until dizziness got the better of me and my foot caught on a pile of bones, sending me tumbling to the ground. Mud clung to my skirt as I stared at the pale bits of what had once been a person, my stomach turning.

Why had I come here? I could imagine Mother's voice now. *You've been tainted by the rain. It should have killed you, yet here you are. Your blood will be black like the devil's by now.* There had been a draw, an insatiable curiosity that had pulled me here but now made little sense. I remembered jumping off a rock into a deep pool in the river once. The older children had all done it, and I hated feeling too small to follow them, so I'd summed up what courage I could find and leapt. The feeling of falling had made me sick, and the drop seemed never to end. When at last I reached the water, it was hard and cold, and not at all like I had imagined. I swam quietly to the shore and slipped away towards home, working to remember why I'd been drawn to do something so impulsive in the first place.

This felt much the same. A foolish deed behind me, with nothing remaining but a sense of uncertainty as to what had led me here.

From the great archway into the courtyard of the castle, I felt – rather than heard – a voice call to me. Something beckoned, something hissed; a sense of being invited into the castle danced along my skin. My lip quivered.

An invisible thread tugged me towards the entryway.

No. Entering these wicked rains, impulsive and ill-advised though it was, had given me enough unease for a lifetime. The castle could wait for another day, or another girl.

The sound of my heartbeat was so loud it drowned out the rain. I gathered myself up calmly, smoothing down my dress. I had come here. What was done was done. There was no use fretting over what was in the past.

I turned and trotted across the bridge, each step faster than the one before it. A need to hurry overcame me, like a dream where danger snapped at my heels but I could not bring myself to run fast enough. *Hurry. Hurry. Hurry.* The word propelled me onward until I'd broken into a run. Despite my rush, I could feel the shaking in my limbs. The quivering of my fingers. I could not present myself back at home in a manner such as this, but I could not think about that now. There was only the need to be away from here, to make myself believe I had never come.

Just before the trees of the great forest swallowed me, I stopped suddenly, feeling eyes close at hand.

A boy with dark hair and muddy boots stood half hidden behind a tree. His eyes were wide and his hands hung limp at his sides. He stared, and I stared back. He had seen me, of course. He had seen me dancing about in the rain.

Dread stirred in my stomach.

I could ask him to keep my secret, but somehow that only felt as though ensuring its escape. I could threaten him, but I'd never done so before, and wasn't sure I knew how.

So instead, I stared a bit longer, imagining all the words I would say to refute his claim if he ever breathed a word to anyone, how I could bury myself in lies and say he was spinning tales about me. People in Zírany knew me well. I liked to think they would take my word over that of a boy I'd never seen.

But the ache of unease wormed its way into my stomach and settled in, making my jaw clench and my heart sink. The boy said nothing, and I wasn't sure if I wished he would speak to shatter the rising panic or if I'd rather he stayed silent and made as if this had never happened at all. In the end, I turned away slowly, walking with measured steps down the overgrown pathway back towards home, half drowning in fear over what might happen if the town learned my secret, and half shivering with unbridled excitement over what I'd just done.

Chapter One

Liljana

Six years later

The lie tasted metallic on the air. Someone had nailed the parchment to the tree crooked, its words staring at me at an odd angle that made me tilt my head. I hung back from the small crowd, comforted by distance and shadows, and read each word once, twice, three times.

Mages of Roșesti, be warned. The Ashen have risen and seek to spill your blood. The king, in his benevolence, has taken pity on those who seek shelter, and offers you refuge in your time of need.

All with magic must present themselves to the hold

9

for safekeeping, by order of King Costel. Your obedience is requested by sundown three days hence.

A hushed chatter kindled in the growing crowd, a general sense of relief evidenced in hefty sighs and grim smiles.

"This is long overdue. I have no good opinion of mages myself, but if the Ashen aren't stopped, we could be next."

"I'd bet all my coin the king is only rounding them up *for* the Ashen, and you can't tell me otherwise."

I clenched my fists until the nails dug deep into my skin. If there was one thing Roşestians feared, it was magic, and with rumours drifting forth from our neighbouring country Marcosza of dark dealings and deadly rains, mages all around Roşesti had begun to turn up dead, drained of their blood. It was their blood that gave them magic, it was said, and it was magic that led to evil. The Ashen were hunting us, and their mantra had spread as a vicious fire around the country:

If you do not take their blood, they will soon spill yours.

Those words had turned friends to foes, lovers to murderers, suspicions falling on neighbours and family alike. Some who had died bore no magic, but what did that matter? To those who blamed magic for all the ills of the world, it was better to be safe than let one slip through.

Magic had little real use these days – or perhaps that's just what we told ourselves to keep from using it. Many born with it lived lives as commonplace as anyone else: working, raising families, dying at a respectable age. It was in the old days that stories about magic were prevalent, when kings and queens slaughtered one another for a throne, using mercenary mages for help . . . until the followers of the Ash God, known as the Ashen for their penchant for burning victims, swept their bloody might across the land and murdered nearly five thousand innocent mages. It had long been whispered that the Roşestian gods reviled magic, as it gave humans too many godlike qualities – and most of all the god of the Ashen, known for ruin and fire and destruction. So when they had begun to murder mages in the name of their god, no one had stopped them, because people would rather keep the gods happy than a bunch of mages.

But the Ashen were magicless, little more than a band of worshippers once upon a time, who let their fear over what such power could do turn them into murderers. And their lack of magic was the only thing the mages across the country could use against them, so decades ago, there'd been a war. Mage against Ashen, common folk joining in on the side of the gods, and though there had been no clear winner, the strength of the Ashen had dwindled in its wake, no true match for the fury and might that awaited them at the hands of a country full of resentful mages.

The Ashen had continued to lurk about the country, but as the few mages left went into hiding to rest and shelter when the countryfolk turned against them, and there was little left for them to do, the strength of the Ashen had waned, dwindling from a blaze to an ember.

However, lately the Ashen's embers had been fanned into flames yet again. It took little. A few heads pointed in the right direction. A single mage who used magic in precisely the wrong way – a Ruiner who'd started a fire without meaning to and burned down a house, killing all its inhabitants. Unfortunate, but an accident all the same. A handful of whispers from Marcosza. Worries were planted about what might happen if the dark power growing within their castle bled into our lands. Seeds were sown in the shadows, watered with murmurs and misgivings, and up sprang a mighty tree whose roots of fear dug deep into the earth. And suddenly those suspected of being mages were turning up dead once more.

Whilst the Ashen *were* a threat to all mages, I could not believe that this paper pinned to a tree was as benevolent as it sounded.

Not all in the country were as blood-hungry as the Ashen. Many managed to spend their lives entirely ignoring the existence of magic, living and dying without worry or fear. But the world was full of many kinds of people.

Those who fear magic. Those who wish for magic. And those who wish to destroy magic.

The paper on the tree before me had all the scent of those who wished to destroy magic. After all, the word *obedience* is rarely used when one has a choice.

And why, after I'd been forced to live in misery for years, hiding my magic, afraid that any person I passed on the street might be one of the Ashen and I would be nothing but ashes by dawn... Why, *now*, would the king take such a keen interest in helping me, and those like me?

It reeked. It stank of plot and suspicion, and I'd sooner feed myself to wolves.

I spun away, a cobblestone digging into my heel through the worn sole of my boots, and fled with quick but careful steps down an alleyway that led away from Tăru's main square. The buildings towered on either side, glowering down as I put one foot carefully in front of the other, eyes forward, meeting no one's gaze. A simple parchment hanging on the Great Tree had flayed my skin from my bones, leaving every once-hidden inner working of my body exposed for all to see. It was foolish, of course, but I swore they could see the magic in my blood. Feel its singe even from across the street. Did that man by the fish cart eye me for a second too long? Did the child hanging on to her mother's skirt stare because she knew what I was? If I rounded that corner ahead, would I find royal guards in rich blue cloaks here to seize me and drag me away to the hold?

The gods knew I would never go willingly.

I had been careful since childhood, since I realized the reason my mother and father had been murdered was because the Ashen had suspected them of magic. Maybe they had been mages. I'd never know. I'd been off for a walk in the arms of a neighbour girl, newborn as I was, when they burned my mother and father alive. Luck had spared me, and then it had forsaken me.

I'd been sure to play with other children as I grew, to fall and skin my knee, to laugh and cry at all the right times. To avoid suspicion at every turn.

But now those suspicions were catching up to me, and the angry Ash God snapped at my heels.

On the surface, mages were difficult to tell apart from others. We looked the same, sounded the same, acted the same, for the most part. But we did not fall ill – at least not with the illnesses that befell those around us. If we overused our magic, our cheeks would sink in, our eyes turning a bit grey, and it would be difficult to leave the bed. But we did not fall prey to fevers or colds like so many around us. I knew not what the Ashen had seen in my mother and father to warrant their murder, or whether they had known the same magic grew within me. Perhaps they felt a spark in my touch, or saw a glistening in my newborn eyes. I liked to think as much, but it mattered little now, eighteen years later. What mattered was that my secret stayed hidden from those who did not already know; such was the hatred of mages in Roșesti.

It was mid-morning, and the streets of Tăru were crowded with peddlers, shoppers, visitors from around Roșesti and beyond. Silken scarves in myriad colours were proudly displayed on ropes hung above a cart. Rich wines from the vineyards of the Bacil region were selling quickly, the dark, plum-coloured nectar the drink of choice on these long, late summer days. A cart piled high with dried herbs imbued the air around it with an amalgam of scents that was somehow both alluring and repulsive. Clothing and linens hung on ropes overhead, drying in the rising sun, and now and then the splash of dishwater being dumped from a window into the street echoed off the stone walls.

I slowed to the pace of those around me, taking in the hubbub of life in the market, pausing now and then to examine merchandise while paying no mind to the vendor who rattled off numbers close by my ear. I'd passed through this market a hundred times before without stopping, but today, the desperate need to blend in was suffocating. Around every corner, I could see my body posted somewhere high, pale, empty, nothing more than a grim reminder for others of my kind, if they didn't burn me first. How many of those in this very marketplace bore the same magic in their veins? How many other hearts raced with fear and uncertainty, hands curled into fists to stop the shaking?

I realized then, as I held a set of carved wooden spoons in my hands, that they weren't trembling. They should have been, of course. The Ashen were gaining ground at the rate of a wildfire, and the king was gathering all mages for *safekeeping*.

Even remembering the word – the lie – set my teeth to grinding.

I looked up slowly to the market around me, dropping the spoons back into the basket from which I'd taken them. There were smiles, laughter, money was exchanged. They had no reason to fear for their lives, because their lives were not on offer. The followers of a dark god were not coming for their blood. The temptation swelled within me to lay a hand on one of the spoons once more and transform it to a knife so sharp it could draw blood from a glance. Give them a reason to fear like I had to fear, to scream and run and see all the possible futures that had once loomed large before them crumble and burn to nothingness. I wanted them to truly know what it meant to fear like I did.

If they were so ready to inflict death and terror on others, they should taste it themselves. That was only just.

It gave me little satisfaction, but to ease the need I felt, I slipped one of the wooden spoons up my sleeve and spun away, leaving the market as fast as I dared.

The gilded portion of the city bled down from the great castle, through the hilly alleys that led to and around the marketplace, and a little ways beyond. A few minutes' walk to the south, and it was akin to having left Tăru entirely and walked into the ruined edges of some godsforsaken hovel of a town that not even the royal guard would spit on. Refuse sat piled in the streets. Pale, too-skinny children stared sullenly from half-open doorways – so unlike the ruddy-cheeked youth thriving so close at hand. The streets were narrow, barely wide enough for a cart to pass through without its wheels scraping along the walls, which made the sun seem little more than a distant memory.

Years ago, I would slip into the well-kept parts of the city to admire the flowered window boxes. The clean streets. The colourful clothes worn by people who could wear something new every day. Who would never have to steal thread just to mend a hole in their stockings. I would stop and smell the baking bread wafting from open windows. If I tried hard enough, I could imagine myself eating it and then feel full for an hour or two. It sometimes worked to take away the pangs of hunger. But I'd stopped going when the sidelong glances and *tsk tsks* reminded me too strongly that I would never belong.

When I was younger, with endless hopes and dreams and energy, I would use magic to alter my dress, make it a bit cleaner, turn some string into a beaded necklace. But being an untrained mage meant that anything I altered would usually return to how it had once been too quickly, sometimes in minutes, sometimes hours, depending on the effort it took to change. I'd heard from other mages that if you went to be trained by your respective magical Order, you could learn enough that the things you changed might never change back.

But wherever the Orders were, no one seemed to know. The knowledge surrounding them had died out to the point that no one was quite certain if they'd ever existed.

And I'd even heard it said that they could no longer be found in this world.

A boy with sunken cheeks and empty eyes watched as I made my way down the close street. I held his gaze until I rounded a bend and he was lost to sight, my chest tightening. If I could work magic without fear of a swift and painful death – or, indeed, if I had ever been taught how to hone it – I would turn the broken stones lying about the street into bits of bread for him, or the puddled dishwater into sweet juice from an apple. Sometimes it was the only way I fed myself, when Iulia Filiṭa drank too much brandy at her own establishment and forgot to feed the serving girls who worked for her. Food, at least for an untrained Alterer, took more energy than other things, because I had to use enough magic to ensure the rocks would not change back after I ate them. Other things I liked to play with – changing the colour of a woman's dress to a hideous yellow green, for instance – would always change back. I hadn't the training or the energy to leave them changed for long. But food, that was different. I couldn't change rocks into bread and then let them change back to rocks in my stomach, so I'd found a way of infusing enough magic into the bread to seal the change – which, of course, was exhausting. It was a last resort. The risk of being seen hung heavy around every corner, and the strength it drained from me weakened my other senses, senses I needed to keep sharp.

There were two of us, Miha and me, both mages

whose secret she had found out, and whose servitude she demanded in exchange for her silence.

I'd toyed with my options. I could spread my secret around for myself, so she would have nothing to hold over me, but the Sage – a wise mage knowledgeable in all branches of magic and happenings throughout the world – whom I sometimes visited in secret had warned me against it. While mages might once upon a time have lived amongst the others in peace and even prosperity, those times were gone. After what had happened in Marcosza, the castle sending out bloodied corpses and murderous rains gathering overhead, all the wrong things any mage had ever done came crashing back to memory, and trust slipped quietly away.

I could leave Roşesti entirely – but no. Of course I couldn't. At least here I had safety in numbers. In the wilds beyond, where the Ashen lurked with fire and hate, death would stretch its bony fingers and find me all too soon.

At night I would lay awake listening to drunkards in the streets, and dream of watching the life drain from Madam Iulia's eyes. It wasn't always for the same reason; once it was after she slapped Miha so hard her cheek stayed red for half a day. Once it was when a patron left the tavern without paying, so she locked the two of us outside for the night. The reason mattered little. What was constant was that it was always me who killed her. Miha was too gentle. Kind in all the ways I wished I could be. So the task of Madam

Iulia's undoing always fell to me, in my dreams.

The weather-beaten sign for the Regina greeted me with a slow, irksome creak as I pushed open the door of the tavern.

There was never enough light inside to see much of anything – candles took coin, and fires were unthinkable in the brutal heat of late summer days. A single lantern with a single candle hung from the centre of the room, burning low already and casting a faint orange glow over the faces of the patrons who had already begun to filter in. The tables were worn, marked by tankards being set down and drawn up too hastily, drink igniting clumsiness. The remnants of a broken plate, or perhaps a bowl, haunted one corner. A number of sconces lined the walls, unlit, little more than piles of white wax collecting dust.

Madam Iulia leaned over the bar, chatting at close proximity with Grigore, a frequent patron who was both married and hideous, but wealthy enough to catch her eye. She cut me a look as I passed by, making for the stairs to prepare for an evening of work. Miha, if she had heard the news from the king, would be lurking somewhere nearby, worried and seeking advice. I wished for her thoughts, to hear what she would do. Would anyone surrender themselves willingly to the king, even with the promise of safety?

"You've heard the news, I'll warrant," Grigore said, and though my back was to him I sensed the words were for me.

"The whole city's alive with it."

I turned slowly, expressionless. I worked hard to ignore Grigore's existence – and, truly, the existence of everyone who walked through the doors of the Regina. My coldness today was only expected. "From the castle. Yes. There is a sign in the market."

"And what say you of it?" He clasped a hand around a tankard of ale and leaned one elbow on the bar. Madam Iulia's eyes glistened in a way that raised hairs along my neck.

Fear flickered, but I hid it with a surly smile. "I suspect it will take more than a parchment to marshal mages. They're a bunch I'd hate to agitate. You know. A hive of bees accidentally kicked. . ." I met Madam Iulia's gaze with a blend of cool indifference and pointed meaning. My words would mean more to her, knowing of my magic. I liked to give her cause to worry sometimes, because although I still feared day and night that she might tell my secret to interested ears, I sometimes felt as though her terror over what I was kept her from doing anything of the kind. In a way, we both held some small power over the other.

Grigore's face bore a thoughtful smirk, then he shrugged with all the ease of someone numbed by drink. "There are more Ashen and normal folk than mages. It will not take long to rid us of their kind. Roşesti will be better for it, mark my words."

I saw myself launch across the distance between us and

take hold of his neck with every ounce of strength I held in my body, squeezing and squeezing until the last gasp escaped his lungs. My fingers twitched with desire, but instead, I smiled. "Perhaps you are right." Again, I flicked my gaze to Madam Iulia. "And perhaps not."

The simpering grin she'd worn since before I'd entered the establishment vanished like an extinguished candle. Without looking away, she felt around the counter with messy grasps until she found Grigore's empty tankard, and hurried away with it to the kitchen.

Satisfied, I ascended the stairs to our living quarters, if the dusty, dark room with piles of old clothes that were musty and riddled with holes could indeed be called living quarters. It was a single attic room that Miha and I shared, a small window on either side, the ceiling tapered and low. The piles of clothes had once belonged to Madam Iulia – still did, though she'd worn through them and left them to rot above stairs, so we used them as bedding to keep from sleeping on the hardwood floor.

Dust spiralled upwards when I shut the door behind me. Miha sat gazing from one window down to the street.

She sent me a small smile when I entered. "You've heard," I said, a question that came out as a statement.

"Heard what?" Miha asked. I moved to my pile of bedding and sat down heavily, dust making me cough.

"There's been a decree from the king." I recited the words I had seen in the marketplace, bitterly, and her eyes grew wide as I finished. *"The king, in his benevolence, has taken pity on those who seek shelter, and offers you refuge in your time of need."* I repeated the words through my teeth, an angry beast growling somewhere within me.

"It's a kind thought," Miha said with a small smile. "The hold offers far more safety than the city. Funny." She swept an arm to the window. "You'd think with all this stone and all these faces you could hide, but I heard. . ." She cleared her throat. "I heard they found another one. Took him from his home down by the docks. Took him screaming from the city."

"The Ashen?" I asked.

She nodded. "If the king was trying to kill us, wouldn't they have taken him to the hold instead?"

"It's a trap," I said sharply. "Luring in mages? It reeks of plotting. I'd rather take my chances in the outside world."

Miha bit her lip, silence settling in for a long moment, then she nodded her chin towards the tiny fireplace. "I made a fire. I know it isn't terribly cold today, but my feet got cold overnight."

That was the other thing about Miha: she was a Ruiner. *A Ruiner.* Her magic was for fire and stone and undoing. It was an odd match to her gentle personality, like a mouse with a pitchfork.

"Well done." I lay back on the pile of clothes and stared at the low ceiling for a moment. "We have to get out of the city. We've waited long enough. Too long, even."

"Why tempt death in the wilds rather than trust that people can be good, and that the king might be true to his word?" she asked quietly. "It's worse out there. In the outside world."

She was not wrong, but that did not change my suspicions one bit.

"It's only a matter of time until Madam Iulia sells our secret off to someone," Miha went on. "We are left with precious few choices. Leave the city, like you say, and hope the country folk are less fearful, but that's a gamble I don't wish to make. We could wait in the city and hope for the best, but this storm has been gathering for a while. I believe it will end poorly for us. All of us."

A cold wind seemed to course through the room at her words. I plucked at a loose thread on the hem of my sleeve and sat up.

"Not all mages will go, surely," Miha said presently. "But the choice must lie with each of us."

"The wording left little room for a choice," I replied. "If anyone *chooses* not to go, it will be at a cost."

Miha returned her gaze to the window, her shoulders slumping forward. "It's bad fortune, being born what we are," she sighed. "But I suppose the time has come to pick our poison. I'd prefer the one with some semblance of hope. I like to believe the king is good, no matter what people say about him."

People did say things about the king. He wasn't hated,

but he was far from liked. He spent countless coins throwing grand dinner parties for royals and wealthy revellers, hoarding away food like a miser anticipating a famine, even when the lands were dry and grain was scarce for his subjects.

And then there was the fact that Miha had once been a servant in the king's kitchen until she was caught using magic to keep the fire going through long winter nights, and was immediately cast out into the streets like dishwater. That was back before the fear of mages had grown so strong that, had the same thing happened now, she would likely have been killed.

"I should like to go," she mused, but I knew her well enough to know she'd made up her mind. "Many of them might remember me. I'm sure they'll take pity on me."

I looked at her, deadpan, stony. "You think the same castle who sent you to the streets for your magic will take pity on you and welcome you back with open arms. Miha, honestly."

"Well, if I were as cynical as you maybe I'd live on a boat in the middle of the sea where no one could find me, but I haven't had the chance to learn how to sail." The words were quick, harsh for someone so gentle. "I'm sorry, Liljana," she said quickly, but I stood, shaking my head.

"Maybe I'll do just that, then, if I live long enough." I left the room, slamming the door behind me.

Night cascaded over the city beneath a sky that smouldered

orange and purple. The grand portion of the city smelled of hearty food and rich perfumes, laughter and chatter sprinkling forth from open windows. A loaf of bread sat cooling just inside a window, the cook slumped over asleep in a corner chair. I reached in with silent hands and grabbed the loaf, tucking it under my arm and tearing off a piece to eat.

With slow steps, I made my way towards the castle, watching, listening. No one around me seemed to speak of the king's decree, or of the mages that had begun to seep in from around the country, drawn by the simple hope of safety. The city folk might not have noticed them, but I could feel them if I drew close enough, feel the singe in the air between us as our magic recognized the other. Invisible yet visceral. Sometimes I thought about seeking out the Order of Alterers, wherever the hell they were, and honing the untamed magic in my blood into something worthy. Something strong and formidable. But with fear choking out Roşesti – and the countries around us – and all within it who bore magic, I dared not abandon what dismal life I had here in the city for what might be in another, better life.

Though now I was dreadfully tempted to climb up the city walls and gaze at the beyond. Imagine all the possibilities that lurked a stone's throw away. Perhaps steal a boat and learn to sail, as Miha had said.

I shivered darkly.

Clouds shrouded the stars on the distant horizon, visible as I climbed higher along the hilly city streets towards the castle walls. A lightning streak split the sky. I paused to watch awhile, nibbling the bread, savouring the cooling air as the storm drew closer.

Peace. Quiet. A beautiful night that came far too infrequently.

A distant scream splintered my thoughts. Muted, almost imperceptible, and perhaps only audible to me through the magic, it sank into my bones. *Miha. I would be able to tell that voice anywhere.*

The bread slipped to the ground and rolled away. I stared at the castle, heart pounding as a drunken fist on a locked door. The imposing stone walls of the hold sat tall and silent, no other noises springing forth.

Had I imagined it? The night was warm, and I was tired. My suspicions over the king's decree had been growing all day, and it was possible those worries had grown flesh and bone within the confines of my mind. But then I heard it again, distorted in a way that nearly mimicked the call of a bird. Miha's scream. Undeniably. She must have left straight after our fight, and presented herself at the castle. She'd followed her mage kin into those unforgiving walls in search of safety. But safety had not been waiting for her.

A drop of rain kissed my eyelash.

My untamed magic simmered in my veins, hungry for escape. I donned the hood of my cloak, steadied myself with a long breath, and hurried with quiet steps towards the castle.

Chapter Two

Béata

Death came with the fall of night. The sun crept lower, a taunt that made the townsfolk cast about uneasy glances as the shadows stretched long. The sound of shutters closing echoed off the streets, locks clicked in doors, candles were lit in the windows. White candles, to be prayed over in hopes that the gods would spare those in the home. As the light outside faded from a warm gold to a deep blue, fear crept into the evening air, thickening it. Filling up every available inch of space until there was so much we did not know where to put it. Fear slipped in through the cracks around doorways, ran down our spines like sweat, stared back at us in the reflection of a water glass.

For every time as we shut our eyes, locked in our

homes, we wondered if perhaps this might be the last night. If tomorrow, our bodies would be found rotting in the poisonous rains that fell over Castle Vyesta, called to our deaths by a spell that sought to see us all perish. Streets that were safe and ordinary during the day became avenues of death by night, conduits to the great castle on the hill under the veil of darkness. Sleep had long ago become elusive as I listened for the sounds of footsteps in the streets as neighbours walked towards oblivion, awake but unaware. I could go and try to wake them, shout in their faces, splash them with water, but Castle Vyesta would keep calling, and anyone who stepped out of the safety of home might soon find themselves at the mercy of the rains.

Gentle drops pattered against my window as Father extinguished the candles in my room one by one, slowly, thoughtfully. I listened for the sound of my brother returning from his trip to Devolos for new barrels. He should be back by now, even despite the storm.

"He will return," Father said. He must have sensed my thoughts. I made no reply. "I will not sleep until he is home." A sigh. "And neither will your mother."

Words felt necessary in the heavy silence, but I had little to offer that would provide any solace. Filep was late, and in these dark times, we knew what that could mean.

Father cleared his throat and made for the door. "Right. Sleep well. Do not worry about Filep. He knows what will happen if he is caught outside after dark; he will have found shelter elsewhere." He offered a quick smile before he shut the door, an effort to seem calm, but his eyes were wild with unbridled worry.

Uneasiness weighed me down, pulling my body further into the bed. I stared at the ceiling. A flint was struck somewhere in my heart. A spark leapt out, and something caught fire. Anger began to singe my body. Prisoners. That was what we were. Prisoners of the castle that sat a mile away, plucking us to our deaths. Something – or someone – wicked had found its way into Marcosza, and into Castle Vyesta, and made itself a home there. Set itself up as though this land were never ours. As if the lives that had once occupied the castle meant nothing.

I could not understand such evil. I could not comprehend the continued executions by way of the poisoned rains. To what end? We'd learned how to survive, to stay indoors at the fall of night. To turn the locks and close the shutters and hide away until morning. This way, we had managed to keep as many townsfolk as possible from dying in the rains and hadn't lost anyone from the town for nearly a year. Bodies still found their way to death: the passing traveller who grew too curious, the passer-by who did not know enough to stay away. But our own people had stayed safe.

I slipped out every day in the early morning, to lurk in the trees around the castle and look for the dead. Each time I saw one, slumped and lifeless on the muddy ground,

I found it hard to look away. Every time, I was taken back to years ago, to that time I stepped foot into the rains and frolicked about like a child on the Eve of Midwinter. And each time I remembered it, all these years later, my stomach turned over.

A lump in my straw bed dug into my back. I rolled on to my side and stared at the wall, picturing Filep's footsteps on the streets of Zírany, hurrying home. He would worry that he'd given our mother cause for alarm, rushing and stumbling to ease her discomfort as soon as he could. That was Filep's way: work too hard, but worry all the while. As Mother's eldest, it had been his task to help raise both me and Alíz, our younger sister.

Pit. Pat. Pit. Pat.

I sat up slowly, staring into darkness. Raindrops, perhaps, but something told me otherwise. Filep finally returning? A weight in my chest said no. Someone walking towards the castle, drawn to their death? Frost crept over my heart. I swallowed, rooted to my bed but desperate to fly to the window. Dare I look? Whoever it was, I might be the last person to see them alive. There was a responsibility in that I didn't think I could bear. People would always ask me later, "How did they look? How fast did they go? Why didn't you shout to stop them?" As if shouting had stopped anyone before. Once they had been called, nothing could be done. Lock them away, perhaps, but if we went out of doors to reach them our own names would be whispered by the castle. By the time I decided to steal across the silent room to look down to the street below, the owner of the footsteps was gone. Now I'd never know, but a small rush of relief washed over me. There was nothing more to be done.

I placed my fingers against the cool glass of the window, the little bit of safety that kept me from the same fate. The glow of candlelight was dampened in the windows of nearby houses by drawn curtains, townsfolk shutting out the darkness and evil that crept about in the night. What a life, shut away like ill-kept farm animals with freedom just beyond reach. Now and then, I entertained quiet thoughts of the world beyond Zírany, of a place outside the forest where there was no castle, no blood-soaked history, no locked doors after sunset and bleached bones unreachable by those who would bury them. Then I would quench those thoughts, send them back to the shadows and stand a bit taller. History was brimming with stories of people who refused to turn their backs in a moment of need. Who would I be if I ran off now, when Marcosza most needed someone to love it?

The footsteps had long been silent, but I stood in the window for what felt like an hour, watching as raindrops fell faster and faster until the water ran in rivulets down the window. I leaned my forehead against the glass, half lost in the memory of that first time in the rain, and half ordering myself to forget it ever happened. Sometimes I found myself wondering if it ever truly did. I'd spent so many years working to never breathe a word, to convince even myself that it had only been a dream. A lie told enough times appears as the truth. In a way, I think I wanted to believe the lie.

Sometime later I must have found my way back to bed, for I fell into dreams of bones with glistening, jagged teeth chasing me through dead trees, and a disembodied voice close by my ear welcoming me to the underworld.

When I woke, dawn was well under way, and I'd sweated through my clothes.

"Sleep well?" Alíz asked me in the kitchen, a subtle stab at me being the last one to wake. I didn't answer her.

Father stood very still before the kitchen window, staring out with glassy eyes, and Mother sat staring at a tumbler of water on the table, her face red and blotchy.

"Filep?" I asked, and my voice broke.

Father turned slowly to face me, and shook his head. Something unseen punched me in the gut.

"He'll have spent the night in Devolos," Mother whispered. "He would not have risked being out after dark. He would have sent word, but the storm, and the hour grew too late..." A sob bubbled up in her throat. "He would not leave this world without saying goodbye to me."

I met Father's eyes, where tears glistened back at me. His face spoke all the words he would never utter in front of my mother. *He did not spend the night in Devolos. He did not find shelter.*

Words felt weak, inconsequential at such a moment. I felt for a chair and fell into it, my legs giving out and my body convulsing with a suppressed sob. The room blurred, and fell utterly silent.

The pain bled into me like water soaking into parched earth; choking, writhing, desperate pain that consumed everything down to my soul. Air seemed foreign, unreachable. The light darkened. I was somehow both floating above myself, my own body strange and unfamiliar, and sinking through the floor into a black abyss. There was everything and nothing. Heaviness and weightlessness. Light and dark. I no longer knew how to be.

The sound of a sob from my mother wrenched me back to myself. I stood abruptly, wiping a hand frantically across my face, my sleeve missing most of the tears. There was a time for me to hurt, but not now. Not when my mother was being crushed under the weight of it.

"I'm – I'm sorry. I'll be back." Where was I going? I stumbled from the kitchen and through the tavern's dining room, finding myself in the street before I remembered opening the door. The morning was cool, but the air felt far away, as though I was living in someone else's body. The street I'd lived on every day of my life had lost its sense of comfort. I might as well have been dropped in the centre of a distant city and told to call it home. My feet chose the direction before I could think. Buildings passed by, cobblestones tripped me up, then gave way to grass and earth and fallen twigs from trees. The world blurred, all green and brown and blue now and then when I caught a glimpse of the sky. Moss and dirt filled my nose, fresh and hearty and right, and I felt more a part of myself. More like me despite the pain that gripped at my heart.

The path beneath me was a well-trodden one that had seen recent overgrowth, vines and grasses creeping along where footsteps had deserted. Whatever life had once traversed this part of the forest was nothing more than an echo, a memory that would soon be lost. But I'd come here, and more than once. The forest was still foggy to my teary eyes, but some part of me knew the way without seeing. Some part of me could walk it in my sleep.

The stones of the castle glowed red in the morning light that filtered through the rain, and all I could see was blood. Flags that had once flown bright and proud hung limp and tattered in the rain, the whole place a ghost of what it once was. My steps slowed as I approached the bridge, afraid to look at the ground. The world was all pain and water and stone, and I feared I might fall from the bridge into the river.

The bridge was behind me now. I should have worried over who might see me here, but the hour was still early, and I was too broken to care. So what if people saw that I could survive the rains? What did that matter any longer, when there was such pain as this in the world?

He hadn't made it much further than the bridge. I saw

his green cloak and worn boots before I saw his face, which lay with one cheek in the mud. His eyes were half open, and I was certain at any moment he would turn and look at me, laugh at what a good joke this had all been. Follow me home and apologize for frightening Mother. He still looked so lifelike, so real and whole and familiar. But there was no life in him. His eyes, though open, were as dead as autumn leaves.

I slumped to the ground, my knees sinking into the soft earth. "Filep," I said, but the rain washed away my words. It took everything: my tears, his life, our future. I hugged my knees with one arm and placed a hand on his shoulder as if I could wake him. "Filep," I said again, shaking with sobs. "Look at me. Look at me."

But he did not look at me. He lay there, silent and still while the rain fell over us, and my pain slowly grew into an anger so violent it blackened the world around me.

Chapter Three

Liljana

"Mage?" One of two guards standing before the small door to the left of the grand gates shot the question at me, surly and uninterested. I nodded. "In you go." He turned a key and kicked open the door, gesturing me inside with a quick nod.

A loud clank echoed in my bones as the door shut behind me.

I found myself in a large stone courtyard. The walls of the castle rose up overhead, black and imposing against the night sky. Here and there, lean trees grew out of the ground, whispering gently in the breeze. They were alive somehow, witnesses to whatever deeds took place within these walls, and they urged me away.

A series of guards, two at a time, stood along the courtyard, forming a pathway of armour up to the gates of the hold. I moved forward slowly, looking behind me every few steps, but I was the only other person in sight. The guards said nothing as I went along, only nodding and pointing at intervals to keep me moving towards the hold.

The realization that I had rushed in here without any hint of a plan struck me like cold water as the impenetrable – and inescapable – stone walls rose up overhead. I'd thought only of Miha, of our quarrel back in the Regina before I'd stormed out. I couldn't let that be the last time we spoke. I couldn't let that be the end.

So I had come here, with vague thoughts of freeing her, which now felt foolish and damnably irreversible. Miha was dead, or about to die. If I went back in, I would die as well, and there was little use in both of us dying.

A few yards before I reached the inner gates, another scream rent the night air. The sound sliced through my flesh, nearly severing the bones. I jumped back, turning to run, but all the guards I'd passed in the courtyard melted into a line, sealing off my exit. An impenetrable, wordless wall of metal and sword. I squared my shoulders and swallowed.

My magic quivered.

"This is no inn," said one of the guards, his sword and helmet more ornate than the others'. "There's no coming and going as you please. I said in you go, and *in* you *go*."

Whatever audacious thoughts I had entertained of breaking into the king's hold and freeing Miha and the other mages disappeared through my trembling fingers. My ill-planned rescue mission had become a bid for survival.

A fourth scream raised hairs along my neck. Freedom was just brushing against my fingertips, but had never felt so far away.

"I'm looking for someone. A mage girl. She came in here not long ago."

They all chuckled. "A mage is a mage," the captain said. "How can I tell one from the other?"

I bristled, but stayed calm. "She has very long hair. In a braid. She liked to smile. She—" I cleared my throat. "She was probably smiling."

The captain tilted his head. "Sure. Rings a bell. Came in maybe an hour ago. But I'm afraid, little lady, if she's gone through those doors, she's dead. Take it from me. I just came back from doing the rounds in the hold." He put a hand on his heart. "It's a touch grim in there."

"She's dead." The words came out hollow, lifeless.

"Dead as dead can be. They all are. Sorry to be the bearer of bad news."

My chest shuddered with a raspy breath. I shifted on my feet, staring up at the hold, wanting to cry, but too empty for tears. And slowly, that emptiness began to fill with anger, pooling, running over, drowning everything.

"You should step aside," I said, my voice as unyielding as the stones around us. "I am in no mood to show restraint."

"Sweetheart," the man said, sliding his sword from its sheath with pointed meaning and grace, "the executioner's axe inside that hold would have been your chance for restraint. Thank the gods, King Costel has finally taken a lesson from the Ashen in weeding out magic from Roşesti. Your time has come, and I am honoured to play my part." I could not see his face, but there was a smile in his voice. "Out here, you're just a dead girl walking. I have no one to answer to, and all night to watch you suffer."

The other guards said nothing, moved not an inch. The captain – or so I assumed – held his sword before me with both hands, his stance effortless and offensive. I let out a long, controlled sigh, searing with desire to rip him apart limb from limb, but allowing enough time for my magic to build and boil and rush to my fingertips with that delicious, blistering burn.

"It's a shame, really," I said. I'd never had a moment when I wanted to both weep endlessly and scream in rage until my throat bled. "I can't see your face, but your voice makes you sound handsome. I suppose now I'll only get to see it when I take off your head, which ruins the effect. But that's how it goes." Quickly, the magic in my blood boiling to the surface like an overfilled cauldron, I snatched the two sticks I carried in my belt and transformed them to knives, flinging one at the man before me with such force that, though it glanced off the gap in his armour at the neck, it carried on in its flight until it clattered on to the stones a distance behind him. Stunned, he stood still for a handful of seconds, blood running from his neck.

With a vicious growl, he threw himself forward and swiftly crossed the distance between us. I had underestimated his height, feeling suddenly small and weak before such might as him, but that sense of insignificance only stoked my fire. I growled back and met him with a clash of blades and force, both of us jolted to a sudden halt with the impact. Another guard moved forward to join the fight, but the captain hissed at him.

"Stay where you are. This fight is mine alone."

He had succumbed to pride, needing to prove his worth to those around him after being challenged by a girl – and a mage, no less. Perhaps he was new in his station, or perhaps he had always been proud. It mattered little to me, but I could use it to my advantage. Play on his need to impress.

"If I went to the marketplace," I said between clangs, "I could find a child milling about who's a better fighter than you. I've met babes fresh out of the womb with more grace."

The captain roared and hurled his body weight towards me, anger turning him clumsy. I smiled through the searing pain that travelled up my arm at his next blow. I'd learned long ago that fights against men twice my size could be more easily won by wounding their pride than their person.

"Tomorrow, you can make up some story" – I fought to catch my breath between words – "about how you were attacked by a burly mage twice your size, with tree trunks for legs and boulders for fists." My knife caught his wrist, but only barely. "You could, but you won't. You've already seen your last sunrise."

He hesitated, but only slightly, a brief pause that betrayed his sudden uncertainty. Perhaps now he was regretting his choice to pick this fight, or to decline help from his comrades, but he could hardly accept it now. That would be a mar on his name he could not easily bear.

"You are a rat," he spat, renewing his attack. "A feral, mangy rat to be feasted on by crows and scavengers. The king is too kind only taking your heads. He ought to burn you alive one by one as a spectacle for all to see."

This time, it was his words that froze me. I stumbled, staring into his helmet and mask for a second too long, until his next blow sent me tumbling to the ground. *The king is too kind to only take your heads.* Now, as I rolled across the ground, I glanced up at the hold, where Miha's screams had echoed moments earlier. Those doors had closed behind her, her heart filled with hope and kindness, as it always was, and death lay waiting to claim her.

How could anyone be so cruel? Who had time to grow such venom?

I scraped my nails across the hard ground and curled my hands into fists, a growl rising up from deep within me.

It rumbled forth and seared my throat, so loud that for a moment I wasn't certain I heard anything at all.

Whether my scream had startled the captain to stillness, or he was merely waiting for me to gain my feet once more for a fair fight, I didn't know, but I was given enough time to slowly, deliberately rise, spinning to face him with tears stinging my eyes. "I hate you," I whispered, wiping the back of my hand across my face. "I hate all of you. Hunting us down like rabbits. Forced to hide in holes and crevices in the world, always looking over our shoulders. Always afraid. Always sad. One day, I hope every mage in the country comes back to seek their vengeance, and I hope they take their time with you all. I wish you pain. I wish you suffering. I wish you fear."

One of the other guards took a step back, but the captain remained. With a heavy sigh, he raised his sword once more. "I hear much talk from you, little rat, but not much action. I have things to do tonight. Please do get on with it."

Like a poorly fashioned bowstring pulled too far, something broke. There was no longer a man standing before me, flesh and bone and a beating heart. There was only shadow and evil, the impression of what had once been human. Whatever thing kept me good was blown away by the wind, so far I might never find it again. It was wrong in a moment such as this, in a place stained with blood and sorrow, but as I gripped my last remaining knife, I smiled. I couldn't help it. The pride of the man before me was so wildly large and misplaced, it sat as a cloud over his head, weighing him down. Everyone could see it but him. My body was tired from the fight, but the anger sent a new wave of energy coursing through me, and that was all my magic needed for a final, heavy push. Something fleeting that would only remain altered for a few moments, so I had to make it count.

Air roared around my ears as I launched at him, quicker than I thought I could move. It was as though the magic in my blood wished him dead as much as I did, as though it sensed a danger to its existence and sought to destroy it. He arced his blade towards me, but ducked simultaneously, and the motion ended awkwardly and sad. The guards around him backed away even further as I leapt, plunging my knife through the gap in his armour at his shoulder. It wasn't deep enough to kill him, but I didn't need it to. I let my magic do its work, and took a step back to enjoy it.

Each joint of his armour fused together with a screeching sound, the metal melting and re-forming, sealing his limbs into place. He shook as though trying to take a step back to keep from falling, but lost his balance and clattered to the ground, unable to move his feet.

It would wear off in a matter of seconds, so I rushed forward, taking the sword from his immobilized hands, and severed his head from his body.

Blood poured on to the stones. Dark, viscous blood that crept along the courtyard. A few of the guards shuffled towards me, but stopped when I held up the sword. I tossed the hilt back and forth, from one hand to the other, teasing them with what I might make of it. A mace with wicked nails? A knife with a serrated blade? I could see the worry in their eyes, the opportunities of what fate might await them spanning endlessly before them.

Little did they know the magic I had already used had made me so tired I had to force my lungs to breathe.

When I was certain they would not approach, I knelt beside the body.

I knew I should feel bad for what I had done to him, regret the life I'd just taken, but I didn't. The words he'd said about the mages, the way he'd almost laughed them out, echoed off the stones and back to my ears. No, this man's death left one more space in the world for someone better.

I stood once more, the guards standing back uncertainly, swords drawn. I spun the sword around in my hand a few times and smiled. "I would like to be shown the door, please. It's getting late."

"We — we aren't meant to let the mages leave," one of the guards said shakily.

"You aren't meant to let one kill your captain, either, but there he is." I kicked one foot against his still body. "So . . . the door?"

They looked at one another silently. Voices rose up by the hold, where more guards were gathering and heading our way. I shuffled impatiently, itching to be away from this place.

"Go, now," the guard said. He turned to his comrades. "We can say she bewitched us. They won't know any better."

I let out a choking, tired laugh as I trotted to the door out of the courtyard.

The night outside the castle walls was quiet. Dead. I stopped running when I was a good distance away from the walls and then turned, staring up at what could be seen of the hold from outside the castle. My heart pounded. My head ached.

My mind took me back to the Regina, to the room Miha and I had shared for years. I could see her sitting in the window, reading, or sleeping peacefully in her bed. I could see her braiding her hair in the morning, or humming while she washed dishes in the kitchen. No matter how wretched this city was, she always embodied joy. It had to be in her blood. Something she was born with. No life in this world could make anyone so happy.

Sisters. Not by blood, but by choice, and barely. Life had thrown us together, two girls from different lives, with different dreams but the same goal: to live in peace. I supposed, in a dark and twisted way, Miha had found her peace. She may end up alone somewhere in a grave with no headstone, but she would no longer feel fear. No longer have to face torture and death and being hunted by those eager to do her harm.

I, on the other hand... The worry of pain and fear would still haunt me. This city would still crush me. This world would still hate me. I did not envy Miha her death, only the sense of peace I hoped she had found. I began to wonder, cold, angry and alone, if peace could be found anywhere in this godsforsaken world.

Chapter Four

Béata

I had never heard anyone weep as my mother wept for my brother. Even when I left the tavern to sit out under the trees by the river that wound through the town, I could hear her through the open windows. I bore my own pain, of course, but I had cried my tears. They were fierce and they were many, but I had saved them for my own pillow so that my days could be spent helping her. Father was worn thin, gaunt and tired and small, but he fought on without complaint. I had never given much thought to how the absence of one person could so wholly change a family: we kept our eyes from the empty chair at supper, from the bed where he would never sleep again, quietly picked up what chores he used to do that now fell to us. Everywhere we looked he was there – or, rather, he was not. His ghost followed us into the market, sat with us by the fire in the evening, looked through the window at night while we slept.

Filep was gone. Gone. Yet he was everywhere I looked.

When nearly a week had slipped by since he'd died, Father reopened the doors of the tavern. He would have left it closed for longer – for ever, I thought, as his heart was no longer in the work – but money was scarce. Filep would understand more than anyone, what with how fiercely he'd worked to keep us afloat.

It took a day or two for patrons to return to us, and when they came through the door, they cast each of us a sympathetic, understanding half-smile that was somehow worse than doing nothing at all. Every one was a reminder, hammering into place the fact that Filep was gone and everyone knew it. So I started keeping my eyes down, refusing to meet their gazes as they ordered their drinks, and went about my work as swiftly and normally as I could.

"Béata, your hair," Mother whispered on the fifth day since we reopened. I reached up absently to feel it, only to find I had forgotten to braid it. It hung messy and limp down my back. It was the first thing Mother had said to me since Filep had died, a play at finding routine once again.

"Forgive me," I said, and sat down on a stool to braid it. I'd taken Father's brown hair, dark like evening trees, as had Filep. Alíz, though, she took after Mother, with reddish-golden hair the colour of strawberries at sunset. I had envied her when I was younger, feeling her the brighter, lovelier girl I could have been but wasn't. But then I'd grown older – though I wouldn't say wiser – and saw in her only a sister to cherish and love for everything she was.

The squares of rich evening light stretched long on the floor, and the door opened more and more frequently to let in townsfolk whose long days of work had come to an end. I lingered longer than necessary by the door, which I propped open with a chair to let in the cooling breeze, and watched the shadows dance along the streets. There was beauty in the darkened shapes of leaves and branches fluttering about the cobblestones, yet I didn't see it. All I could see were the echoes of Filep's footprints as he'd wandered towards his death.

Why hadn't I gone to the window, or called down to Father? Why had I let him go?

If Filep were still here, he would pull me aside to remind me with firm words that this was not my fault, so stop acting like it. *People die, Béata. That's life. You sleep, you wake up, you remember how to smile, and you live your life until the end.* That was Filep's way. Carry on through anything and everything, no journey too long, no task too hard. It all could be done, with enough effort and will. It was exhausting just to be around him, though now I would give anything for one more glimpse of that unending energy.

As the horizon slowly beckoned the sun, the evening air grew ever cooler. "Béata, lay the fire," Father called from across the room. His hands were full of empty tankards. This was how he was coping, I had come to realize: by keeping life so busy he had no spare moments to let the sadness in. I swallowed, and nodded. The fire had always been Filep's task. I'd learned how, of course, but had rarely needed to do it. I moved towards the hearth with slow steps, as though hunting some flighty prey that would flee at the sound of a breath. The kindling sat waiting in a basket, and a handful of locals watched my reluctant steps curiously, but I pushed their prying eyes away. All I saw was the hearth, Filep as a young boy carefully laying the fire, me watching from a nearby chair and committing every move to memory. One day I would do it myself, I remembered thinking – when Filep had gone off to get married and live in a house far away. Not like this.

The kindling caught quickly, having sat out to dry all summer. The twigs snapped and crackled and sent sparks flying up into the chimney. Warm memories descended on me, of pleasant evenings by the fire, snow falling in the dark night outside, stew bubbling in a pot, and Mother humming songs quietly to herself. Those days had seemed so simple back then, so ordinary in a way I never thought I'd miss so fiercely. Yet miss them I did, with all the intensity of a winter wind.

Those in the tavern moved gradually closer to the fire,

its warmth and comfort a draw after a long day's work. I didn't understand it; a sweaty day in the fields or hunting in the forest, and they came here to sit by a fire. It seemed only a reminder that, though autumn was lovely and fast approaching, the harsh days of winter were edging closer.

Poking at the fire kept me out of the kitchen and away from my other duties for a few precious minutes. The blaze had already caught, the wood slowly blackening away, but I sat and stared for what could have been hours, lost among the flames.

"Was just this time of year back then," an older man behind me said. I didn't look at him, listening without moving. A beetle crawled towards the hearth, then, sensing the danger of the fire, turned and disappeared into a crack in the wall. I wished I could fit through that crack. Disappear from the world for a while, somewhere dark and quiet. "I think I was sitting just here when I first heard the screams."

"Ján, do not speak of it. It can do little good," another voice rebuked.

"Fat lot of good not speaking of it has done," Ján retorted. "Here we are, all these years later, no king or queen to speak of, bodies piling up outside the castle, and what's worse, I heard some folks from the outer edge of the village saying the rains are moving."

"Moving?"

"Moving. Growing. Coming this way. Whatever's in that

52

castle wants us dead, and if we won't go to it, it'll come to us. We should have abandoned this town a long time ago."

"You wouldn't leave this town if you were the last man alive, you fool," someone said, a hint of jest in their voice despite the mood.

"Perhaps not, but there are others who should. Get out and build a life somewhere, even out of Marcosza. What's left here but death, anyway?"

"Hope, I reckon," the same voice replied. "Precious little of it, maybe, but there is still hope."

"Hope's deader than the king and queen, Eugen, and you know it. You saw 'em. We all saw 'em. Deader than dead. The boat was so full of blood it was half sunk. It still turns my stomach just remembering it, and that's saying something. I think I was sick for a week after that."

"I did see," the other muttered, and I heard the sound of a long draught being drunk.

I'd heard the story a hundred times, but each new person to tell it seemed to have a detail I had never heard before. It almost made me wonder what was fact and what was fiction. One day, life in Marcosza was as it had always been, and the next, the mangled bodies of King Aurel and Queen Tabíta were sent on boats from the castle grounds, the rains had gathered overhead, and that was the end. Our history, our world, had been rent in two, leaving only before and after.

I'd never known the times before, only the after. Only

the broken world their deaths had left behind. My mother had had the misfortune of delivering me the day before, and though our town would often come together to celebrate a birth, mine had only been met with wails and sorrow after the killings.

People whispered of black magic and sorcery, of devils and the castle being a gateway to the underworld – in quiet corners of taverns or behind the closed and locked doors of homes, lest the castle should hear them. Some packed up and left our small town of Zírany altogether, the rains and the rumours too much to bear. I hardly blamed them. Like the rains that drenched the ground around the castle, evil had seeped into every nook and cranny it could find, turning our dreams dark and our hearts cold.

Others could not bear the thought of gathering everything they owned and leaving the only home they had ever known, so they stayed, but they locked their doors day and night, and prayed faithfully to the gods, lighting candles every noon and midnight in the hopes that they would be smiled upon.

"There's been enough sadness in this place," said a voice that wasn't Ján's, quietly, as if I wouldn't hear. "It does not do to dwell on the dark parts of the world."

"I'm sure Izsak's doing his best. It can't be easy, being flung into ruling a country in chaos and told to make it right."

"Izsak has had years to make it right," Ján retorted, his

words slurred with drink. "I grew up a farmer's boy, and I reckon I could do better than him."

Izsak was a baron who lived in Szaliri House, a small castle in the walled city of Dungléd in the far north of the country. It sat in the Oroszom Mountains on the border with Sovažska, distant from our own town but vital to Marcosza for trade and travel. They said it was the one place in all of Sóar where mages were welcomed – ever since our castle's devilry and anyone with magic had put a sour taste in the country's mouth. Dungléd, where the Weavers – mages who could create and build and design – had long been known to live and work, had become a sort of beacon for anyone magical in Marcosza in the years following the death of the king and queen. People would quietly disappear from towns and cities, off to seek safety and a new life somewhere they would find others like them.

Baron Izsak was second cousin of the late King Aurel and senior in the court thanks to his knack for foreign affairs, which largely concerned dealings with Sovažska. Having been fortunate enough to have been one of the only members of the court who had not been in Castle Vyesta at the time of the murders, he had naturally been assigned rulership of Marcosza in the fallout all those years ago. I'd heard it said that he resented the position, though I couldn't think why anyone wouldn't wish to be king. He'd refused the title, insisting he keep only his former title of baron.

Then again, I couldn't think how overwhelming it

would be to have a broken kingdom with an unstoppable killing rain thrust into your hands with no hope of righting it.

"Then perhaps you ought to go knock on the gates of Szaliri House and tell him so yourself," said the other voice with a sigh. "You're full of talk in your town local, but that's all it ever is. Just talk." There was a hint of a smile in his voice.

"Least I got feelings on the matter, Elek," Ján shot back. "I don't hear you offering anything useful. Then again, if you ran off to save the world, this poor old place would go out of business without your coin coming through these doors every morning, noon and night, so I suppose you're good for something."

"You're a bastard, Ján, and you've drunk too much. Best get you home to Nadett before she comes in here to drag you out herself. Wouldn't want that . . . again."

I rose slowly and slipped into the kitchen, the hubbub of chatter and movement growing suddenly quiet when the door closed behind me. Alíz stood scrubbing dishes, but stopped when I entered.

"Finally." She untied her apron and flung it towards me. "It's your turn." She swiftly exited into the dining room. I didn't mind so much. Dishwashing meant time alone to think and wonder, and the past few minutes had given me much to wonder about.

Were the rains truly growing? It was difficult to believe

words uttered in the tavern under the spell of drink – though I couldn't say it would surprise me.

I *could not* wait for another dreadful thing, and then another, until one by one we'd all been picked off like rabbits. Filep could not simply be another name gone. Another soul taken for nothing. There had been years for something to be done. For someone to make it right. Many had tried, yes, but all had failed, and since Filep had died, the knowledge that I was one of the only – if not *the* only – person who could enter the rains without dying had weighed on my mind like an infection with no cure. There was more at work than the rain around the castle. Some greater goal none of us could see. But I had every intention of finding out.

There was a sudden stir outside the kitchen. I laid aside the tankards I'd been washing and shoved the door open so quickly it knocked against the wall. A crier stood in the dining room, all eyes fixed on him. He wore simple brown robes and a pendant with the Marcoszan symbol engraved on it: two griffs with their talons locked together.

I hadn't realized we still had criers, with there being no court and all.

"I bear news from Szaliri House," the man said, his voice loud but tired with travel. He unfurled a scroll and read the words slowly, clearly, for all to hear. "Let it be known that Baron Izsak of Dungléd has offered a reward of five hundred gold coins for anyone who may enter Castle

Vyesta and bring an end to the rains. Let darkness and devilry have no more hold over our country. May the gods go with you and smile over your way."

Chapter Five

Liljana

After escaping the castle, even more than before, I felt forced to hide my face. To slink between shadows and keep out of sight. The night was pitch black and brisk, the air thick with mist following the rain. When I'd escaped the courtyard and gathered my thoughts, there was only one place I could think of to go: the home of Petre Borduva, the Sage that only us mages knew lived in the crypt below the Old Church near the centre of Tăru.

The sky grew further and further away as I traversed the close streets, slow and careful, each step calculated. The buildings grew taller, the cobblestones smooth from frequent passage, the ropes far overhead, flung between buildings to dry laundry in the hot sun, seeming as large and graceless spiderwebs against the dingy grey of the night sky. Whatever sense of home this city had ever given me had vanished. Now the streets were foreign, unfamiliar, frightening in a way I didn't know they could be.

There were precious few other souls about at an hour such this, for which I thanked whatever gods had yet to forsake us. Those I did pass were too drunk to notice me slipping quietly by, and even then I gave them a wide birth. Word of the mage who'd slain the castle guard would not stay secret for long.

Somewhere in the city a voice shouted, echoing off the buildings. I froze and listened, but all was silent. In every whisper of my cloak, every patter of my feet on the cobblestones, Miha's voice was there to encourage me. Her gentle, relentlessly gracious voice. I saw her sitting in the window again, like she had been what felt like moments ago. Looking down on the street. Watching life in the city go by.

And I spent every second trying not to picture her headless body lying somewhere within the hold. An ache that hurt more than a broken bone, more than my body after too much use of magic, set in, so agonizing I was forced to stop now and then to double over and breathe. But then a voice in the corner of my mind would urge me on, remind me I hadn't the time to rest. Not yet. So on I went.

The heart of the city was ancient. I didn't know when it had been built, but the stories went back hundreds of years, before any of the kings we knew of had ever sat on the throne. There had been repairs and new buildings as time wore on, but one footstep in the rounded city centre and the tired stones and moss were unavoidable. The Old Church was aptly named: its roof bore patched holes and broken stained-glass windows that no one had bothered to touch in years. I couldn't even be certain what gods had been worshipped within its walls, but if I had to hazard a guess, I would have said Senža, the Sea God. I rarely found my way down to the docks, but without the sea, Tăru and Roşesti would have been nothing. Fishing and trade had kept the country going since time immemorial.

The old bell tower looked ready to fall, even in the dark of night. A dead tree stood in the graveyard, all angled branches and gnarled points. The gate to the graveyard hung open, various ropes and chains lying useless on the ground from previous trespassers. Eventually, whoever had once made a show of the church's upkeep had given up. I couldn't blame them. Why waste the time when the only feet to pass the threshold in recent decades had been those of vandals?

I crept quietly to the shadow of the large tree and stopped, turning slowly to take in every alley and window nearby. No other bodies moved. No other eyes looked on. Just me and the dead, long buried in the graveyard of a church returning to dust. When I had convinced myself that no one was looking, I adjusted my cloak and moved with crouched, hurried steps to the tombstone marked Petre Borduva. Well, it only said Petre Borduva to those with magic. To anyone else it just bore the name of some long-dead chap no one came to see.

Anyone who wasn't intended to would never know it belonged to a man who still lived.

With limbs that shook from the weight, I pushed aside the unadorned stone to reveal a steep, dark staircase leading down into the earth. I had no light, and there was none nearby to aid me, so I stepped into the darkness, balanced myself on a narrow step and slid the stone as closed as I could manage.

I used to come here more often, back when things were simpler and I harboured dreams of training my magic, of leaving Tăru and seeking my fortune. Every year, Petre would invite mages around the city to gather with him, share news of the magical world, of those struck down by the Ashen. It made us feel like we weren't alone. The visit with him that stuck out to me the most was one from two years ago, when I had gone with Miha when she wished to enquire if she could rid herself of her magic. The answer had been no, of course, but it meant something to her to hear it from Petre.

As I descended the stairs once more, I remembered how endless they felt, one after another, surrounded by nothing but darkness, my fingers catching on spiderwebs along the stone walls. I moved slowly enough to keep from tripping, but each second felt an hour in this grave, the dead lying all around me. I could feel them, even if I couldn't see them, keenly aware of their bones lying only feet away, separated by earth.

Three hundred and twenty-five steps later – though I hadn't realized I'd been counting until I reached the last one – I entered a dimly lit room. Decorum perhaps would have suggested I avert my eyes from the vaults lining the walls, filled with the coffins of those who had lain here for centuries, but I always stopped to stare, rapt. Logic told me why Petre had chosen this place for his hideout – no one who didn't carry magic would be brave enough to descend into a dark, forgotten crypt without a very good reason, and most knew nothing of its existence – but to live down here, surrounded by the dead and their untold stories, their silent memories and lives lurking just beyond reach, was unthinkable to me.

Single candles dotted on various surfaces lit the way down the hall of the crypt, and ahead I heard shuffling and humming. Petre was an older man with grey hair and beard, smile lines etched around his mouth, though he smiled rarely nowadays. I had wondered more than once about his past, but I knew that knowledge was dangerous, at least when it came to mages.

Webs clung to bits of broken stone in the corners. The shadows of what had once been ornate carvings to adorn a place of rest now danced with vicious glee as my passage set the candles to flickering. The statue of an angel now stood chipped and run-down, more nightmarish than calming. Her hands reached out as though offering solace. I stopped before her, staring into the blank stone eyes that I was certain watched me, whispering words into the total silence that I couldn't quite hear. Lifelike. It was far too lifelike in a strange, shadowed way. Drawing in a breath, I ran my fingers along the carved hair – just to be sure.

Stone. Nothing more.

Swallowing, and irritated with myself for wasting time, I spun and moved faster along the hall of the crypt, keeping my eyes forward. There were Seers somewhere in this world; the dead were their business. Mine was simple. Make one thing into another. Feed myself. Sometimes form a knife where I once had a stick – I smiled subtly to myself at the memory of escaping the courtyard, and then quickly ceased when I imagined the streets above me now crawling with guards.

"Petre." He turned from where he'd been hanging a kettle over the fire. It was late, the middle of the night, really, but I supposed that was the only time he received visitors. It was best to always be ready. "I see you knew I was coming."

He smiled. "Liljana Vahani. Welcome." He proffered me a bit of bread, which I declined. "I sensed someone would come by tonight, and thought you might like tea. Can I offer you a cup?"

I nodded, and seated myself on a small round stool. Despite the bones lurking only feet away, he'd made this crypt quite a home, with stacks of books, baskets of food, a bed with a blanket so warm and vibrant I gave it a long second glance.

"It was a gift," he explained, catching my gaze. "From another mage. It has been a busy summer, no doubt about that. The Ashen, those bloody fools, they've spooked all the mages within five hundred miles. Sometimes I think I ought to get out of the whole business myself. Retire to Savenče or some other small, quiet country with a knack for good wine. Or perhaps Dungléd. Find others like myself. Somewhere safe and removed." He cocked his head, thinking.

He spoke so quickly he stumbled over his own words, clearly eager for conversation. Perhaps these years below ground with corpses for company and the occasional fretting of an unsettled mage had worn him thin. I had given little thought to what his life must be like, but, then again, I had given little thought to him. He was there to help. To answer questions. To support us however he might. His happiness and well-being had never crossed my mind.

"Why do you do it?"

"Do what?"

"What you do. Help mages. I wouldn't bother. I would run as far from this place as I could."

"Then why haven't you?"

The question caught me off guard.

"Where would I go?"

"The world is great and wide, and you've seen this much of it." He held his fingers close together. "If you want to, you could leave."

My mood soured a little. "I live and work in a tavern, Petre. I hear detailed stories of what the Ashen do in the countryside when they find a mage, without the king or the guards pretending to keeping them in check."

"You're afraid."

"I'm terrified."

He sighed a little, then returned to my question. "Do not think I haven't thought about it. I have my own dreams, of course. But if I ran away, who would help them? You, I mean. And those like you. You're all kittens, tottering about the nest, but the world is large and cold, and you need tools to survive. I can't give you those tools, but I can help show you how to find them. That is my job. It's all I know."

I cleared my throat. "In the castle, they're killing all of the mages. All of them. They killed my friend. Miha. They almost took me as well. I had to kill a captain of the guard just to get here." My words came fast, tumbling forth with a suppressed sob. Despite my efforts, tears stung my eyes. I resented every one of them, wishing myself stronger than this.

"I feared as much," Petre said after a moment, laying

aside his teacup. "I had a sense, you know. I didn't want to believe it, but I suppose I should have. Things have been changing around here for a long while. What a shame."

There was a sadness in his eyes, as though he'd felt it was his duty to save them all, and had failed. But there was only one on whose shoulders their deaths rested: King Costel, safe and well-fed and comfortable in his stone fortress above us. Well, him, and everyone who followed him. I had seen him a few times, traversing the city on a great white horse who wore a gold mask. He had smiled and waved, bidding us all a good day, but the smile looked fake. Hollow, as though someone had told him he must do it to please us, but he hated every second of it. I had hated that smile even back then, though I had far less reason to hate him than I did now.

"Why have you come here tonight?" Petre asked softly. "To seek refuge? Are the king's men after you?"

"Yes," I said curtly. "They are." I pulled one knee up to my chest. "But I didn't come here to hide. I came for your help."

"You're chatty for a murderer on the run." It was meant as a joke, or perhaps a subtle chastisement, but the weight of his words pushed my heart into my stomach. "And what can I help you with?" All spark of contentment had gone from his eyes, leaving only a growing hopelessness that worried me. Petre was always balanced. Always strong and calm like I imagined a father to be. He was the foundation on which us mages could build ourselves, and that foundation was cracking before my eyes.

"I don't know," I said finally, staring into the fire. "I need you to tell me what I need help with. I need you to tell me what to do. How to survive as a mage in the world above." Tears burned my eyes once more, but I had given up trying to be strong. "Everything is falling apart. The mages are dying. The king is against us. The Ashen are everywhere. I think Madam Iulia would sell me out to the king if I went back home, if she hasn't already. The guards are hunting me all over the city. I have nothing." I sighed. "I envy the folks in this crypt. The world they died in must have been far less wicked than this one."

"Do not envy the dead, Liljana," he told me quietly.

"Why shouldn't I?"

"Because death is the only thing that lasts for ever. Everything else is temporary. Even this."

I spun around to face the direction I'd come, certain I had heard a noise. Petre glanced about us, then shrugged.

"You are unhappy, Liljana. You can change where you are, who you are with, what you do, but you cannot change who you are. You must learn to love yourself, magic and all, or happiness will never find you." He put a comforting hand atop mine, and offered a small smile. "Sometimes life is a murmuring brook, and sometimes a waterfall. The only way to be happy is to love the fact that you're water, and not the course you take."

I turned again, a noise sounding closer this time.

"You hear many strange noises down here," he explained. "It usually turns out to be a rat, or a bit of stone that fell." There was an edge to his voice I couldn't quite place.

"Is that what you believe we just heard? A bit of falling stone."

He swallowed, then sipped his tea. "No."

My blood ran cold. I stood, then sat back down, frozen with indecision.

"You asked for my help," Petre went on, quicker than before. "I have little help to give you. What things are afoot in this land are not easily stopped without an army, and a lot of untrained mages can hardly be called an army."

I bristled.

"It's a fact, Liljana, not an insult. And it's not only in Roşesti, but further afield. In. . ." He fell silent for a moment, hugging his teacup and staring at the fire, which had begun to die down. "There is much happening in Marcosza. Dark things are awakening there. Things that have no place in our world. The hatred you see around you has grown from the fear it has caused. Spread out like an illness and infected our homeland. If peace and safety are what you desire, then they cannot be had until that darkness has been quenched." His eyes glanced behind me, an urgency lighting them in a way I'd never seen before. "I've had word from a Seer in Marcosza. Their castle has

69

been consumed by something evil. It killed their king and queen years ago. No one can enter through the poisonous rains overhead. It has claimed life after life to no end. If it is a world of peace you are after, then destroying that evil is the only way. No one will trust magic while that darkness sits festering."

Another sound made me jump, followed by a distant shout.

The king's men had found me.

"What do I do?" I asked quickly, tying my cloak on tighter and moving across the room. My hands shook. Everything shook. The crypt had felt safe. I needed more time with Petre, more time to delve into the things he'd just said, but death had come calling, and I hadn't a moment to spare. I didn't know the way out of here, other than the way I had come, but there must be another. Petre would never have trapped himself down here with only one way out.

"I cannot tell you what to do," he replied, "because I do not know. That question must be answered in person. You have enough magic in you to achieve something in your life, Liljana. Do not waste it. But remember, if you do choose to go there: there are others like you. Others who feel the way you do. You may dislike people, but you might do well to learn how to get on with them, if you are to succeed."

My lips twitched, but there was no time to unpack his comment. "Marcosza. Where? Where do I go?"

The shouts grew louder. The sound of swords being

drawn rang out against the stone. I backed away, further down the dark hallway.

"To Castle Vyesta," he said hastily. "First get to Marcosza. Then your magic will lead you to the castle. You will hear of an Order in Dungléd. They will not help you. Get to the castle by yourself instead." He pointed quickly, glancing once over his shoulder. "Now, follow this tunnel as far as it will go until you reach the stairs. Hurry."

"Will you not go with me?"

He smiled, though it seemed strange and out of place in the moment. "My work is finished," he said gently. "The Marcoszan Seer said there was a girl with enough power to either build a queendom or tear the world apart. I believe he was speaking of you. I have played my part. Good fortune to you, and all others like you. Better days will come."

Perhaps I ought to have stayed to help him. To fight off the guards and force Petre to join me. But I could already see the shadows of the men along the walls, and the resolve in his voice told me he would not easily be swayed.

"Thank you, Petre," I said, and I fled down the hall, hot tears running down my face.

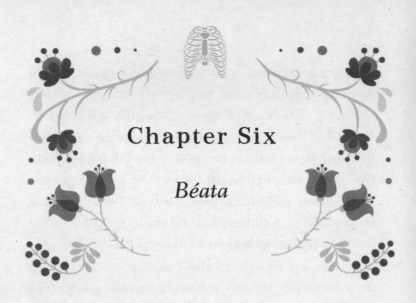

Chapter Six

Béata

For days after the crier had left, there was talk of nothing but the reward for entering the castle. At every table, on every corner, by every well and through every window people spoke of it, shared ideas, wondered who might be the lucky soul to at last breach the murderous rains and find what lay within.

As if five hundred gold coins would keep anyone from dying in the poison rains.

Anyone other than me, that is.

I could not help but wonder if talk of Filep's death – the first in a long while – had made its way across the country to Dungléd, and all the way to Baron Izsak's ears. How strange it would be, my own brother's name on the lips of the baron and members of his makeshift court.

Despite a castle that wanted us dead, we had learned how to survive. Lock the doors. Stay inside after sunset. Only out in the open air could your mind give in to the draw of whatever dark magic haunted that wicked place. Perhaps Filep's death worked as a reminder to Izsak that things were still dire. That something had to be done.

Shame he'd chosen a route that I could not see ending in victory, but I supposed there was some goodness in finally working to bring an end to the castle's evil.

It was a cool morning, with dew gathered on every surface and a clear sky taunting us with the idea of how perfect things could be, as though the vicious rains that fell so close at hand were nothing more than a bad dream. I volunteered to make the walk to the well for Mother, swinging the bucket back and forth as I went, avoiding the gazes and sympathetic glances of all whom I passed. This morning was too beautiful for such reminders. I wished only to take in the fresh air, stretch my legs and gather water. Everything else could wait.

I hooked the bucket to the rope and lowered it down until I heard a splash. The river murmured away nearby, light mist clinging to the surface. Birds darted between the branches of the trees that grew by the water's edge. Life felt whole and beautiful, even for a fractured moment, and I breathed it in deep.

Then the river disappeared. The well was gone. The birds and trees and blue sky vanished. It was late evening, and around me was a courtyard with a river. Stars shone overhead, and someone's hand held mine, gently, but with the firmness of what could only be love. Laughter rang out through the air – my laughter, with a kind of light-heartedness I had never had the luxury of knowing. I skipped over stones and up a set of winding stairs to a tower that overlooked the land, the hand still in mine, yet I couldn't quite see the face of its owner. Every time I tried to see it, there was only shadow and fog. We stood there on the tower for so long it felt a lifetime, and each moment was not long enough. If it could have gone on for ever, I would have cherished each second as though it was my last one alive, fallen in love with such a beautiful evening and a perfect companion over and over again. The world was right and whole and good again, perfect, if such a thing were possible – until it wasn't.

The evening breeze around us vanished, replaced by screams and frantic, pounding footsteps. Fear gripped me, the kind I'd never felt, even with the rains. Even with the castle's incessant call of death. Fear that was real and writhing and alive, and coming closer with each horrifying second. Nowhere was safe. Wherever I looked that fear was waiting, staring back at me in the shadows of the nothingness all around. Death was close at hand, waiting, watching, haunting.

The screams eased away, and the world around me settled back into view. The well sat silently before me, the river meandering by. A street or two over, the murmur of the town carried on, as though nothing had ever changed. I fell to the ground, dirt and rocks digging into my skin through my dress, and leaned one shoulder against the stone of the well.

What had overcome me?

This was not the first time I had been swept away on a torrent of someone else's vision. The first time it happened was when I was ten years old, wandering the forest close by the town with Filep, collecting kindling, and without warning, I was on horseback, riding through a part of the forest I had never seen before, headed somewhere unfamiliar. Filep hadn't noticed because he had drifted further ahead, and I'd never said a word, because what would I say? I couldn't even explain to myself why it happened, let alone to anyone else.

One moment I was me, and the next, I was overcome by a dream, a memory I knew was not mine. And it tormented me and drained every ounce of energy I had until all I could do was fall and rest on the ground until I was again strong enough to stand.

I would have stayed sitting beside the well for hours, until the sun dragged itself to bed and the shadows came calling, but other folks eventually came towards me, whether to check on my well-being or to get water for themselves, so I rose slowly, shakily, and fetched my bucket from the well.

My best guess was that they were memories of dreams I did not remember having. They possessed the intensity that only ever accompanied a dream, that bone-deep dread, that need to run but feeling rooted to the ground. I could force all the broken pieces together until it very nearly made sense in my mind, though I could never quite find the answer for why I would be dreaming them again, and during the day. I needed more time to think on it. An answer was out there, certainly, yet there were too many fractured pieces of my heart and mind to put back together first.

Another day.

I smoothed both hands over my hair. Took in a breath of the clear air. Watched a bird fly from one tree to another, a worm in its mouth. Extraordinary, how there could be such turmoil in the confines of my mind, yet the world around me knew nothing of it.

The water felt heavier than usual, splashing around as I hauled it back to the tavern. The sky seemed less blue now, the air less fresh. Everything seemed tainted somehow, as though the waking dream had sucked all the beauty from the world. I stared at the ground so I wouldn't notice the change, my shoes slowly growing sodden with the spilled water.

The afternoon saw a busy tavern. The door opened and closed almost constantly, bodies bustling around, the air outside cool and beckoning all from their homes. I scurried about doing my work almost without thinking, forcing nearly all thoughts from my mind. If I didn't, I might slowly be consumed by them.

As I delivered a loaf of bread and a refilled tankard to a table, I paused for a moment to survey the room, my eyes meeting with those of a young man seated alone. He had only water and a slice of bread before him, and a notebook in which he was writing. His dark, grown-out hair was stuck together in places, a few strands clinging to his forehead. He was neither in the garb of a farmer nor a shepherd, rather in a blue tunic with boots that seemed too heavy for the season.

Seconds passed, and still we stared.

"Béata," my mother said, shoving a tray of tankards into my hands. "You can daydream after we close." She pointed to a table and hurried off.

As I slowly delivered the tankards, I kept my gaze on the boy. He had looked back down to his book, but glanced up and met my eyes. Looking away felt strange now. Impossible. New faces came through these doors almost daily. Travellers, merchants, visitors curious about the castle. Why had this particular boy transfixed me so? His lips twitched with a suppressed smile that both excited and infuriated me. I could feel his gaze on me as I crossed the room, and suddenly my every step and every breath felt artless and off, as if I was doing it for the first time and didn't quite know how.

I shook my head, strands escaping from the knot in

77

which I had tied my hair at the back of my head, and set wildly about my work. Collect those empty tankards, bring more if they wished, pull bread from the large oven while my mother's hands were full, tell the man trying to leave that he still owed us coin for his drink. Everything and anything but glance at the boy seated by himself with a notebook.

"Béata, that young man there requires more water. Do see to him." My mother hurried by, arms full of dishes needing to be cleaned. Her pain at Filep's loss seemed to be masked only by furious work, scurrying about the tavern and the town as though exhausting herself might cloak her agony. I wasn't sure it was working.

I looked towards the young man in question, and our eyes met again. Without breaking his gaze, I took the glass from his table and then turned away, striding into the kitchen.

My sister threw a quizzical look my way, from where she stood with a glistening face, washing dishes. "You're a bit pale, Béata. Has someone died out there?" Her voice carried an edge of hope, as though a dead body would be far more interesting than the mountain of dishes still waiting to be washed.

"No."

I refilled the water glass while staring out the window. Until this moment, I had struggled to place my feelings, but the longer I stood there, staring without seeing, the more certain I became that it was anger setting my ears to burning. In a quick movement that splashed some of the water on to the counter, I grabbed the glass and exited the kitchen back into the dining room, my footsteps heavy as I approached his table.

"Who are you?" I asked, my voice solid but too quiet to travel far. Some part of me startled at my boldness – rudeness, even.

Amusement toyed with his face. He closed his book and leaned forward, arms crossed and elbows resting on the table.

"My. I have little time or money for taverns such as this, so I'm unfamiliar with the customs. Are the owners always so polite?"

"I know most folks in Zírany, more or less. Lived here my whole life. I've never seen you before." I sat down opposite him, on the edge of the seat so I could stand quickly.

"But you feel like you have." He finished the thought for me.

I swallowed. "Who are you?" I asked again.

"My name is Benedek, from Kupesno. I came to see the castle."

"Ah. The reward." It had begun to draw strangers from far and wide, all standing about outside the rains and staring, as though if they waited for long enough, the sky would clear and the ground would dry up, and they could wander in uninhibited.

"Word gets around," Benedek said. "Even to Kupesno."

"I've never heard of it."

"Kupesno? Unsurprising. It's like the piece of a town that broke off long ago and no one bothered to look for it. You only find it by accident."

"Charming."

"It is, actually. I recommend a visit."

"Why were you staring?"

"Why were *you* staring?"

"I wasn't."

"You were."

I paused and looked around the room, checking for my family. "You. . . I thought I knew you, but I don't. That was all."

"It's a shame." A false wave of sadness pulled at his face. "I'd hoped it was the good looks." A moment of hesitation, and then he cleared his throat. "In truth, though, yes. I thought I knew you, too."

Uneasiness wormed its way into my heart. I thought back to the memory I'd had at the well, the one I was certain couldn't be mine. Today had felt off in every way, tilted, angled, incorrect, though I couldn't place how. "Hmm." I sat back, drumming my fingertips on the table. "We've passed each other on the road, then, or found ourselves in the same marketplace. We might never know."

"What's your name?"

"Béata. Rovedosi."

His eyebrows furrowed. "You seem worried."

"I'm not. Just confused."

"Well, Béata Rovedosi, if you find a spare moment to chat about your castle, I'd be grateful. I've come quite a way to get here."

"I. . ." I cleared my throat. "I don't wish to talk about the castle."

He studied my face. "I'll be around for a while, if you change your mind."

I shrugged, and pushed my chair away from the table. "I won't, but do enjoy your time in Zírany. There is so much more to it than the castle."

He smiled and nodded, and I stared again. I had seen that smile before.

The room seemed to tilt as I turned to walk away, shaking my head. The warmth I felt at his smile and friendliness was quickly hampered by the uneasiness that settled in. *How could I have seen him before?* A chill raised hairs along my arms as I hurried into the kitchen.

Twilight was settling in. Night-time drained away the light of day, and the call of crickets and the like rang out against the walls and the trees. The whole world was bathed in orange and blue, shadows stretching away until they melted together into a grand, creeping darkness. I wandered the streets slowly, taking in everything, toying with the danger of being out so late. I couldn't see the horizon, but any moment now, the last of the sunlight would disappear behind it, and the call of the castle would grow stronger. I should turn and walk home, and hurry my steps, but I couldn't. My mind was too awake to slip back into the tavern and into the life that awaited me there.

The vision that had overcome me.

Benedek.

The day had been filled with uncertainties that would not be quieted. Mother would worry. Father would be angry that I'd worried her. But still, I did not turn back.

"Béata."

I whirled around, but the street was empty. I looked up to the windows of the buildings around me. Nothing.

"Yes?" I called. No answer.

Try as I might, I could not find the source. A town child playing some great joke on me, most likely, but I couldn't shake the feeling that it was something greater.

You always think that, I reminded myself. But how could I not? The world around us was dark and crawling with wicked things. It was not beyond reason to worry.

"Béata."

I turned again, and stopped walking. "What?" The anger that came out with my voice was rich and heavy. "Who is it?"

But there was no response.

I ran both hands along my dress, then smoothed down my hair. Fear would do me little good. So I did the only thing I could think to do, and I turned and ran the whole way back home.

Chapter Seven

Liljana

I should have gone back to save him. There was a part of me that knew that, yet I didn't. I heard the moment the guards entered the room where Petre was waiting. I heard their voices, I heard swords clanging, but then I was too far away to hear anything more. I could light no candle to show me the way, instead stumbling along the dark hallway, feeling for the stairs that would lead me up to the gods knew where. Now and then my feet kicked something, sending it skittering across the floor, and I winced in horror.

An age had surely slipped by before I, at last, stumbled over the first stairs. Scrambling to gain my footing, I rushed to climb them, steep though they were, up and up and up until my hands fell on a wooden trapdoor that was creaky and rotted with age. I lifted it slowly, peeking through the crack to see where it led to, but the night was too dark, and wherever I was seemed too far from the nearest lamps to offer any light. Taking in a long breath, I slowly pushed the door open enough to crawl out on to the grass, then let it quietly close.

The glimmer of distant city lights faintly illuminated a grassy courtyard, around which stood the crumbled walls of an old building I didn't recognize. Though I felt as if I had walked for miles, I was still in the old town, a quiet reminder of just how vast Tăru was. A few wanderers lay sleeping against the remaining pieces of wall, wrapped in tattered blankets and cloaks. Placing a large fallen rock atop the trapdoor, to buy myself what extra moments I could from the guards who pursued me, I slipped quickly from the courtyard and into the empty street.

Exhaustion beat down on me, harsh and unrelenting. It took time to gain my bearings, creeping from wall to wall, shadow to shadow, looking behind me, hearing things that weren't there. A battered old sign read Piarcă Way, the old word for market. So if I travelled this road, it would eventually find me in the market, and beyond the market, I could – with any luck – make the winding journey down the layers of the city to the port.

And beyond the port lay the Bay of Morța, another old word, but this time for death. The perilous cliffs and invisible rocks lurking just beneath the surface of the churning waters had sent many a sailor to their grave. I had never, not in my entire life, set foot on a boat or touched the waters of the bay. I'd spent enough time in the Regina hearing tales of its bloodthirsty sea gods to dare. But with the streets crawling with guards hunting the mage girl who'd killed the captain, there were few other options available to me. I needn't go far – finding someone who would take a few coins just to drop me a few miles to the north, where I could disappear into the Hills of Ariu, hardly seemed an impossible task. Although with how the past day had gone, I kept my hopes in check.

The empty market opened before me. It felt smaller, somehow, without the endless carts and sea of people milling around to make it feel as though it went on for ever. I hated this city with everything in me, despised every morning I woke up in it, and every night when I closed my eyes. I wouldn't miss it, certainly not – yet a sudden longing overcame me as I stood in the familiar marketplace, about to leave it for what could be for ever. A younger me would have given anything for a reason to leave. To see the world I had heard waited beyond the city walls. But wishing for a thing and facing a thing, it turned out, were very different.

But a shiver of something cool – excitement, maybe – travelled slowly up my spine.

Things were changing. My life was reinventing itself, after years of being stuck in one place. The old and well-worn trails were crumbling away to reveal new and untrodden paths that might take me anywhere. And as long as they led away from Tăru, familiarity notwithstanding, I could be as close to happy as I might ever be.

I still didn't know what I wanted: to follow Petre's words and make for the castle in Marcosza, or to simply stow away, sail across the bay, and disappear for ever. Maybe Marcosza did need help. Maybe all of magekind needed help. Maybe they needed *my* help. But maybe all *I* wanted was to live my life the way I wanted to, not the way the world told me to. My life, on my terms. It was a dizzying thought.

I pushed myself forward, each slow step dragging my feet across the cobblestones growing faster, energy rising. I knew little of what lay ahead, only of what lay behind, and it was hardly worth looking back. If the future could be no worse than the past, what was to fear?

So I crossed the marketplace, and I did not turn around to see it once more as the narrow streets of the city again closed around me.

The smell of the sea grew stronger as I descended the streets of the city to the bay. Now and then, I'd heard the distant shouts of guards, seen torches moving swiftly through streets too far away to spark true alarm, so I had carried on, quickly but quietly, following the scent of the water and the signs for the docks. By day, the waters were a blue so deep I'd wondered darkly if it had been stained by all the blood. By night, the water seemed black as the wings of a raven. Ink-dark and beckoning. It lapped hungrily at the edges of the docks, the voices of the sea gods whispering for bodies in the rush where a wave sent spray over the edge of a boat.

The way the small wooden skiffs thumped intermittently against the docks slowed my pace. Perhaps it was the time I'd spent in the crypt with Petre, but the sound reminded me dreadfully of bones.

Liljana, you craven fool, I scolded myself. Mages were being slaughtered – beheaded – within the walls of this very city, and I was fretting over the sounds of empty boats. I stamped my foot to ground myself and right my mind, then looked around quickly, worried I might have drawn attention.

The docks were largely abandoned at this hour, the moon cresting the sky, the stars fierce and bright so far from any street torches. Yet one small boat sent forth a glow that beckoned me closer, so closer I went. There was a small lower level down two steps, from where the candlelight shone. The boat bobbed around a bit from movement within, and the mumblings of a man who was speaking either to himself or to someone else reached me.

Glancing about once more, I rapped my knuckles on the open door and waited. A moment later, a man with dark hair that fell nearly to his shoulders emerged, his face twisted with confusion.

"An odd hour for visitors to the docks," he said, eyeing me up and down.

"These are odd times."

He shifted from one foot to the other, leaned one arm on the boat railing. "What're you after?"

"A boat to take me up the bay, to the Hills." I'd spent the entirety of my descent through the city remembering the sounds of the king's guards as they'd found Petre, his final words to me bouncing off the narrow walls. *You have enough magic in you to achieve something in your life, Liljana. Do not waste it.* Why couldn't I have just been an ordinary mage, with little power and even less desire to use it? I wanted a chance to be selfish, to find somewhere I could build my own life and not worry about anyone else's. But Petre's words had sunk in, eating away at me. Finding their way through the defences I had built around my heart.

The man sniffed and tilted his head, clearly thinking. "Odd," he echoed. "Heard there's lots happening up in the castle. Mages and the king and all sorts. You running from something?"

"Aren't we all?"

"I'm not. Not today, anyway."

"Well, I am. Will that stop you?"

"Depends on what you're running from."

"The king, mostly. The castle. The guards. The city, if I'm being honest. Shall I go on?"

A long pause. "This smells like trouble."

"You don't seem like the sort to let trouble stop you."

"Some trouble sticks. You got coin?"

"I wouldn't be here if I didn't."

A pause.

"When do you need to leave?"

"Now." I turned, distant shouts reaching my ears. Torches made their way down city streets above. Windows began to light up as citizens were disturbed from their slumber. "Immediately. I'll pay you extra for your speed."

He eyed the moving torches, standing up straighter. "I'm not so sure. I don't much like this."

I was tired. Any use of magic would be utterly exhausting, but I could wait no longer. I pulled one of the sticks from my belt and transformed it into a knife. "I would much appreciate your cooperation."

He bristled, but after another pause, a wild, worried look in his eyes, he stood aside and motioned me on to the boat. "It's little wonder there isn't much love for your kind," he muttered as I walked past, holding his gaze. "There's a polite way to ask for things."

"That was the first way I asked," I reminded him, ducking behind sails to remain out of sight. "Now hurry. I'll pay you when I leave the boat."

With a grumble, he set about readying the boat to depart. "I hope you know I'm meant to be hauling some cloth up to Anastadt tomorrow," he said as we drifted away from the docks. "You best hope I'm not late."

"I don't mind so much if you're late," I told him. "I'll be

gone by then." He sniffed again. "That seems like a long haul up to Anastadt. How long?"

"Two days, if I sail through the night and the winds are good. Three if not. Four if I skirt far away from Marcosza, what with all the rumours I've been hearing."

"Marcosza doesn't have a coast." I tried to remember what maps I had seen.

"Perhaps not, but the coastline of Savenče that separates Marcosza from the sea is only a few dozen miles across in places. Even that's too close for comfort."

"I'm going to Marcosza."

He spun to look at me as the docks faded further and further away.

"Why? You'll go to your death, mark my words. Nothing good has come from that country in years, and no good souls go there to ever return."

"Perhaps I won't return." I shrugged. "I have my reasons."

"I'll never understand your kind. Always mysterious. Always after something. Never just living. No wonder people don't trust you."

"We can't just live any more, or we'll be killed. Because of people like you."

He drew back, angry. "I've never killed a mage in my life. I take offence at that."

"Not you, exactly. People like you. The days of mage freedom are as gone as yesterday's sunrise." The cold

90

reminder was a punch in the stomach. I hugged myself and changed the subject. "What's your name?"

"Miloš."

"Liljana."

"Didn't ask. I suppose it's nice to meet you."

I fell silent for a time, watching as the lights of the city grew smaller and smaller, the once vast and sprawling layers of Tăru now distant and insignificant. The problems, the worries, the fears grew lighter as the boat drifted away, out into the black bay where a new set of doubts had the room to take hold.

I drew my knees up to my chest, just barely making out the rugged cliffs that fell away to the sea below. The horizon, dark as it was, hung so far away, opening up a world that had, until moments ago, felt closed and small. These waters, I had heard, had claimed thousands of lives over the years. They were peppered with unseen rocks, shipwrecks, hungry creatures that never rose above the surface.

"What is the darkest story you've heard about the sea?" I asked.

Miloš was silent for a long while before answering. Small waves crashed against the boat, the only sound in the utter quiet. "Beyond the bay," he said softly, as though someone or something might hear, "in the Sea of Senža, I heard my father talking of things out in the water, big as mountains, even from a great distance. Like whole islands moving about in the fog – only in the fog. Never in the daylight. Just distant shadows, moving slowly through the sea to the gods know where." He touched his temple and his heart, a quick blessing, and shuddered. "You hear many things on the water," he said, louder and more chipper. "The hard part is knowing what to believe."

"What stories do you believe?" I was determined not to spend this journey, however long it may be, in silence. There would be no one to talk to as I made my way through the Hills. Let now be the time for words.

He shrugged and shifted his weight, hair bouncing in the breeze. "Not many of them. They're nice to tell to land folk who don't know no better, but they're just words, mostly. The shapes in the fog, though, I think I believe that one. I think they're the gods, the sea gods, and that's why they never let us get too close. And I think I believe that if you drown at sea" – again, the sign of a blessing – "your soul is surrendered to them. I don't see how that couldn't be true, you know?"

I stared at the dark bay and didn't reply, gloom seeping back into my heart. Petre would be dead by now. The thought struck me like a cold wave. In just a few short hours, I'd lost both Miha and Petre. Everyone was dying. Death lurked around every corner. But I was still here.

Lonely as that felt, it was but one more opportunity to do what I seemed to do best: survive.

"How much longer?" I asked, wishing suddenly to be away from the dark waters and back on my feet, hurrying towards Marcosza.

He shrugged. "Another four hours, I think, and you'll be on your way."

Four hours. The sun would be up by then, and prying Ashen eyes would be roaming about the Hills. Creeping through Tăru, I hadn't had time for thoughts on how I would get through, what my crossing into Marcosza might look like. How grim a thought, that I might have escaped the hold and the city only to die in the wilds, freedom almost within grasp.

Although whether the evils hiding within Marcosza could be considered freedom, I wasn't certain, but being far from the clutches of Roşesti seemed free enough.

"I wish you hadn't threatened me to take you," Miloš said with a resigned sigh. "I could have liked you."

I shifted. "You wouldn't have taken me otherwise."

"Perhaps not. Even still."

Our conversation dwindled, a candle slowly burning out. I sat holding my knees, watching the dark horizon in the dim glow of the moon as the boat gently rocked about, until the sky grew grey and the stars grew softer, and the wild Hills of Ariu rose up along the coastline like waves of some vicious storm bringing on uncertainty and change.

Chapter Eight

Béata

There was a cemetery beyond the river, in a clearing on the edge of the wood. The rush of the water was just loud enough to be heard, and the golden sunlight trickled through the overrun treetops above. I stood beside Filep's grave – well, the mound of earth that held what things of his we'd managed to part with. His body could not be recovered, but having no ceremony at all felt sick and wrong, and a way to anger the gods. So we had buried his things, and it at least gave us somewhere to go to, somewhere to visit to feel like we could be close to him again.

I stood alone, staring at the grave, pondering the finality of it all. How had this happened? I looked towards the north-west, where the castle stood somewhere out of sight, and my body shook with rage.

"Filep's life was not yours to take," I whispered. "You owe me a life. You owe me a debt. And I will send my soul to the underworld if it means taking you with me."

The castle didn't hear me. And if it did hear me, it wouldn't believe me, of course. What would it find to fear in a village girl with an unkempt braid and a dress in desperate need of mending? Its walls were haunted by devils and darkness – if the rumours were to be believed. I knew little of such things, but the unchecked rage that burned my insides seemed, in that moment, strong enough to face it. I had been given a tool to stand up to the castle, and whatever lay within it: my ability to survive the rains. Why that was I could not say, and it mattered little. I could survive. And that was that. If there were others like me I had yet to hear of them. Who would I be if I did not use that to help my poor Marcosza, to stop anyone else ending up like Filep?

The thought of what it had been like to see Filep's body rotting away in the brutal rains punched me in the gut, making me double over. This was it. This was my beginning, fashioned out of a painful ending. I would gather what scraps of myself his death had left behind and forge a weapon in myself so powerful that whatever evil lay hidden in the castle would go limping back to hell.

But how? What could I do? Dive headlong into the

bloodthirsty castle? Entertaining thoughts of facing the evil hidden inside alone seemed a quick way to end up like the other poor souls sinking into the mud outside the castle. Dead. Gone. A chance wasted. And yet, I knew not of a single other soul who might be able to help. No one else could breach the rains as I could, at least not to my knowledge. No one else could live.

Which left just me. Simple, solitary me, and a castle hungry for bodies.

Presently, I turned away from the graves and made my way with slow steps back into town. It was a quiet day, warm and misty and a final nod to summer. I drank it in, trailing my fingers along the stone wall of a building, wishing every day could be like today. I had grown to love neither summer nor winter, but rather the seasons that fell in between, the ones that were neither here nor there. Days that felt too warm for the cool nights, and frosts that crept over us before dawn. Now, as summer slowly and grudgingly began to die away, I felt ever more alive. Bonfires would be lit, shawls would be donned, graves would be visited as the veil between us and the dead thinned, and homes would glow with the warm yellow light of candles and hearths. It was those nights that my grandfather used to tell us stories, the darker ones that did not suit the warm air of summer. Stories of the dead walking the land after nightfall, bones rising up from the ground to dance under a starless sky.

I stopped walking in the town square.

"Béata."

Again. The voice called to me again.

But the square was empty, save for two men walking slowly through, chatting with one another and ignorant of my presence.

Your imagination. Nothing more.

I took in the buildings, forcing thoughts of simplicity into my mind.

The houses were narrow and colourful, painted in mustard yellow or a rich umber. They stood vivid and glowing in the summer sunlight. Birds danced along the thatched roofs, and window box flowers frolicked against the vibrant colours, stirred by a light breeze.

"Béata."

I bunched my hair into my fists and shouted, "Who are you?" The two men, who'd nearly exited the square, stopped and turned, exchanging uncertain glances. I spun away from them, shaking my head. "Who are you?" Quieter this time. I searched every alleyway, every window, every shadow where someone might lurk, but found nothing. I moved to the centre of the square and sat down on the cobblestones heavily, frustrated.

She's just buried her brother, passers-by would think. *She's broken.*

The voice came from no one around me, a thought that slammed into me with the force of a waterfall. "There's no one around you," I said a few times to myself. "No one around you." *Breathe.* So I turned inward.

I closed my eyes and reached out, searching for the voice.

I felt for anything I could. What direction it came from. To whom it belonged. The shadows of my mind closed in, worries leaping out, fears looming large. I tried to shove those worries and fears aside and lock them away so I could focus, but they kept finding ways to set themselves free.

Béata.

Memories were everywhere, ones I cherished and loved, and those jumped out at me like a dog delighted I'd come home. Warm summer afternoons lying in the shady grass of the forest, watching birds dance about amongst the leaves. The bright red dress my mother made for me on my tenth birthday, and how alive I had felt when wearing it.

But hidden amongst the joy and familiarity were dark places I had never traversed, a murky fog that wriggled its way into everything.

The voice that called my name, though, it came from those shadows. There was no mistaking that.

I opened my eyes and leapt to my feet, startled.

The voice came from somewhere within. These recent days had been too full of tears and pain to learn what that meant. I smoothed down my dress. Adjusted my hair until it was tamed. Watched as a bird hopped along the roof of a nearby house. Life had a habit, lately, of throwing rivers at me that required a bridge to cross. This was one more bridge, but I could build it another day. I could build it tomorrow. Today, I wanted nothing more than to be with my family.

The streets grew more and more busy as I made my way home – slowly, each step a drag. I had resolved to think no more of that strange voice, only of family and hope and love. But it was everywhere I looked. In every doorway. Down every side street. Resting on the branch of every tree. As people emptied from buildings or made their way in from the fields for the day, the hubbub of noise and chatter grew loud enough to drown out my thoughts until I was forced to think of each step, to turn sideways to avoid that cart, to apologize for elbowing that woman in the side. My breathing grew shallow, forcing me to pause every few steps to catch my breath. I had told myself to stay calm, to ground myself in happiness and familiarity, but fear had found its way in and sprung up into something great and terrible.

Anyone who recognized me gave me a wide berth, that cursed look of sympathy plastered on to their faces, but to everyone else I was just another body taking up space on the street. Someone to push aside. To avoid. I preferred it that way.

Two mothers spoke quietly to one another, each with a hand firmly on their child's shoulder. The children chatted, too, close enough that I could hear.

"Mátyás's father said we're cursed," one said, a young

boy with a wooden horse in his hands. He stared at it while he spoke. The girl's face turned white. "He said this is how the gods punish us, by letting the underworld in. Eventually, the darkness of the castle will take over all of Marcosza, and we'll be gone." He snapped his fingers. "Just like that."

"I want to leave, then," the girl said, her voice shaky as though on the brink of tears.

"You can't," the boy told her. "You can't get away fast enough."

I spun around to say something, but someone pushed past me, momentarily jolting away my attention. Feeling a strange weight in my hand, I looked down to find a tiny, folded piece of paper in my grasp. I looked around the busy street to see who had bumped into me, but it was impossible to tell with so many bodies milling about.

I turned my shoulder away so no one nearby could see, and I slowly unfolded the note.

I know where I've seen you before. I saw you in the rain. We must speak soon. Meet me later today, where the stream forks, beyond the birch glen. – Benedek

The busy street disappeared. The children's voices faded into silence. The daylight vanished, the sun withered, and the only sensation known to me was the pounding of my heart, as though it might escape my chest.

I had been seen.

I had been seen.

Slowly, the memory of the boy in the trees as I had left the castle all those many years ago came crawling back, and a shiver danced along my spine.

The voice in my head called again.

The vision I'd had that I was certain couldn't be mine came rushing back.

My dance in the rain felt as recent as if it had happened yesterday.

And in the space of a heartbeat, it was all too much.

I crumpled up the paper into my pocket, turned, and ran through the street as fast as I could force my shaking body to move. I did not stop running until the dense brush of the old forest surrounded me, and I dropped to the ground, out of breath.

Chapter Nine

Liljana

The coast was wild and unruly. The closest Miloš could bring me to land was a short swim from the slippery rocks that climbed up and disappeared into the hills. The water was frigid, and I swam as quickly as I could, keenly worried of what might be reaching for my heels beneath the dark waves. I had never swum before, but as Miloš pushed me from the boat, he had shouted, "You will figure it out! Everyone does!"

I stood watching as the boat grew smaller and smaller in the distance, back towards Tăru and everything I'd once known. Spray from a wave landed on my skin. I shivered, both cold and excited like I had never been before. Miloš's company had been at least some small bit of familiarity, another voice, someone to speak to.

Now I turned to face the rich green Hills of Ariu that separated me from Marcosza, and I sighed. I knew nothing about them, how to cross them, what lay within them, but each step would be a step closer to peace. To safety. To building the life for mages that Miha and I had always deserved. But first lay evil, and the unknown. The air seemed colder suddenly, as the knowledge of what awaited me sank in. There hadn't been many things to make Petre go pale, but he had, when he'd told me of the castle.

I breathed in. Like Petre, I would play what part I could in this story for as long as may be, until the task fell to someone else.

A warm breeze hit me, and for a moment, I felt at peace.

Behind me, back in the Bay of Morţa, the boat was almost too small to see any more. Miloš was gone. Tăru was nothing more than a memory. And before me stretched adventure.

The thick trees set in almost immediately past the coast. The land rose and fell sharply, the Hills climbing ever higher towards the sky. Each climb left me wildly out of breath, and each descent nearly saw me tumbling along the earth. The way would have been much easier had the ground not been blanketed in shrubs and vines that sought to throw me from my feet at every step. I picked my way along, sometimes slower than the marketplace at high noon, and sometimes swiftly when the forest opened up and the only things to dodge were the large trunks of trees that stretched up to the sky. Here and there, I came to a clear path that was well worn by years of travel, but I crossed it and slipped back into the underbrush.

I knew little about the Hills, but it was common knowledge that the Ashen walked these ways. Those paths belonged to them – I could feel it in my magical bones. Their hate and evil had curdled the air in their wake, the stench so strong I held my breath for a moment.

So I kept out of sight, watching every step, stopping now and then to look and listen and ensure I was still alone.

Roşesti had been my life. Out here, birds sang, rabbits scurried between bushes, bugs landed on my skin and flew away. Everything was alive, moving, breathing. Despite having lived in a city of thousands, somehow out here I felt less alone than before. Branches creaked. Spiderwebs stuck to my face as I slipped by. Disturbed moss at my feet sent an earthy aroma into the air I'd never smelled before. It was a new world, unfamiliar and beautiful in every way.

By the time the sun reached the top of the sky, I realized I'd given little thought to food. My stomach grumbled as I made my way along, and I contemplated the dangers of transforming something in my current state of sleepless exhaustion. In the land of the Ashen, my wits were my defence.

Though starvation would do me little good.

So I stopped and found a solid rock, took in a few deep breaths, and called on that fire hidden within me to transform it into bread. The loaf felt heavy, and smelled freshly baked. My stomach grew louder, so I picked at it and ate slowly as I walked, my eyes heavy with tiredness after using my precious reserves of magic. Despite the strangeness of this forest, I required sleep, or the rocky start to this journey would have been all for naught.

When I'd eaten half the loaf, I came to an area of dense shrubs that bore large, heart-shaped leaves. It would do as well as anywhere else, so I crawled inside and wrapped my green cloak around me. Passing eyes would never notice my presence without looking for it, and it would offer enough shelter for a quick sleep. I kept my eyes forward, afraid if I looked too closely around me I would notice what other leggy creatures had made this underbrush their home.

The shadows shifted as the day wore on, and one moment I was still staring, wondering if sleep would ever find me, and the next, I opened my eyes to find the world had gone dark. The day had slipped by while I slept, slumped over on my side with my shoulder against the stump of an ancient tree that had probably toppled over a century ago. Still waking, I stared at its large, gnarled shadow against the dark forest, wondering distantly what had felled it. One of Miloš's gargantuan shapes, perhaps, or a battle had been fought here by people we'd never know about. Or perhaps it had simply died and fallen in a summer storm, and lain wasting away ever since.

With no sounds but insects nearby, I crawled slowly,

stiffly from the underbrush and stretched my aching limbs. It had been far from comfortable, but I'd slept as soundly as if I'd climbed into the king's bed and nestled down among his layers of furs. Now, with my sore body and chill bones, the thought of a comfortable bed sent a jolt of longing through me like a kick in the stomach.

With no buildings or street signs to use as guidance, I soon learned the difficulty of finding my way through the forest and remembering which way I'd come. In the end, the fallen tree was my only landmark – it had been on my left when I had arrived, if I remembered correctly, so I set it to my left once more and picked my way through the trees more slowly than before. In the dark, the sound of critters scampering away set my heart to racing every time, and I'd stop and stare into nothingness until there was only silence left.

An owl called nearby, sounding so like a person I froze and waited. It called again, then the beat of wings signalled its departure. I let out a breath and slumped my shoulders.

I had managed to escape a city filled with guards hunting me like an animal. I'd survived my whole life in a land that grew more and more hostile to those who bore magic. I had survived, over and over again, when the world had tried to crush me. This forest would be no different. I stood taller, shook the dirt and leaves from my cloak, and smoothed loose hairs away from my face. I had at least one tool at my disposal: magic. I was rested and ready, though I'd need to be careful when choosing a time to use it. The journey ahead of me was still long.

The ground beneath my feet grew sodden and cold, the nearby sound of a creek reaching me through the trees. The earth stank of rotting vegetation and stagnant water, and my boots were soon soaked through.

Something snapped.

I stopped walking, staring down at my feet as though I could see more than a few inches from my face. The sound hadn't come from below me, but then again, it could have bounced off the trees and come back from a distance. The forest, it would seem, enjoyed playing tricks.

I waited, unmoving.

Underbrush rustled nearby. Footsteps, or a rabbit? I'd heard too many creatures since entering this forest to believe it might be anything other than human. They were definitely footsteps now, in quick succession, one after the other, drawing nearer and nearer. I could move to hide behind a tree, but the sound of my movement would only draw attention. So I stood perfectly still, staring into the darkness, my hand on the stick I carried at my waist.

A figure, barely more than a piece of the blackness around me that moved of its own accord, came into view. The footsteps changed from the rustling of shrubs to the squelching of the swamp. I drew the stick from my belt and held it out, ready to transform it.

A body brushed against my hand, and a yelp rang out. My magesense flared to life.

"Be quiet!" I hissed to the figure, still veiled by darkness. "Who are you?"

"Who are *you*?" The voice of a young man.

"Answer me first."

He hesitated. "My – my name is Marek. I don't mean any harm. I'm just trying to cross the Hills."

I didn't answer for a moment, my hand still closed tight around my stick. "Why?"

"I have my reasons." I heard the shuffling of clothing, and the sound of rocking back and forth from one foot to the other, as though the evening chill had got to him.

"Are you alone?"

"Just me, I'm afraid." Sadness tinged his voice.

A subtle sting ran along the arm closest to him again, and I stood up straighter. "Are you a mage?"

He was silent for a long while. "Y-yes. How did you know?"

"I can feel it."

"Ah. I thought that was only the cold."

"It isn't that cold."

He sniffed and said nothing.

"Where are you headed?"

"I'm not certain. Away from Roşesti. That's all I know. I'll slip through Marcosza, perhaps. Into Sovažska, maybe. Hell, I'll take a boat across the Waters of Hlór and disappear into the frozen wastes of Kölm if I have to. I just want to get away."

The edge of desperation in his voice rang out all too familiar. I lowered the stick and quietly hung it back at my waist. "From Tăru?"

"Segrata. Maybe an hour's ride from the city. The Ashen burned down a number of our homes a few days ago. I left with two others, but they were picked off along the way. I'm the only one left." Sadness weighed his voice down, deep and dark and endless. I knew that kind of sorrow. Years ago it had been little more than a seed, but now it'd grown roots and vines that split my bones and worked to strangle me.

"Well." I fiddled with the cloth of my trousers, eager to be off again. "I wish you good fortune on your journey. These hills are far from safe, but they're on the road to safety, I hear."

He was quiet for a long moment, shifting about uncertainly. "Why can we not travel together?"

I bristled. "We don't have the same destination. There's little to be gained."

"Just until we cross the hills. Strength in numbers. I'm not even certain where I'm going. Just anywhere out of Roşesti. Anywhere has to be better than here. I'm a Ruiner, by the way – well, I could be a Ruiner. I can start fires and crack stones, with great effort. If the Orders hadn't disappeared from the world I'd have sought training to make it useful. What's your skill?"

I sighed, leaning from one foot to the other, and back again. "Alterer. And I would prefer to travel alone. I'm not friendly. I do not have friends." Miha's death, Petre's death, the captain of the guard I had killed to get away, any sort of closeness to other people, at least for me, seemed to lead only to heartbreak or trouble. I would get into Marcosza, do what Petre had told me to do, and I would do it with my own two hands. No one else's.

"No one said we have to be friends."

"You so clearly want a friend, or protection at the very least. You go your way, Marek, and I'll go mine. All the best to you on your journey. I hope Sovažska treats you better than our own land." I took a few steps away from him, the land growing solid once more.

"Please," he said softly, and I heard tears in his voice. "I don't wish to be alone. It was never meant to be this way. We were all to travel together."

I flicked an insect from my face. "You can't find the extent of your strength, Marek, if you've always someone to lean on. Now is your chance. Do great things with the opportunity you've been given." I hurried away before he could say anything more.

Hours later, when the rushing of the Somis River rang out for miles all around and the lights of the Ashen illuminated the only bridge across it, I wondered if perhaps I'd been too stubborn when I had denied Marek my company.

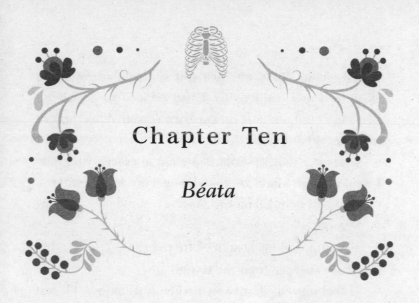

Chapter Ten

Béata

The rain started during the night, and by morning had become a downpour. I stared out at it, wondering how we might know the difference between the usual summer rains and the spreading of the deadly rains. I tried not to, but I felt as though I saw it out my window. I saw the raindrops falling on friends and neighbours. Saw them falling to the street, never again to rise. I saw all of Zírany as nothing more than a ghost town, talked about around the world, written about in books but utterly forsaken.

But the birds still moved about, and the streets still held the occasional drenched passer-by. Just rain. Normal rain. Nothing more.

I couldn't point to a specific moment when I'd decided

what I would do. It was just sort of there, in my head, all formed and ready to go. I had decided to meet with Benedek. Find out how he knew my secret. When he had seen me. What I could do about it.

And after that, I would figure out in exactly what way I would rescue Marcosza from the evil inside the castle.

A knock sounded on my door.

"Come in."

Father poked his head in. "Are you joining us?" A kind jibe at my absence from the tavern.

"I feel unwell," I answered without thinking. "I'll rest today, if it won't be an inconvenience."

He sent me a half-hearted smile. "Of course not."

The door closed softly.

Although my attic room was high, I had learned years ago that if I carefully hoisted myself out the window, I could wedge my toes on to a certain beam that offered just enough width to support me, and from there I could push off, with great care, to reach the branch of a tree that was not otherwise accessible. This feat could only be accomplished under the guise of rain – safe, ordinary rain – for our tavern had the misfortune of being off one of the busier streets in the town, with enough eyes that would make any hope of going unnoticed impossible. Night would be better, of course, but that was out of the question.

I left a note on my pillow, partially hidden. If they worried and came looking for me, they would find it, but if things changed and I returned soon, I could dispose of it without them ever knowing. It was simple, because I didn't know how this day would end. I knew how I wanted it to end – with me storming the castle and not leaving until we had rid the world of its evil – but that was unlikely.

I am well. Please do not worry. I have something I must do. I will return soon. I promise. Love, Béata

I tied on my old boots and debated staying home. But then I braced myself for the chill of the rain, and I carefully pushed open the window.

Slowly, I eased myself out, and, after closing the window as much as I dared, without preventing myself from getting back in, I began to lower myself down. Within seconds, my right foot slipped, and I dug my nails into the ledge to keep from falling all the way to the ground. Rainwater poured from the leaves of the tree as I jumped and caught the branch, finding its way into my hood and down my neck. The cold made me shiver, but I clung to the branch as tightly as I could, as I fought for footing on the slippery tree. My heart thundered; I saw myself tumbling to the ground, limbs shattering. But after several tries, my boots finally found purchase on a branch just below me, and in a quick movement over which I had very little control, I crouched on to it and leapt to the ground, rolling over a few times in the street.

I lay still for a moment, listening for any footsteps or shouts that might signal someone had heard me, but there was only the rain beating against the cobblestones. No faces came to my window, and no nearby doors opened to investigate the commotion. When I was certain it was safe, I climbed to my feet, adjusted the leather bag and hurried off in the direction of the forest.

The moment I entered the relative shelter of the trees, the rain lessened somewhat – or, rather, the myriad raindrops became large, cold droplets that fell from the trees when the leaves grew too heavy. I shook out my cloak and kept well away from the river, the ground around it thick with mud. I followed the sound of it instead, letting it guide me along in the darkened forest where little sunlight found its way through the storm clouds and treetops. The feeling of darkness and vulnerability, of anything unseen having the freedom to quietly slink up behind me, made my footsteps faster and clumsier.

Though I worked to fight off thoughts of demons and shadows from the castle moving silently through the trees, breathing down my neck, reaching out for me in the dark, they found their way in. More than once, I jumped and turned to look behind me, convinced of a whispering voice or a cold hand brushing mine, but there was only ever trees and falling rain.

It wasn't just talk of the castle that had instilled in us a fear of the dark. No, my people had enough grim stories to tell around harvest time fires to give pause to even the most stalwart among us. My mind drifted, as the call of a bird cracked the air, to thoughts of the nitraka, an eyeless blackbird said to eat young children. I was no child, but the gruesome thought hung sharp in my mind, a warning to keep my wits about me.

Some of the shadows seemed to depart the nearby trees, moving towards me and then away in the filtered light, a phantom taunt that left me chilled.

As I drew closer to our meeting spot, a sort of premature defensiveness sparked to life. Benedek seemed nice enough. Smiling. Friendly. Not someone I had any particular reason not to trust. Except that he knew my most carefully guarded, heavy secret that I thought only I had carried all these years. And with that secret, he carried the power to destroy me. Or at the very least, the power to put me into harm's way. What would the village say if they found out? Suspicion would grow, because for reasons unbeknownst to me, the rains saw fit to spare my life. Anger would rise that I had long known this, and had done nothing to save others. Done nothing to collect the bodies piling up in the grass.

And what if Benedek did not understand the importance of such a secret? What if no one but me could fully understand the guilt, the pull, the need to use such a gift as being able to survive the rains to put an end to our nightmare?

I want to.

I have to.

I need to.

I thought of a hundred ways to explain myself, but those doubts melted away the moment I saw him again.

My feet slowed as I entered the birch glen. He stood waiting, leaning against a large tree, a long, dark overcoat reaching to his knees, and what hair was long enough to be tamed was tied atop his head. A light flashed, a match being struck, and a lantern in his hands flickered to life. In the dim light and shadows cast by the flame, his eyes were pools of darkness.

"There's no one else?" he asked, looking behind me and holding the lantern aloft.

"Yes, I beat a drum on my way out of town," I answered drily.

He shot me a look through narrowed eyes, then beckoned for me to follow him to where some large rocks ran down to the water. Between one rock and a fallen log stood a makeshift tent, small but relatively dry, and lit by a second lantern. The ground was covered with blankets, and a few satchels of books sat in a pile.

I slowly followed him inside, torn between wishing to be close to someone after the dark journey through the forest, and sense telling me to keep my distance from a stranger.

He dropped to the ground and sat cross-legged, clapping his hands together in a way far too chipper for the moment. "I know my note must have caught you off guard, and I am sorry for that. These are desperate times." He shrugged.

"We can get into that, but how about I put something out there first, eh? To show you I mean you no harm."

I tried to speak, but stopped, unsure. I hadn't expected this.

He pulled a sketchbook out of a leather bag, the same sketchbook I'd seen him with in my father's tavern. He threw a glance briefly over his shoulder as his fingers unwound the twine keeping it shut, and handed it to me. I bristled slightly at his closeness, but moved my eyes to the sketchbook. "I can trust in your discretion, I should hope," he said softly, searching my face. "As you can trust in mine."

I met his gaze without wavering, finding only honesty and hope written there. Relief, warm and assuring, began to wash over me. I took in a long breath, and nodded.

He opened the sketchbook to a page filled with drawings, all of which looked to be of the interior of a grand building. Long halls. Rooms with painted walls hung with tapestries. Arched doors carved with the crest of Marcosza. A drawbridge, and a courtyard.

My heart flickered, whispering with a growing certainty that I knew these halls. I did not know how, but every corner, every door frame was familiar to me. The castle. It was undeniably the inside of the castle. Questions rushed in. How had Benedek come to have such intimate knowledge of a place he couldn't have been? Unless he too could walk through the rains. Excitement pierced me at the thought, but he was still a stranger. . .

"Are you planning to build a house?" I asked.

He let his head loll to one side, casting me a look through his eyelashes. "Charmed as I am by your wit, no, I'm afraid not. It is the castle."

"The castle," I repeated, eyeing the drawings to pull my attention away from him.

Benedek turned a leaf over to show a map of hallways, all with startling detail that made my breath catch, locations of doors and great statues, positions where guards used to stand. "I can see it all, up here," he said, tapping his temple once. "I've been there, I know, but at the same time, I know I haven't. Perhaps I entered it once, and my mind made me forget. Or perhaps it was a vivid dream I can't forget. Whatever it is, it is consuming. Overwhelming. It eats away at my mind until there's nothing left."

His voice had taken on such a heaviness, such a weight, that all my worries and thorns melted away. Tormented, that's what he was. Tormented – and I knew what that was like.

"I can see it, so clearly." He stared off towards the river. "I see myself walking the halls; I see the door to the throne room, ornately carved with the scene of an ancient battle. The stairs down to the kitchens, winding and narrow, with one arched window that looks out over the river. I see the statue of King Gasper, and the flag of Marcosza hanging in the Great Hall. But I don't see myself entering, or leaving. Whatever devilry is at work in the castle has robbed me of my memory, and I can't find it again."

Eyes returning to the sketchbook, he turned a leaf over once more, to a drawing of the great throne, wolves carved into the arms, and a cushion of rich green velvet. Each detail was so vivid, so stark.

I pushed the book away suddenly, startling him a bit. I hardly knew this boy. He'd been right earlier: these were desperate times. People would do anything to get inside the castle. Some to stop the evil, and some just for the reward. Surely I was being drawn in by a good face and a gentle wit that pulled at me in all the right ways. How he smiled sideways, like he was suppressing things I desperately wanted to hear. The way his eyes searched mine sometimes, as though trying to truly understand my thoughts and words, not just hear them. I had managed to survive by trusting only myself, and I could not let that change now.

"Your note said you saw me in the rain. I need you to explain that, or I will have to leave." I laced my fingers together and spun my thumbs around one another. "We haven't the luxury of trust in this world."

He sighed and closed the book, holding my gaze. "I did see you," he said softly. "I've never spoken of it. Even now it feels wrong, a secret I've sat on for years and years." He glanced out of the tent and into the rain. A shiver ran over me at the reminder, searching the trees for a rabbit or a squirrel to be sure the killing rains were still far away. "I came with my father to this town when I was a boy. He had trade to do with a local. I can't remember who. Everyone always talked about the castle, so I snuck away when he was busy to see it for myself. I remember thinking how large it was, but unimpressive. I suppose I'd always pictured black stones and red eyes, devils slithering about." He laughed a little, barely shrugging his shoulders. "I didn't have the nerve to leave the trees, but I saw you. I saw you go in. I saw you crouch over a body. I saw you dance about like it was a summer festival. And I saw you see me before you left, silently, your dress soaked and your shoulders shivering."

I stared at him. Stared at his lips that had just spoken the words. At his face that watched mine, awaiting a response. He *had* seen me. No one else would know that I danced. "How did you know it was me?" I whispered, and then found my voice. "In the tavern. How did you know that I was the girl from the rain?"

His lips twitched thoughtfully to one side. "I can't say, really. I just did. Something in me recognized you. That's all I can say. And I know how that sounds."

I took the sketchbook from his hands and leafed through a few pages, marvelling at the detail. Distracting myself. How foolish I felt about the dance now, more than before. It was so long ago, but why had I done it?

"A good storyteller," I said, handing the sketchbook back to him. "That's all you might be. I can't know if these are true to life without having seen the castle myself, you know."

He took the book and ran a hand over the cover. "There

is little I can do to offer proof," he acknowledged, any tinge of confidence gone from his voice. "But I saw you in the rain. I could think of no one better to tell. Other people with secrets seem like the best to tell secrets to."

Every bit of me wanted it to be true. Someone with knowledge of the castle, someone who could work with me to find a way in, to bring an end to all of this. Yet there was such a thing as too perfect, and this reeked of it. The castle's trickery at work, perhaps, luring me to my death. What could be believed at a time like this?

"I thought... Well, I suppose I hoped, though I have little by way of a plan, that— What I mean to say is, you can walk through the rain, and I *somehow* know the castle. It seems a bit like we ought to combine our efforts, don't you think? If not us, then who?"

I looked away towards the river, though I couldn't see it. "Béata?"

"Yes." I turned back to him. "I just... I can't know if I can trust you. I can't. How could I? I've spent so many years thinking this secret was mine, and mine alone, and trying to figure out how to use it for the good of the country, and now here we are, talking about it as though it had never been a secret at all, and I do not know how to feel about that."

"I can give you only one reason to trust me," he said quietly. "That it's been six years since I saw you in the rains, and I have never breathed a word to anyone."

I watched his face, and he stared back at me,

121

unflinching. The intensity of a thousand thoughts pressed behind his eyes, and I wanted to hear each and every one.

"How can I know that?"

He scoffed a little. "Do you not think you would have been hunted down by now? Used as a tool for someone else to enter the castle? Especially now, with the reward. You would not be free, as you are. You know that as well as I do." He snapped a twig between his fingers. "There are enough hungry, desperate people in this land to find your . . . gift desirable." He threw both pieces of the stick out of the tent. "I'd never do anything like that."

"*You* find it desirable," I reminded him, a little harshly. "I can survive the rains, so you sought me out like a priestess for a blessing. How is you using me any different than anyone else using me?"

Benedek had to think for a moment. "I don't know you, Béata, even if I feel like I do. Of course we're all a little selfishly motivated, but it's not like I'm trying to break into the castle to take the throne. My mother could use the reward money, certainly, but I . . . I *have* to get in. I can't stop seeing its rooms and passageways. They're everywhere I look, in everything, even at home. At night I dream of it. By day it follows me around. Maybe it's calling to me. Maybe it's signalling me somehow. I'll never know if I don't go in."

Questions rose on my tongue, but now did not feel like the right time to ask them.

"I believe you," I said firmly. "I believe you. It won't be easy. Whatever is in the castle has grown stronger, and surviving the rain will not mean much once I'm inside, but I think we can work together."

He brushed the hair from his face and smiled, holding out a hand to me. The smile was deep and genuine, lighting up his dark eyes like I hadn't seen before. A warmth blossomed between us, and all the weight of our secrets lessened until we could finally breathe again. "You are the girl who can walk in the rain, and I am the boy who knows the way. We ought to be unstoppable."

His words were light-hearted, but given what I knew of the castle, no part of me believed them.

Our conversation fell towards entering the castle, wandering now and then as he explained some room or hall, and where it led, and I asked questions I didn't directly need answers to, just because I loved the way his eyes lit up when he was talking.

"But what I don't know," I said presently, staring at nothing, "is how you would get in, if you cannot survive the rains."

He tilted his head, thoughtfully. "I have thoughts about that, but they're unclear. Foggy. I think there's something I'm not remembering, but I'm trying to find it. It's up here somewhere." He tapped his temple a few times. "And if I'm wrong, then all I can do is arm you with knowledge of the castle. If it's as riddled with dark magic as the rumours say it is, then it will try to trip you up before you've cleared the main door. I can help you with that, I think. Tell you where to go. Where to hide. Hidden hallways. That sort of thing."

Once again, I flipped through Benedek's sketchbook, musing aloud at various details, questioning him when something struck me, or just silently taking it in.

"Béata."

"Yes?"

Benedek looked up at me. "What?"

"You. . ." I swallowed. "Didn't you just say my name?"

He shook his head. "No. And I don't think anyone else did, either." He looked around us to be sure.

I breathed deeply and set aside the sketchbook, closing my eyes.

"Béata."

What?

"Béata." When I focused, there it was again, inside, hidden amidst the fog that haunted my mind. *Béata, time is running out. The evil is growing. You* must *find me.*

My eyes shot open. Benedek sat watching me, curious, but respectfully quiet.

Time is running out.

Until what? My hands shook. I shut my eyes again.

Béata. I wished they'd stop using my name. *Follow my voice. Be swift. Your time is almost up. You cannot enter the castle without my help. They took your brother. Do not forget that. You must follow my voice.*

"How could I forget that?" I screamed out loud. Benedek jumped. "I'm sorry." I closed my eyes again. *Am I going mad?* I wondered, trembling. Between the vision I'd had back in town, and now the voice I could not escape, doubt began to take hold.

I don't know who you are. I will not send myself into the unknown when the castle is so close at hand.

If you enter the castle without my help, you will die.

I swallowed. Breathed in, and back out.

Follow the voice. To where? To the castle? Was this the devil's work, trying to lure in another soul to murder? If it was the devil, it didn't sound like I'd imagined. It was a gentle voice, with a hint of well-meaning and honesty. And when I really listened, it didn't come from the direction of the castle, which, from where we sat, lay due east. The more I listened, the more it pulled my face to the north.

Hurry. You need my help.

How could I think to do this? How could I think of setting off into the wilderness in search of a voice that existed only within the confines of my mind? But, I told myself, though we had good intentions, Benedek and I still had hardly anything resembling a plan. And though leaving to find the voice might delay our entering the castle, would that not be better than simply diving in to our deaths? What if this person truly *could* help us? I would be foolish to deny us that help.

"I have to leave." The words came out suddenly,

thoughtlessly. I couldn't remember the decision to speak them, yet there they were, ringing out through the air around us. I was going. I was going, and that was that.

Benedek leaned back, his head tilted again. "To go where?"

I swallowed, and traced a finger along my boot. "I don't know, exactly. There's someone I have to find. Someone. . ." I tapped my head a few times with one finger, keenly aware of the foolishness haunting my words. "Someone up here. I must have met them before, or heard them somewhere. I can hear their voice. I think they can help. I can't wait any longer."

Benedek stared at me, his mouth open. "Béata, that. . . You – you, uh. . ." Falling silent for a moment, he let his hair down, then smoothed it back up into a knot. Lantern light flickered in his dark blue eyes, darting all about the tent to everything but me. "When shall we leave?" His eyes twinkled.

The question caught me off guard. He'd been about to chastise me, or question my rationality, I was sure of it. "That's – that's all you have to say?"

He shrugged and laced his fingers together. "I've heard far stranger things these past few years. If there's someone you think can help us get into the castle, then we would be foolish not to take it. The gods know we'll need it."

I could think of nothing to say. The silence stretched away for several long minutes.

"How certain are you that you can find this person?"

"Not terribly."

"How long of a journey?"

"I can't say."

"Do you have a name?"

"I don't."

His head tilted to one side, and he cast me a look beneath furrowed eyebrows. "You inspire little confidence, you know. Perhaps lie to me next time."

"I never agreed to let you come."

"Oh, I'm coming. There's little use in splitting up when we've already agreed to work together."

I smiled a little facetiously. "Look at you, speaking as someone with authority you don't have. If I wish to go alone, Benedek, I will go alone." My voice carried the edge of a freshly sharpened knife — just to be safe. I had agreed to work with him on entering the castle, but though his smiles and kindness made him feel like an old friend, I had to remind myself that I had only just met him.

He leaned towards me, resting his elbows on his knees. "Béata." There was something captivating in the way he said my name, the gentle lilt of an accent from another region, the heaviness of his tired voice. "How badly do you wish to set off from your hometown and seek a stranger in the wilds beyond this forest?" A laugh that was more like a quick rush of air, sceptical. "You may go, of course, and I won't follow you, but I could help you, be your companion, someone to speak with, another set of eyes to watch the road when you are tired. Can you really, truly, turn that down?"

I sighed, long and slow. I hated to be alone, deep down. I'd never truly had to be. There had always been Filep, and Alíz, and Mother and Father; the tavern was always filled with people. And when no one else was around, I would sometimes speak to our cat and imagine he spoke back. The only true loneliness I'd ever known was the secret I carried with me always: that I could walk in the rain, when others could not.

"I don't know how long we'll be away." I spun a loose bit of hair around my finger absently.

Silence closed in. Presently, I mused, "The day is getting on. It must be close to noon. If we leave, it must be soon. We will need distance between us and the castle before nightfall."

Benedek drew in a long breath and climbed to his feet. "Then off we go!" He sounded far too excited for such a grim time. "No time to waste."

"Wait," I said, patting the ground again. "You can see the castle in your head. You don't know why. I understand that. I understand that you want to lay your worries about it to rest. But you mentioned your mother. Said she could use the reward. Why?"

He sat slowly back down, staring off through the trees. For a moment, I regretted asking, but it felt important. A layer of him worth knowing if we were to work together.

He plucked at a loose thread on his trousers. "She gave a lot to care for me. It's long past time I returned the favour."

There was far more to the story. The weight of it hung between us. "Where's your father?"

"Gone."

"Dead?"

"No. Yes. I don't know. Maybe."

"I don't understand."

"He left five years ago for a trip to Anastadt. A trader. Everyone told him not to take the Wöernz Pass so close to winter, but he said it was faster. The worst part is that we'll never know if he died, or if he just decided life was better in Anastadt. I hear they have nice food and drink, after all."

"I'm sure that's not what happened."

"You don't know. But we were poor after he left. Poor as poor could be. My mother grew skinnier and skinnier, and it took me too long to realize it was because she was giving me her food. This reward from the baron... I mean, I'd do anything to help Marcosza, of course, but the reward could change everything for us. I need it. She needs it."

I lifted a hand to comfort him in some way, but dropped it again.

"I couldn't confide in her about the visions, obviously. She had too much of her own pain and worry to bear. So it's been a weight that's built up all these years, until now, when I feel like I might burst."

I nodded. "I'm sure that was awful."

"Why do you want to do this?" Benedek asked.

"Because the castle took my brother. His body's still out there, just lying in the rain. We can't move it. Well, I could, of course, but then there'd be questions, and I don't have answers."

Benedek nodded solemnly. "I suppose there's no time like right now to set off, then. The rains will wait for no one."

I stood slowly, my limbs sore from sitting on the ground for so long. Somewhere, that voice called to me again. I glanced back in the direction of the town, and though I couldn't see it, longing tugged at my heart. How easy it would be to slip back home, take up my place in the tavern and carry on with life as though nothing had changed.

But everything had changed, and everything would carry on changing. The poisoned rains would soon creep over the tavern, the one place in the world that had ever felt quiet and safe. Death had come calling for Filep. Soon it would come calling for us all. Our corner of the world would ring out with cries and screams, until the last echo had vanished into oblivion. And I was sure there were only two souls on this earth who stood even the smallest chance of stopping it. So I squared my shoulders, set my back to the town, and struck off through the trees.

Chapter Eleven

Liljana

I sat cross-legged on a stump in a particularly dense part of the forest on the opposite side of the river from the Ashen. Now and then, I'd see one of their forms pacing the bridge, a torch in one hand and a spear in the other, clearly hoping to catch mages as they tried to flee from the king's decree. I dug a fingernail deep into the wood, itching to get my hands on the patrol if it wouldn't cost me my life.

The bridge was the only way across the river and into Marcosza. I had walked up and down the bank a good long way, only to find white, rushing water in both directions without any hint that it might settle if I walked further. It crashed around large boulders and thundered through ravines, cut through rocks that begged to break my bones.

So the bridge was the only way. And the Ashen clearly knew it. Either I would find a way to cross it, I would journey along the river for who knew how long until I hopefully found somewhere calm enough to swim across, or I would abandon this journey and return to Tăru to live out what precious few days remained to me.

I hated each option open to me.

So I sat, and I sat, and I sat, half expecting something to change, or a fourth option to smack me in the face. Deep down, I suspected I was waiting for nightfall, when my chances would improve, if only slightly, but I had nothing by way of a plan. With so much time to rest, and magic simmering in my veins, I transformed my cloak from green to black to better blend in with the night, in preparation for whatever I was about to do. When I grew tired again, the green would return, but I'd have a few hours at least.

Clouds had covered the sky all day, so nightfall came early with the sun hidden behind them. When the darkness had settled in, wrapping itself around everything and bathing the river in shadow, I slipped off the stump, stretched my legs, and made my way slowly along the water towards the bridge. The lights of the Ashen encampment across the Somis River flickered, branches of trees swaying before them, the occasional outline of a body moving about. Every so often, when the breeze was just right, I heard the echo of a voice over the rushing water. Each time it sent a talon tearing along my spine.

I stopped walking maybe thirty yards from the bridge, well-hidden between two large trees that bent oddly over the water. Another patrolling Ashen wandered the wooden planks of the bridge, a torch in one hand, a sword in the other. His ash-grey cloak swayed behind him, the stride of a lazy, careless man out for a walk with little to fear. My fingernails dug so far into my palms they threatened to draw blood.

"Who goes there?"

I froze in place. I hadn't moved to begin with, and my cloak hung limp around me. What could have given me away? A sudden worry gripped me that perhaps they might have a captive mage who could sense me so near, or that I had failed to notice a scout wandering on this side of the river – but the man was not looking at me. His eyes were focused on some dense shrubs on the other side of the road that led to the bridge, and even without seeing anyone, my heart sank.

I knew who it was.

Bodies swarmed on to the bridge, a sea of torches and shouts coming this way. *They still haven't seen you,* I reminded myself, standing perfectly still. *They still haven't seen you. Do not run. You'll give yourself away.* But panic gripped me at the sight of an angry swarm of the Ashen running towards me, swords and spears at the ready. My legs shook with the desire to flee, but I knew even if I used every ounce of magic my untrained body could hold, it would never be enough to free me. Not from people whose only purpose was to destroy mages. The only defence I had left was to remain unseen, so I shrank against the tree trunk, my face hidden behind a branch full of leaves, and I watched.

They pulled Marek out of the brush like a baby bird from the nest, so roughly his feet left the ground. He screamed and writhed around, but they held him fast, all arrows and spears pointed directly at him.

I ached to help him, but I was sure that if I did, then we'd both die. There was no way around that. Either Marek died, or we both died. I told myself that over and over again, but it didn't take away the ache of guilt that nearly made me vomit – the harsh and unrelenting reminder of how I'd had to leave Miha behind, even though she had already been killed. *What if I had arrived at the castle sooner? Would it have been enough time to save her?*

"Where you running off to?" one of the men asked Marek, holding a knife against his neck. "What do you think waits for you in the north?"

"I just wanted to be free and away from you," Marek pleaded between sobs. "It isn't fair. It isn't fair."

"I don't understand. You didn't even try to use your magic to hide. Do you want to die?" another man asked.

"No, he's just a whelp. One of those untrained pups who couldn't work magic if their life depended on it. And his does! Pity."

Marek sobbed again.

An inkling of an idea tickled the back of my mind, but the thought of it made the ache even greater. I could use the capture of Marek as a distraction. The only other options left to me were to turn back and give up, or try to free him. Those both led to death. If I made a run for it, at least I stood the smallest chance of surviving.

But I was also Marek's only hope.

It was time to pick my poison.

I stood straighter, ready to run – but before I took a step, Marek looked directly at me.

He could sense my magic.

"Aren't you going to help me?" he shouted through tears.

My stomach clenched. The shriek of terror in his voice was almost too much – almost. It was now or never, help him or leave him, and I knew that this decision would haunt me for the rest of my life. I didn't want another mage to die, not if I could help it.

But my job was not yet done.

If I waited another second, the Ashen surrounding him would have enough time to understand his meaning and come for me. My only window of hope was in this moment, before they learned of my presence. I needed them confused and uncertain, and maybe even a little disturbed at the thought of two mages so close together.

So without giving it another thought, I departed from the trees and ran as if the ground was straw and a wildfire chased my heels. The shouts and yells and cries from

Marek all melted together, lights from torches blurring and the rushing of the river little more than a dull roar somewhere far away. I ran and ran and ran, bodies looming before me, hands reaching out for me. An arrow whizzed by my ear and clattered somewhere on to the stone. And then the end of the bridge was before me, and the trees closed around me, and the only sound I was aware of was Marek's cries echoing off every trunk in the forest.

But I was free.

It must have been hours before I stopped running. Every muscle ached with a kind of pain I'd never known, and my vision grew so blurred I had to feel around before me with a hand just to keep from walking into trees. My heartbeat thundered in my temples; my lungs were full of sand. Eventually, I fell to the ground and stopped moving. I had no way to know if I was still being pursued – I'd run too frantically to pay any attention to what happened behind me – but I doubted very much that they would put too much manpower behind chasing down one lone mage when they'd already caught another.

Marek.

As my vision returned, I stared up at the trees silhouetted against a greying sky. He was probably dead by now, or soon would be. Could I have saved him, if I'd tried? Probably not. There were so many of them, and only two of us. It would have been little more than a final stand, a show of strength before they put out our fire.

It had to be this way. In my heart, I had promised Petre I would reach Marcosza. Reach their castle. Find what evil was growing within its walls. If I didn't, no mage would ever be safe. Marek shouldn't have had to die. But he had died, which meant that now, more than ever, I had to use my life to save every mage I could. To give them the safety they so deserved.

The trees swayed. The sky grew lighter. Birds began to sing around me, heralding the coming dawn. I should find somewhere safe to hide, I knew that, but my body refused to move. So I lay perfectly still and stared at the sky until a deep, black sleep came over me.

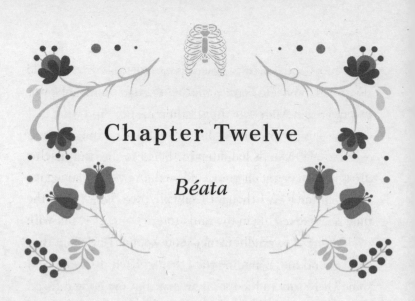

Chapter Twelve

Béata

Deep in the forest, summer had already begun to die away, bringing in the autumn. Tiny, brilliant fires, by way of flaming leaves, had begun to light the trees here and there, while green still clung to life all around. There was beauty everywhere, but also strangeness. There was a stark difference, I noticed quickly, between traversing the woods with the intention of shortly returning home, and traversing the woods with an unfamiliar destination. It made the trees seem wild and odd, and even the sounds of the birds and woodland creatures rang out with a peculiar note.

The shadows were deep and rich, and the large trunks of the trees felt as walls to keep me in. I had always loved the forest, growing up. I recalled thinking that if I could grow roots and leaves and rise up towards the sun, I would do so, and I wouldn't give it another thought. The forest was as peaceful a place as I could think of.

But not today.

As my footsteps led me past the castle, even at such a great distance, the air grew cold, and bumps rose along my arms. At my feet, I thought I saw phantom bodies like the ones that lay rotting in the rain around the castle, but with eyes wide open, watching me. I shut my own eyes, but they were there again when I opened them, rotted still more, and their fleshless mouths begged for me to help them.

The moss-covered rocks became cracked and bloodied skin, fallen logs and branches transformed into decaying limbs, and the dewdrops clinging to leaves and grasses were glassy, unseeing eyes that somehow watched my every footstep. Everything that was gentle and beautiful in the forest around me became something great and terrible, until even the soft call of birds and the singing of nearby bugs was nothing more than garbled screams and final gasps for air. If this was what became of me by merely passing through the forest, what business had I in entertaining thoughts of entering the castle? What would become of me there?

My feet stopped walking, and I turned, almost unbidden, to stare through the trees to my far left. Somehow, though I couldn't think how, I knew I faced the castle, and beyond the endless trees, the cursed shadow of what lay within was watching me. A shiver, small at first, snaked its way down my spine, setting my whole body to trembling.

"Béata?"

Benedek's voice seemed far away.

"I'll return soon," I whispered through the trees. "And I will bring destruction with me." Impossible though it seemed, a gentle breeze in the leaves around me whispered back, *I will be waiting.*

I turned and quickly resumed my walk, holding both hands up to cover my ears. Benedek followed me, asking questions I couldn't hear. Nothing else existed, only one foot in front of the other, the roar of thoughts slowly quieting the further from the castle I walked. I would stop now and then to close my eyes, to listen, to focus on that voice pulling me along. To fix my course if I had strayed too far until the voice was once again loud and clear. But always, the castle worked to cloud my mind, shadows finding their way in, unintelligible voices murmuring by my ear.

What could have been an hour later, I finally stopped. Worry was etched in every line of Benedek's face.

"Are you well?"

"I don't think so."

"What happened?"

"I can't say. I think the castle knows about me. I can feel it sometimes, sensing me."

He ran a finger along his eyebrow, lost in thought. "Do you know if we're headed in the right direction?"

I closed my eyes and reached for that dark fog, listening for the voice that beckoned me. Slowly, I lifted an arm and pointed in the direction I heard it the loudest. It was stronger here than it had been back home. "That way."

Benedek nodded and carried on walking. I followed.

Stripping a leaf from a branch as I passed, I asked, "Ben. Does anyone ever call you that?"

"My father did."

"Should I?"

"No."

"Why not?" I dropped the leaf and grabbed for a new one, realizing suddenly how much I enjoyed the sound of his voice. Smooth, but with an edge that whispered of heavy thoughts and dark memories.

"It reminds me of him."

"Still painful?"

"Still angry."

"Why angry?"

"He had no business dying and leaving us behind."

"I'm not sure it was his fault. People don't know when they're going to die. Not usually."

He scoffed a little. "He didn't have to leave, and he didn't have to take that route. More than one person tried to tell him that." He ran a hand over his hair. "I look like him, I

141

know that, but I hope I don't have half of his stubbornness. As does my mother, I'm sure."

I let a few heartbeats slip by to give him some space. In the quiet moments when we were merely walking without talking, I watched him subtly, wishing to hear him speak again. He was interesting, friendly, and I wanted him to find me interesting, too. I wanted him to be talking when he was quiet, and I wanted to keep him talking when he was.

At any rate, it was a pleasant distraction from every terrible thing that filled the rest of our lives.

"You said he took the Wöernz Pass," I said presently. "I don't know what that is."

"Mountain pass in eastern Anastadt. Cold. Precarious. Perilously high. Slippery. Foolish. Need I go on?"

I brushed my fingertips against his shoulder. "I'm sure he didn't mean to leave you. An accident. You can't begrudge him an accident."

"I can, when it was avoidable. I've had years to let this heal, and it's refused. You won't change my mind so quickly." His hands were jammed rigidly into his pockets, his shoulders hunched forward in a way that reminded me of someone about to retch. He was angry, sad, torn up inside, all these years later, and an ache found its way into my own heart at the sight.

We both watched as a squirrel darted through the clearing and disappeared back into the trees, a reminder that the forest was alive and thriving around us, despite the images that flooded my mind. Away from the more commonly trodden paths of the forest, the trees grew thick and free. Underbrush and deadfall clung to our feet and legs as we traipsed by, and I couldn't help but think of them as slender fingers and hands working to pull us under. Leafy ferns grew nearly to my waist, shrouding the roots of trees that often worked to make us stumble. Now and then, my feet would sink into parts of the ground that had gathered water and detritus, and my breath would catch as, just for a moment, I imagined being sucked beneath the earth and suffocating. Tree limbs groaned as a breeze bent them this way and that, and sometimes the birds would sing to one another from treetop to treetop, while at moments, there was nothing but an eerie silence. The scents of fresh moss and new growth mingled with the heavy stench of damp earth and rotting leaves. As we walked, I caught sight of narrow, worn paths through the brushwood, no doubt left over time by the passage of forest creatures. I imagined great antlered harts picking their way delicately through the trails.

On occasion, we would cross a gurgling stream, the growth all around it thick and rich, a kind of green I never knew to exist. Bees and bugs hummed around the flowers that grew near to the water, our presence all but ignored as the denizens of the forest moved about their day.

Benedek removed his coat to carry it in the warmth, his

white undershirt loose and partially untucked. I tried not to stare, but the way he had let his guard down brought me joy. On a whim, I reached up and pulled at the ribbon that tied back my hair. It tumbled down in a mass, reaching past my shoulders in a way my mother wouldn't approve of. He glanced at me, but only very briefly, like he had witnessed something private and didn't want to pry. I bit my lower lip and stared at the ground, feeling a little bit foolish, and a little bit exhilarated.

What was he thinking, just now?

Evening was gathering itself around us when the trees cleared some. I hoped we had put enough distance between us and Vyesta so that if it were to reach out with those invisible hands and draw us in, we would have to walk through the night to reach it, and find ourselves there when the sun was up and we were safe.

I wanted to celebrate that distance, to revel in the knowledge that I could enjoy some evening air for the first time without fear that it might be my last, but the frustration of leaving the castle so far behind when it was the one place on earth I wanted to be had grown strong. Something within me, perhaps common sense, whispered to me that it was the right thing to do, that whatever force was beckoning to me now would armour me in my foray into the castle. I could not rush into a fight when I knew so little.

Orange light speckled through the canopy above, signalling a vibrant sunset I wished I could see. But we were deep in the forest now, swallowed alive. If I didn't focus to find that voice hidden somewhere inside me, I would have no way of knowing which way we'd come, and which way we were going.

My grandfather told a story once about the forest, one my mother refused to let him ever tell again. He insisted it was a cautionary tale to keep children from wandering towards the hungry castle. About how even the air around it couldn't be trusted. Mother had told me and my sister to forget it, but I didn't. I remembered every word, and they came back to me now, whispered amongst the leaves of the trees.

The road is long and winding. There are no shadows, because there is no light to cast them. I've walked for hours. Every time I reach a turn, I'm certain I'll see the end of the forest. But always it winds on. "Never leave the road," I was told, yet my feet are sore, and the fallen leaves within the trees look soft.

I come to a gnarled tree with a wide branch low enough that I could climb it and lie down. My feet hesitate, but I walk on. "Never leave the road," I was told.

Another bend. Another hour. More trees and darkness.

I come to a gnarled tree with a wide branch low enough that I could climb it. "Never leave the road," I was told, but my feet are sore, and I can't deny them a rest. I climb the tree and lie down on the branch.

"Never touch the road," a voice whispers.

145

The story was simple, meant to illustrate how the winding ways and underbrush of the forest could trick and confuse you, and wear you out until you no longer knew one direction from another – especially with the castle's devilry lurking nearby.

I did not like to make room for fear; they said it made you weak, and weakness led to cowardice. I would stay up happily on the Eve of Saints – an ancient holiday begun by the hands of the gods, when the dead were welcomed back and celebrated for one night a year – waiting by the window for the spirits to find me. They never did, but I waited all the same. Now, though, with my grandfather's words whispered in my ears, and the rumours of the castle looming large, fear slipped a cold, ghastly hand around my heart.

Our steps slowed together, until we stopped completely. The stretching shadows from the falling day darkened the clearing we'd found ourselves in – and a handful of derelict, overgrown gravestones stood haphazardly in the ground. It wasn't a clearing so much as a cemetery.

Cold fingers trailed along my arms.

"Ah. Bit of a shame, really." Benedek brushed his fingertips along the top of a gravestone. "So deep in the forest, with no one to visit them."

"We're here."

He shrugged. "Quite by accident. That's hardly a visit."

Movement drew my attention to one of the gravestones on the far edge of the clearing, a milky-white shimmer that fluttered in and out of visibility. It took the shape of a person, the height and size of a woman, and she swayed this way and that, arms waving about in the air as though dancing to music I could not hear. A spin, a twirl, arms up, arms down, a smile so rich I felt it everywhere.

"Béata?" Benedek's voice came from a distant land, as though he'd whispered it to the wind and it had carried its remnants to my ears.

A man joined the woman, rising up from the ground as smoke from a fire and gathering himself into a figure so pale I wasn't even certain I could see him until I looked away. He leapt and danced and joined hands with her, then darted away again, and suddenly there were eight of them, all bounding around the clearing, passing through the gravestones like they weren't there at all.

"Béata, you've gone so pale."

"Shh," I whispered. "I'm watching them dance."

He looked slowly around the clearing, spinning in a circle, and then back to me. "Watching who?"

"The people." I pointed to the first woman I'd seen. "She looks so happy." And she did. Her smile never faded, never changed. Her silvery, intangible hair bounced at every spin and turn, and though she was too ghostly to see properly, everything about her seemed young.

Ghostly.

I pulled a hand to my mouth, suddenly petrified, as Benedek's words came back to me. *Watching who?*

"Benedek, do you see those people?"

He looked around us again, and I knew what he would say before he answered. "What people?"

A scream erupted from me, though the dancers didn't seem to notice. They saw me, I knew that. Their eyes would meet mine for just a fraction of a second before darting away, but they never fell on Benedek. I hadn't noticed until now.

They danced on.

Just as when I'd first walked into the rains and learned I could survive, the weight of knowledge came crashing down. I could see what Benedek could not. And I did not know why.

Bringing both hands up to shield my vision, I ran. I ran as fast as I could force my body to move, and did not stop until the shaking in my legs became too much and I fell to the dead leaves below me.

The graveyard was far behind me now, but all around I still imagined I could see dancing bodies bathed in white, clothed in things no one had worn for centuries. They'd been dead, and dead for years. Why had I seen them when Benedek had not?

He caught up to me in a matter of moments, wildly out of breath, and dropped to his knees a few paces away. When he'd caught his breath, he said softly, "What happened?"

It took me a long time to reply. I watched the dancing leaves above, my heart slowing, the visions, the frolic in the rain, and now the dance of the dead all spiralling about in my mind. "I don't know," I finally whispered. "There were people in the cemetery, dancing and revelling. Pale, young and old, I saw them come up from the graves."

Benedek's silence spoke volumes. I fancied I could hear his thoughts, the trail of worries winding endlessly away. *The madness of the castle has ruined her. Too many dark tales have done their work.*

I could hardly blame him. Somewhere within me, I worried the same.

But all he said was, "I know what it's like, Béata. Not exactly what you're going through, but I know how it feels to be tormented. Even here, now, in this forest, I see the castle everywhere. In a grove of trees, I see its hallways. In a hole in the trunk of that one over there, I see the window that looks down over the courtyard from the kitchen. I see it in everything." He breathed deeply, calming himself. "This person you're seeking. They seem to wish only to help you. I don't know what that help will look like, but it must be invaluable if they are beckoning you from so far away. Magic, maybe. Something more than what we have. Perhaps they will be able to explain the people in the graveyard, too. Don't worry yourself too much." And he brushed my shoulder gently with his hand, only for a moment, but in a way that left a lasting impression of his fingertips.

I looked over at him, silhouetted against the falling day,

shadows framing his tired but elegant face. There was no sympathy there, no patronizing air of tenderness such as one would show to a child. Instead, I found only genuine worry and a small, kindly smile that wrapped my heart in a warm embrace. In that moment, overwhelmed, exhausted, and uneasy as I was, that smile was exactly what I needed.

So I smiled back.

Chapter Thirteen

Liljana

The rising and falling of the ground made for slow going, but eventually, the hills began to decline, and the forest just spread before me like a wall warning me away. It was mid-afternoon when I splashed my way through a cold creek, and passed an ancient wooden sign nailed to a tree that read, in barely legible letters, *Nárovar*. I paused, then I took in a deep breath of the new air.

I knew only vaguely that it was an ancient border town within Marcosza's limits. Whether anything remained of the town I didn't know, but it was the first realization I had that I was, in fact, in Marcosza. The border had likely been back by the river, but I'd been too consumed with running and thinking of Marek dying to think of it.

So now here I was.

I had never left Roşesti in my life. Never even imagined I would. I turned and looked back across the creek, waiting for the pang of sadness to settle over me, but my heart only raced with excitement. I'd made it. I'd left my old life behind, and never-ending possibilities stretched before me like the open sea.

Madam Iulia's tavern and the king's hold seemed so small now, with so much distance between us. If only Miha had had the chance to see what a wide-open world awaited her beyond the confines of the city. Why hadn't we left years ago? A pang of guilt punched me in the gut, but I pushed it away furiously.

I spun away from the creek and hurried on, keen for Roşesti and every second of my past life to be far behind me.

With nothing around but trees, with the addition here and there of a brook, a fallen log so large I had to traipse my way around it, or the ruins of what looked to have once been a house, it was difficult to know which way to go. I kept an eye on the sun so I wouldn't get too turned around, but a life spent in a city had left me ill-prepared for a journey through a dense forest.

But now and then, when I stopped and listened, I felt something pull me along, the slenderest spider's silk guiding me to somewhere unseen. My magic, perhaps, but taking me where? Did it know I wished to reach this mysterious castle? Was another mage nearby calling to me? With no map and little to go on, I followed it, keeping a keen eye on the forest.

Presently, I came to a small farmhouse tucked away in a clearing of the great forest. Smoke curled up from the stone chimney, set into a thatched roof, and horses and sheep grazed lazily in a small paddock. Somewhere out of sight, a rooster crowed, though the day was already waning.

The farmer, or so I assumed, sat on his knees in a garden bed far across the clearing by the line of trees, picking something from the ground. An orchard grew lush and dense to my left, the branches laden with apples, and hens pecked their way around the farmyard, eyeing me now and then suspiciously.

I stood and thought for a moment, the farmer's back turned to me, and made a decision before I could find a reason to talk myself out of it. Slipping quietly to the paddock where two horses stood munching lazily on hay, I opened the gate and spoke quietly to the horse nearest me. She was simple and brown, with gentle eyes and a few grey hairs giving away her age.

"I'm sure you have a lovely life here," I whispered, running a hand along her neck. "But I need your help now. We're going on an adventure." She nuzzled my shoulder and reached for more hay. She was old and lazy, not easily enticed away on an adventure with a wayfaring mage, so I coaxed her away with a pebble turned into an apple.

I'd never ridden a horse before, though I'd been around them many times. Sometimes patrons left them outside the Regina, tied to a post, and I'd sit on a stump and talk to them. Once, when the owner had grown irritatingly drunk and rowdy inside, I'd set his horse free and watched her trot away down the road.

Climbing on to the fence for some height, I slid carefully on to her back, gripping her mane unsteadily.

A voice called across the farm, and I whirled. The farmer was running this way, arms waving wildly in the air. "Get away from my horse!" I heard in a thick accent.

"Let's go," I said quickly, urging her on with my heels. She broke into a brisk trot, soon giving way to a quicker pace, and we made swiftly for the line of trees, leaving the farmer behind. Clinging on to the back of a horse proved to be far more difficult a task than I'd anticipated. We were barely into the forest again when she leapt over a small log and sent me flying to the ground. Groaning, I rolled over and tried again, this time managing to keep her at a slower, steadier pace between the trees.

All the following day I journeyed through the great forest, sleeping in a copse of trees against a large rock stuck into the ground. The mare stayed close by, dining on what grass found its way up through the leaves carpeting the ground, and I slept better having a companion than I had since leaving Tăru.

The sky was heavy and grey on my third day in

Marcosza. I began to wonder vaguely if this forest ever ended. If all the tales of life beyond Roşesti were but fables and yarns, and in fact the world was nothing but tree after tree until it fell away into the stars. That wouldn't be so bad. I could think of worse places to wander for the rest of my life than the silent, peaceful forest. But I kept in tune with the thread within me, following an invisible map to wherever my magic would take me.

As twilight began to make itself a home, my magic flickered. I stopped the horse and examined the woods around me, listening, reaching out with the sense that told me something was amiss. I'd grown too comfortable in my own company. Hairs stood on end along my arms at the sudden interruption in my quiet thoughts.

I turned back to face the direction I'd been travelling and stopped breathing.

Two black shadows, the size and shape of men, moved towards me side by side, a few yards separating them. They bore no faces, and their edges danced like smoke from a smouldering fire. Their hands were crossed before them, and they moved without a sound. About ten yards away, they stopped.

A black stag stepped out from behind a fallen tree and moved to stand between them. Its white eyes cast light like a lantern would, and the way it cocked its head to stare at me spoke of something all too human.

"Greetings, Liljana Vahani," said the stag.

Suddenly, nothing mattered more to me than hiding the fear that roared to life. The things Petre had said about the dealings in Marcosza roiled about in my thoughts, dark power dripping forth from the castle, casting fear as far as its neighbouring countries. I forced the thoughts away with a smile. "And to you," I replied, thrilled at the calmness I managed.

The stag smiled. "Your show of strength is endearing, but it will fool no one."

"I have places to be," I said with a sigh. "Who are you, and what do you want?"

"Down to business," he said, arching his head up high. "I like it. I'm in need of a favour."

Beneath me, the mare stomped about, a sound somewhere between a low whinny and a growl escaping her. I tilted my head. "Everyone likes to ask favours of mages."

He smiled again. "I do not bargain like a human, Liljana, so do not treat me as one." He paused, then spoke each word slowly. "I can offer you what you have always wanted. A life of magic, safe, away from those who would wish you harm. A life so far from this world you cannot find it by map. Is that not what you have always wanted? A life away from Roşesti" – he rolled the word like someone who'd lived in Roşesti all his life – "and from Madam Iulia Filiţa? All I ask in return is one simple favour that will bring you no harm. A few days or weeks, and you will have your freedom. It's a small price to pay for something so dear to

156

your heart. Is it not?"

My thin veil of stalwart arrogance fractured. My mouth fell open, but I couldn't be bothered to close it again. He knew that I was a mage. He clearly bore a magic stronger than anyone I'd known, given his appearance, but knowing of my magic meant little. One mage could tell another as simply as a child could recognize their mother.

But not everyone could tell me my deepest, strongest desires as though reading them from my journal.

"What is the favour?" It was the only thing I could think to say that gave away little of what I was thinking – though I could no longer be sure, given how much he knew, that he couldn't read my mind.

Beside him, the faceless shadows stood still as statues, hands folded, staring forward. Though I saw no eyes, I could sense them watching me.

"There is a girl I need you to find. She has managed to elude me for too long now, and the time has come for this to end. I was. . ." He looked away and let out a long, low hissing sound that sent a vicious tingle along my spine. "I was banished to this world long ago, and my soul confined to the castle. I cannot yet leave it, not without more power, and only now I have pushed my sight into this beast for a few fleeting moments. For years I have sought to lure the village girl into the castle, and for years, she has managed to avoid me. Enough. If you can find her, and deliver her to me at the castle, you will have your life of peace and freedom.

I promise that to you."

The horse shifted below me, calmer, but still on edge. I cracked a knuckle in my hand while I thought. Easy. This sounded far too easy. Convenient. A magician, coming to me with an offer of exactly what I sought, in exchange for handing over someone I'd never even met.

Although... I looked away through the trees, remembering all the times Miha and I had talked about freedom, about finding a life of peace and joy somewhere far away. Yes, I had made a promise to Petre in my heart, but in a way, I had also made a promise to Miha. To find that life. To live it. To love it. And Miha mattered far more to me than Petre.

"Why are you asking this of me?"

He paused for a moment in a way that felt heavy with a meaning I didn't understand. "Your magic is heavy and rich. Even untrained as you are, I believe you can accomplish what I ask. You've come this far, haven't you?"

I looked around us at the forest, suddenly dark in his presence. Night had not yet fully arrived, but daylight already seemed far away. I shivered at a sudden chill in the air.

"Who are you?"

"There's little in a name, Liljana. Ask better questions. I am the lord of the castle, and that is what matters."

A sense of clarity struck me like cold water to the face. He *was* the darkness. He was the sickness plaguing the castle. All the rumours I had heard while back in Tǎru. The evil in Marcosza that Petre had warned me about, told me to find and extinguish. That evil was standing before me, and though my mind warned me to run, to flee, to hide and never enter this forest again, my heart held me in place.

If I had the strength and the magic, I could destroy him right here. That thought seemed just wild enough to be possible.

"This life of safety you offer. Where is it? How will I get it?" My words were quiet, barely above a whisper as all the possibilities danced before me.

He smiled again, and I sensed he thought he'd drawn me in. "Muranj," he said, drawing out the word, relishing it in some strange way. "The Kingdom of Magic. It is here, just beyond reach, so very close, but so far, if you don't know where to look. The only people you will find in Muranj are mages, like yourself, trained, untrained, happy, safe. There are no Ashen, no Roşestian kings, no one out to destroy you."

"Then why are you not there?" The question came quickly, but I was finding it hard to breathe. *A kingdom of magic. A world of mages and peace.* Suffocating. I was suffocating at the thought. Hungry for it. Desperate.

"That is a story I have not the time to tell. Bring me the girl, and it will be yours."

"And what if I don't?"

The stag jutted his chin to the shadows beside him. "I

needn't say more. We will find you. And we will destroy you. I will find another mage with as much magic as you carry, and I will keep finding mages until one of you brings me what I seek."

I paused, staring unflinchingly into the stag's white eyes. "Who is the girl?" I asked.

"Her name is Béata."

Chapter Fourteen

Béata

The land around us had begun to rise steadily, continuing to climb until we had to slow our pace, out of breath. We spoke sometimes, but only of unimportant things, our minds occupied by what had happened in the cemetery. I stared at the ground as we walked, afraid if I looked up, I might see another pale, dancing figure grinning at me with a look that said they knew something I didn't. And that's how it felt: like there was something the world around me knew that I could never quite understand. Like I was in this land, but not part of it. The things I thought I knew began to die away, leaving everything foreign and tinged with a sense of hopelessness.

Before us, the land rose to a high crest and the trees

thinned out where the wind that beat against us would make it hard for them to thrive. Exhausted, we rose to the top of the hill and stopped, the ground falling away into a wide valley with a lake stretching away far below. Only the shore closest to us was visible in the dense fog that clung to the ground like snow.

"Is this right?" Benedek asked, holding his hair out of his face with one hand.

I nodded. "I think so." All day I had been listening for that voice, that thing that pulled me along. And every now and then, when the forest had been quiet enough, I would hear it again.

Béata.

Benedek had ceased to question me about it until now, but he would glance at me when he thought I didn't notice, his eyebrows perpetually knitted with worry. I couldn't quite tell if it was worry for me, or worry that I might lead us astray and he would never make it to the castle. Never find the freedom and understanding his mind and heart so desired after years of torment. Either way, I found myself suppressing a smile each time my eyes met his, and once or twice, I felt very nearly certain that he let his steps slow so I wouldn't notice his eyes watching me.

Though I could feel them.

He was beautiful, in an unkempt, country kind of way. The tied-back hair. The dusty coat. The patched boots laced up to his knees. Everything about him was wild and messy and perfect – so much so that I found it hard to look away. I would watch him when he wasn't looking, admire the way he brushed his fingertips against tree branches, gently, lovingly. Enjoy how, now and then, he would start humming a song I didn't recognize, and then catch himself with a sudden smile and stop.

And over and over again, I found myself smiling for no reason other than the rush of excitement I felt each and every time I saw him. He noticed sometimes, but he pretended not to, and that only worked to captivate me further.

He told me he had dreamed the previous night about the castle again. He said he could see himself standing in a tower, looking down on the rest of the castle. It was a simple dream, with no true reason to spark alarm in anyone, but his visions and dreams of Vyesta were growing more and more frequent, and without an explanation, he was growing more concerned.

"I don't know what to do any more," he had said, his eyes glistening. And in that moment, I wanted nothing more than to embrace him. But instead, I had held his shoulder firmly, and assured him we would find the answer.

And I would. I promised myself that.

The voice calling to me was stronger now, almost as solid and close as Benedek's voice when he spoke to me. There were more words, a never-ending string of them, beckoning to me, urging me to hurry. A man, I thought, though I couldn't quite be sure.

The descent into the valley was tedious, the ground so

steep in places we were forced to slide down in a tumble of dirt and dried leaves, rips tearing open in my clothes here and there, and dust stinging my eyes. When we finally fell below the line of fog, it was like tumbling into a different world. What little of the open woodland we could see around us was bathed in white, the mist rolling about. The grass was short and lush, the trees sparse and trunks light. The tops were invisible, enveloped in the fog. If the voice in my head had not pulled us along, we might have wandered the mists until death found us.

But at last, we made our way along a flat, rocky beach to the lapping waters of the lake, and came to a halt. The voice urged us on, pulling me forward, yet the way had stopped. There was no bridge, no boat, no pathway along the lake. No stepping stones, nothing but water lapping around our ankles.

"I don't understand," Benedek whispered. The disappointment in his voice cut away at me, and I turned to walk the beach and put some distance between us.

"Please," I whispered aloud, and then finished the thought internally. *Please do not let this have been for nothing. Please help me. Please help us.* I didn't think I could bear the thought of having come all this way, dragging Benedek into the wild forest and further from home than we had ever been, all for nothing. Only to have to turn back and make the trek home empty-handed.

Think. I needed to think.

So close now. No time to lose. Onward. Onward.

The words in my head continued tumbling forward faster and faster. My head swam. My stomach rolled.

And then my heart stopped.

Out of the mists of the lake came a single small boat, rowed by no one, making its way slowly towards me. Oars lay in the bottom, untouched, yet onward it sailed until its bow ground on to the beach and it stopped, waiting.

The sound of Benedek's footsteps approached, then stopped by my side. Neither of us spoke.

There were no sounds around us. No people. No instructions. Just a wooden boat, empty, on a lake bathed in fog. I began to wonder again, suddenly and fiercely, if I'd fallen prey to some great plot, and was nearing the end. Nearing my own undoing.

"We've come this far," I whispered, as though worried someone might hear me. "We carry on, or we go home."

Silence yawned between us. The water splashed below. Somewhere far away, a strange bird called. The boat waited.

"We cannot go home," Benedek said softly.

I moved forward and took hold of the boat, pushing it with all my might back into the water, leaping inside when it was afloat once more.

Benedek joined me, dripping from the waist down, sweat rolling down his forehead into his eyes. I stared at him for a long while, and he stared back at me as our oars splashed in the water.

"You look different," he said quietly.

"Different how?"

"I don't know. Just different. Sad, but . . . determined. Like a leader."

I smiled, my cheeks burning at his gaze, and then turned away to the water to hide my joy at his words. The mist had closed in around us. I couldn't see the shore any more, in any direction. All around the boat, there was only quiet, still water, stretching away into the fog. A shiver crept along my spine at the sense of sudden, utter isolation. No land. No people, other than Benedek. No known destination. Nothing but the boat, and the water.

We rowed on. The thread within me felt stronger with each pull of the oar, and the voice was ceaseless now, an endless stream of imploring words. Sometimes I was afraid to speak, lest the words in my head come tumbling out of my mouth. The lines between the voice and my own thoughts had been hopelessly blurred.

"I see something," Benedek whispered after what felt like hours. Time was almost impossible to tell with nothing around us, no sun, no sense of the light changing.

I stopped rowing and turned in the boat, my gaze falling on a large shadow protruding from the water. "An island," I said, "or the opposite shore."

"I don't like it. We don't know who's there," Benedek told me, gripping the edge of the boat. "What if this has all been a trap? What if this is where it ends?"

I stared at him squarely. "Then it's too late for escape." I gripped my oar again and rowed faster towards the land. "If this *is* the end, then I suppose I should have liked to know you better. Perhaps in another life." I smiled a bit, my words intended as a jest, but feeling suddenly heavy once spoken.

Benedek turned his head away, but his eyes lingered on me for a few extra seconds. He didn't reply.

The boat again ground on to the beach – what little of it there was. A small patch of dirt and pebbles perhaps a yard wide separated the water from a verdant bank of grass and reeds. We dragged the boat as far as we could, and climbed the slippery bank to the trees that waited above, falling more than once to the mud beneath.

"It's definitely an island. I'm almost certain," Benedek told me, stopping to examine our surroundings.

"You cannot be definitely almost certain," I replied, eyeing a large, crooked tree unlike any we had back home. The branches grew angled and wide, like a bench to view the water.

"Well, I'm almost certain." He paused. "Funny. I always used to dream about adventure. Like the ones my father had. He was always telling stories of his travels. I don't think I ever quite imagined myself on one. I figured I was more the sort to hear them than to live them."

I tucked a piece of hair behind my ear. "Now you'll have your own stories to tell one day. Like about sailing to an island on a boat that came to find us."

His shoulders twitched with a shiver. "Adventures never sound so frightening when told later."

"Are you frightened?"

"Yes. Are you not?"

"I am. But I'm also . . . excited. Perhaps that's not the right word." I thought. "Impatient. We've come so far. We're almost there. I want to learn what we need to and get back to the castle. End this nightmare."

"I'm sure it's good to be scared, at least a little. Fear makes you care, about yourself, if nothing else."

"Does it?"

"I think so."

We carried on. As we rounded a tree, my hand brushed his, and I remembered the vision I'd had back in Zírany, of walking over cobblestones holding someone's hand. The love I'd felt, so heavy and consuming, came back to me. I suddenly wanted that love. I wanted it desperately.

"Have you ever been in love?" I asked Benedek. The question felt so strange once spoken that I rushed to fill the silence it left behind. "You seem like someone once in love. Maybe not any more."

His eyebrows twitched in confusion, and the edges of his mouth pulled into a small smile. "I don't think so. I think I've cared for people deeply, but not quite love. Love is . . . real."

"Love *is* just caring."

"It isn't."

"It is. I care about my mother and father. I care about my sister. I care about Marcosza."

"I *care* about my boots, but I don't love them." He lifted one foot to demonstrate.

"That's different."

"How?"

"It just is. What is love to you?"

He thought for a moment. "It's paring back the flesh of people, their faults and flaws, and loving the bones underneath."

"Love is bones?"

"Sure. They're strong, but they break, and even though they heal, they're never quite the same again. There's always a mark."

I turned his words over as we walked through the crooked trees. I wanted to love one day, but I also wanted to cross the Oroszom Mountains on foot, dance with the souls of the dead on the Eve of Saints, and rid the castle of the evil inside, and not every dream comes true.

I stopped short when, between the gnarled branches, my gaze fell on a house. A hut, really, small and round with a thatched roof and a tall, angled chimney. Smoke rose up and disappeared into the treetops. Birds hopped along the thatch, darting in and out of a nest. The wooden door stood open, as though waiting, and inside, someone moved about.

"Is this him?" Benedek whispered, pushing aside a branch of leaves for a better view.

I reached inward, searching for that closed door, and nodded. "Absolutely." Nerves shook my limbs, and the fear Benedek had told me was so important yawned large and hungry, but I shoved the branches aside and crossed the grassy clearing to the house.

"Do come in," came a man's voice when I knocked three times upon the door. I swallowed, and glanced back at Benedek, who'd followed me at a distance. "No need to be alarmed," came the voice again. "I can explain everything. Well, most things, anyway."

Without waiting another second, I walked through the door.

The rounded room was dark, lit only by a lazy fire that was all but burned out on one wall. What little light filtered in through the door did not reach much further beyond it. After the brightness of the day outside, despite the fog, it took my eyes a moment to adjust. Benedek stood close to me, rigidity and unease oozing off him like sweat.

A man in a simple grey tunic and white trousers stood by a small table set with water and bread. His hair was the grey of rock that had seen a light snowfall, and he had eyes that harboured secrets.

"I hope your journey was an easy one. I began to worry you'd never find me. I know it can be difficult to follow the Voice when you haven't been trained, but I tried to make it easy. I trust the boat found you on time?"

I said nothing.

"Yes, this is all a bit sudden. I should speak more slowly, and introduce myself. I am Rovaslo. I've been calling to you for some time." He stuck his hand out towards me. I shook it, uncertainly.

"Béata."

"I know who you are. I know probably more than you do." A subtle smile that vanished quickly. "But all in good time. And who . . . who do we have here?" His voice curved downward at the end, as though he had somehow answered his own question while asking it.

"Benedek." The two shook hands, and Rovaslo nodded knowingly.

Slowly, Rovaslo moved towards me, and motioned to a chair. I sat down. Benedek sat beside me. Rovaslo handed both of us a glass of water and a plate each with a slice of bread. I ate slowly, watching his face as he thought long and hard about what he would say. Thoughts and memories were dancing – or mauling – their way through his mind. It was evident in the weight in his eyes, and in the lines on his face. I wished to give him the time he needed to sort through his thoughts, but at the same time, every muscle in my body was twitching with impatience. I had come all this way for answers, so it was answers I wanted.

"I've thought about this moment so many times, yet words fail me now it's here. I don't know where to start except the beginning, but it's difficult to say where the beginning is when everything feels like an ending." He took a sip of water and stared into the fire. "As I said, I am Rovaslo, and I was a Seer in the court of Marcosza."

The words tore through the air and settled like snow around us, cold and conspicuous.

"A Seer." The word felt strange on my tongue.

"A Seer," he said again. "Seers are the bridge between souls and the living. Both can coexist, but you need us to interact. To speak."

Souls.

I had given very little thought to life after death, if there were such a thing. Many in Marcosza held that once you passed away, your soul spent some time in the shadow world, waiting to pass on to whatever lay beyond. I had always just imagined endless darkness, like nights without a dream.

"Souls don't always go to the shadow world," he went on, as though sensing my thoughts. "They can linger. Stay behind. In the castle, the monarchs of Marcosza have long practised the art of soul-pushing, through the use of people like me. People like us. Pushing the souls of the dead into the castle, so that they may stay behind and aid in the country's future. The halls have long been roamed by former kings and queens, their children, grandmothers and grandfathers. They can be seen, spoken to, at any time." The faraway look in his eye spoke of happy memories, of faces he'd long missed, and old conversations that he hadn't recalled in years.

The fire crackled. Benedek's face had gone deathly white. I waited.

"Then . . . then what's in the shadow world?" Benedek ventured presently.

Rovaslo's eyes cut to him. "Souls. Spirits. They could all have gone there, if they'd wished to. But the castle became a sort of large family, lines continuing on, fathers still guiding their sons, mothers still watching over their daughters. No one wished to leave."

I imagined the tavern filled with the spirits of my grandparents, my grandfather still watching over us. A family that only ever grew.

But a darkness pressed against my mind, the knowledge that it wasn't meant to be that way. Souls do not belong in our world.

"That's a scratch on the surface of what I have to tell you," Rovaslo said gently. He studied my face for a long moment while I struggled to sort out my thoughts. Everything was broken, knowledge fractured, things that had once been neat were now wildly out of place. The only thing I could find order in was my breath, so I kept it steady, even, fighting the urge to give way to panic.

"Why did you call to *me*? What makes you so sure that I can do anything about the castle?" It was the only question that seemed to make sense among the hundred thousand others. "And how did you know I was going to enter the castle?"

Rovaslo sighed deeply, the look in his eyes telling me we'd reached some sort of turning point in our conversation. Whatever he was about to say, I wouldn't be the same person after I heard it.

"Magic, to answer that last question. And you are not who you think you are, Béata," he told me softly. I clenched my clothes in my hands while I waited for him to go on. "Well, you are and you aren't. There's so much about you. . . Where to begin?" He stared at the fire for a moment. "This world is full of mages. Perhaps you've heard of them, perhaps you haven't. Some folks think they're little more than myth, and some believe it to be so true it fills them with terror. They used to be everywhere, in every town and village, before the murders in Castle Vyesta. Before the fear of magic settled in like a twilight that never left. In Roşesti, across the Hills, I've heard they're murdering them. *Murdering.*" He shook his head. "And you, Béata, you were born a Seer. Well, you were born with the ability to be a Seer, with some training. Mages are born raw and wild, magic simmering within them that requires honing to be properly used. After it's been honed, that mage can join their respective Order."

"Order."

"Yes, Seers, Weavers, Ruiners, that sort of thing. All depending on what strain of magic they're born with. I am a Seer, as are you. Our duty is to use that magic to commune with those who have passed on, and be the messenger between the living and the dead."

The dancers in the cemetery flashed before me. My hands shook violently. I doubled over to face the floor.

"I hope, in some small way, that answers more questions for you than it raises. I usually find that to be the case."

He was right, in a way, and he was very wrong. Some things made sense – the strange visions now likely had an explanation, the way I so often felt off, as though there were something about me that was not the same as those around me – but at the same time, everything had fallen into confusion. I toyed with the drawstring on my cuffs nervously, thinking. Strange, how such a simple explanation should make sense of all the oddities in my life, and yet I felt as though it had shattered everything.

My heart hurt. My stomach ached. I wanted to crawl into my bed and hide from the world.

"I don't understand what you want from me," I whispered. "Or why it was imperative that I find you so quickly. Why I was so short on time."

Rovaslo cocked his head thoughtfully. "There is only so much you can take in at once, Béata," he told me. "If you fill a glass too full, it runs over. Your questions will be answered in time. Today is a day for understanding who and what you are. You will need time to mull that over, and to learn what it truly means to be a Seer. Autumn, as you know, brings with it the Eve of Saints, when the Veil between the living and the dead is at its weakest. Perhaps you've noticed things around you changing, spirits, voices, unusual things. But don't worry if you haven't. I can help you make sense of it all."

My eyes met Benedek's for a long, lingering moment. The firelight flickered. The shadows danced. "I'm sorry I brought you," I told him.

"Don't be," Rovaslo said, pulling our attention away. "Benedek has a very special part to play in all of this. It will make sense, in good time."

"Do I ... have magic too?" he ventured, both with trepidation and hope.

"You do not," Rovaslo told him. "But that is enough on the subject for now. You must be hungry after your journey. Can I offer you some dinner?"

Dinner. Such a normal, simple part of the day, but food was the furthest thing from my mind. How could I think and act normal when everything was wrong? Things were different; life did not look the same. The world seemed somehow darker. My head throbbed, and for a moment, I thought I might retch.

I stood and left the house to steady myself in the fresh air.

Chapter Fifteen

Liljana

I skirted around the town of Zírany to make for the castle first. I could pay the town a visit soon enough, but for now, the castle was at the forefront of my thoughts. The stag's words had trailed behind me, whispered back at me on the evening mist, echoed off the fallen trees. They were everywhere I looked, in every sound of the forest.

There are no Ashen, no Roșestian kings, no one out to destroy you.

His offer felt as if it were the end of a long journey, finally seeing the destination I hadn't known I'd spent a lifetime chasing. It glistened and shimmered, a feast after years of starvation. And I wanted it. Gods, I wanted it so badly my hands shook.

The castle was much like the castle in Tăru, yet somehow different. The stones were reddish in the twilight, and the rains fell incessantly. I wished I'd asked the stag more questions about the castle, enquired about some of the rumours Petre had warned me about, but I doubted if he would have answered. He'd had a design in mind, a mission he'd set out to accomplish. Allaying my curiosity and ignorance was not part of it.

I left the horse in the trees outside the castle in a lush patch of grass where she could graze. Then, with slow, careful steps, I moved towards the castle.

The bodies were the first thing I saw, limp and slumped in the mud. Here and there, a red hand stood out, or half a blistered face overturned on the ground.

I stopped walking.

The world around me shifted suddenly, the castle and rains disappearing and transforming into a great room where screams rent the air. I could see nothing clearly, but I felt everything, heard everything. Terror ran through my veins as blood, and I was running, running, trying to escape something, or someone, bumping into panicked bodies all around the room. Everywhere I turned there were more, sealing off every exit, every door, every window. Swords clanged, a child cried. I fell to the ground and lay there, a thin carpet separating me from stone. *I'll die here. I'll die here.*

Without a pause, the rains returned. The castle stood

before me, bodies dotting the ground around it. The screams vanished, the carpet slipped into nothingness.

I fell to the ground and leaned my back against a tree, covering my face. The vision – if that's what it was – had gone, but the terror it sparked remained. My limbs shook, my heart raced.

Voices nearby jarred my attention away. I drew in my knees and pressed myself against the tree trunk, peering about until my eyes fell on a small band of young people about my age, making slowly for the castle. Their clothes were far too heavy for the season, furs and leathers piled one on top of the other, shawls wrapped tightly around their heads, cloaks topping it all. As they walked, they pulled on heavy gloves, thick layers of trousers protruding from heavy boots laced up to their knees. In their arms they carried thick blankets and more layers, which, as they drew closer to the castle, they began to unfurl and hold over them as a sort of moving tent.

They stopped just before the bridge that led across the river into the rains, and conversed for a few long moments. I looked from the bodies on the ground, to them, and back to the bodies. One boy, garbed as heavily as the others, stood a yard or two apart from them, pacing nervously back and forth. His hands fidgeted with the hem of his blue cloak, and he took no part in the conversation.

With their backs to me, I leaned around the tree for a better view. Once more, they hoisted the blankets high over their heads, and ran swiftly as one unit into the rains.

They crossed the bridge before the first person fell. They screamed and clawed at their face as the wicked rain kissed their skin, rolling about in the muddy grass before going silent.

Chaos settled in.

The first boy who fell had dropped his corner of the blanket, which sent the rest of the group into disorder. A girl fell to her knees, crying out, while others frantically grabbed at the makeshift tent to keep it in place.

One by one, they died in the grass outside the castle. Their screams were short-lived, the silence following grim and heavy, red marks rising on their skin even in death. I needed to look away – *should* have looked away – but I didn't want to. So I stared and stared and stared.

From under the pile of fallen bodies, clothes and blankets, something moved. After a brief shuffling, the boy in the blue cloak stood and looked around, horror lighting his face. He stood perfectly still, staring down at his hands. Waiting. He was waiting to die. The seconds ticked by. He would fall, any moment now. I waited. He waited. I gripped a branch, fingers trembling. He turned slowly and gazed up at the castle. He didn't fall.

With careful steps, he moved towards the great archway that led into the courtyard of the castle, pausing occasionally to look around him, to look back at his companions to see if any of them might move. He brought his hands to his face, stared at them, turned them over. Dropped them back to his sides.

I left the tree behind and took a few steps towards the castle, then stopped short. My magic flickered.

The boy didn't seem to notice, only pressed on through the poisoned rain, passing beneath the archway and disappearing around the corner.

I eyed the new bodies on the ground, the footprints in the mud left by the boy. He was a mage. There was no doubt about that. I wanted to believe he only survived because of his magic, but I couldn't be certain that none of the others who died hadn't been mages. I knew too little. But the dark, yawning archway where the mage had disappeared called to me. Beckoned to me. Taunted me.

A flare of impulse jolted through me, and I took one step, two steps, broke into a run. The rain drenched me in seconds, soaked through my clothes, set me to shivering. I waited for the pain, for whatever had made the others scream. And I ran on, without stopping, until the archway swallowed me up and I'd entered the castle.

The boy was nowhere in sight, but the large, ornate wooden door stood partly open, darkness inside. I stopped, leaning against a stone wall, and stared at the muddy ground. The empty, drenched courtyard sent me back to the courtyard of King Costel, to the captain I'd killed, to the screams coming from the hold. It felt as little more than a distant dream, so far away. Like a memory that wasn't mine. I was hardly the same girl, changed by so short a time.

A lone dead tree stood on the far side of the courtyard,

ashy brown and gaunt. I pitied it, so alone. So cold. What things had it seen over these long, lonely years? What stories could it tell?

High walls rose up around me, turrets grinning down like jagged teeth, torn flags hanging limp in the rain. The water ran in rivulets through the courtyard, mud inches deep clinging to my shoes. Though thick and humid, the air around me carried something else, a sense of heaviness and dread. The archways that branched off into the castle called to me, their shadows rich and deep. My feet told me to walk through them in obedience, but my mind bid me be wary.

A sound echoed out from the door into the castle. I pushed off from the wall and crept towards it, my steps slow. Careful. If the black stag I'd met in the forest told me anything about the powers here, then I'd do well to embrace caution. Each step could be my last.

I worked to keep my footsteps as silent as possible, as if the castle might never know I was here. As if it wasn't watching my every move. Here and there, open windows looked into darkened rooms, guarded by closed wooden doors. Kitchens, maybe, or servants' quarters. They looked more like the cells of a dungeon. I had never seen a dungeon, but I had read about them before. Dark, confined spaces.

A gentle patter made me stop, shivering. The boy's footsteps echoing around me, perhaps. But I waited for cold, invisible hands to grasp my own, to pull and guide me into oblivion, deep within the castle.

A door creaked somewhere further along the hallway. I waited, breathing myself back to calmness, and then followed it.

Though I dreaded to touch it, the only way through the nearly dark hallway was to drag my fingertips along the stone walls. I stumbled my way up three steps, stiffening at the scraping noise my boots made against the dusty floor.

Ahead, and to my left, a large wooden door sat partially open. It was more ornate than the others, carved on either side with the crest of Marcosza – two griffs facing one another, their large claws locked as if in battle. Old stories used to say that griffs, vile and terrifying as they were, could be ridden between our world and the others. They were said to have red eyes and black feathers that sometimes glistened like burning embers. Now, though they faced one another and were carved from wood, I couldn't help but feel like they saw me.

A voice came from within, followed by another. I slipped against the wall, barely daring to breathe, and ever so slowly, peered through the opening of the door.

More than once, I had imagined what a throne room looked like. Not Marcosza's, perhaps, but certainly Roșesti's. I pictured a great throne with plush cushions covered in velvet. Long tables that were always filled with food and wine, servants ferrying heaping plates back and forth. I pictured entertainers, singers, dancers, all prancing about in their finery, the candlelight glistening off their jewels. I pictured a great fire, warm and roaring, the heart of the castle itself. I pictured a king or queen layered in fine tunics and cloaks, a crown of precious metal resting on their head, their feet propped on a cushion before the throne.

Life. I pictured life.

What I saw was not life. The great room was a dull, dusty grey. Tall windows let in precious little light from the outside, where the dense clouds and rainfall made the sun seem like a myth. Grand stone pillars lined the room, and before each stood a candelabra, old wax melted and pooled on the floor. Yellow and green flags hung down from the roof at intervals, still and limp. Tapestries had been rent in two, doubled over and too dust-covered for their once vibrant colours to shine through. A great chandelier hung from the centre of the room, listing to one side, broken.

And bones littered the floor. Some still took the shape of a person, lying where they'd died and never moved. Others were fractured and scattered, part of a hand here, a leg there. Running along the floor, from where I sat all the way to the far end, was what I imagined was once a rich green rug, but was now faded and old, an artefact that remained from a time gone by. Rich, blackened stains clung to the carpets, blood spilled years ago and left to dry. Much further down the rug, and elevated by a grand dais that was draped in the colours of Marcosza, sat two large stone thrones. Two wolves made up each arm, their claws

184

seeming to dig into the floor. The air was close and dusty. There was a thickness to every breath I took.

Standing on the dais was the boy in the blue cloak, visibly trembling, even from so far away. And before him stood a man in a great, heavy cloak, black as black could be, his face shielded by a hood and thick dark hair that refused to stay put. Behind him, standing on either side of the thrones, stood those faceless shadows I'd met in the woods.

The man in the cloak, I knew with certainty, was the black stag. My magic recognized him in a way that felt like a returning sickness.

"All the others died," the boy was saying, his voice on the brink of tears. "It's just me. I don't know why I'm alive. I shouldn't be alive." He looked down at his hands again, turning them over. "Why am I alive?"

The man reached out a hand and ran it along the boy's cheek. A sentimental touch that made me shiver. "Oh, you ignorant little thing. Your magic saved you. Don't you know that?"

"My magic?"

The man shook his head sympathetically. "Truly, power is wasted on some of you. You know too little too late of what you might be. It's better this way."

"What way?" The boy was crying now.

"Your magic saved you," the man said again, "but not this time. The only good it will do now is feed me, and I'm so very hungry. Thank you for your great sacrifice. I

185

know this can't be easy." He grabbed the boy by his throat suddenly, muttering words in a language I didn't know as a roar began to fill the room. Light poured from the boy, disappearing down the man's mouth, until the boy's body collapsed in a lifeless, colourless heap on the floor.

I stifled a yelp and shrank back against the wall, holding my breath and listening. In the throne room, the man coughed, cleared his throat, and then there was a shuffling sound that made me think he'd sunk into one of the thrones. "Weak," said his voice. "Weak, like a bad liquor. I'll need more. Many more." A sudden flick, like the snapping of fingers. "Báal. Ásta. Find me more. Stronger ones, like that girl in the forest. Bring me someone like her, but not her. Not until she finishes finding me Béata. Bring me someone like Béata, in fact. Someone with the kind of power that gives me a shock when our magic meets. I am fed up with these weakling rats I keep having. I need her power, or that damned door will stay shut for ever. I am unhappy. Do you hear me? Unhappy. And I do not believe you wish for me to be unhappy, do you? Do you dare wish for that?" A distinct chuckle. "Go. Now."

I slipped down the hallway and broke into a run.

Chapter Sixteen

Béata

The fog never left the valley, or the island. I sat outside at twilight, savouring the feeling of knowing somewhere beyond the mist and cloud, the sun was falling behind a violent orange horizon, but the castle would never find me here. There were no doors locking, no feet hurrying along the streets, no fear rising up like bile. There was just the fog, the rich grass that carpeted the island, and the call of water birds I'd never heard before.

Everything was sweet and quiet and beautiful.

I cast my eyes down for a moment, guilt pressing heavy and sharp against me. Mother, Father, Alíz – they were all still there. They were still living in the hell that the castle was building. Living in fear and sorrow. *But you are here to bring an end to it*, I reminded myself. *You are here to get help.*

"My father took me to a lake, once, when I was very young." Benedek's voice came from behind me. He moved to sit on a large rock in the glen of trees where I lay on the grass, eyes closed. "Lake Tízo, I think. It isn't the largest one in Marcosza, but as a little boy, it never seemed to end. I remember walking into the water and soaking my boots, and my father chastising me, but I didn't care. It was worth it, for those few seconds, to be a part of something so great." I kept my eyes closed, enjoying the sound of his voice. Husky, in a gentle way.

"We had little time for travel, other than to nearby towns. Trading, buying, that sort of thing. My father's business is a good one, but consuming."

"Do you wish things were different?"

I almost said yes, on an impulse, but I was struck by the memory of my father sitting with my grandfather, shortly before he died, sharing a drink and surrounded by the tavern his father had built with his bare hands. The tavern meant everything to my father, besides his family, so while it had consumed much of our life while I was growing up, it had been worth it for the joy my father found in keeping my grandfather's dream alive.

I opened my eyes and stared up at the trees, barely visible through the fog. "No. I don't wish things had been different. The past is the past. I can set my own path now. Make my own life."

"Adventure is rarely what it's cracked up to be."

Rovaslo. He stood a few yards away, a book tucked under one arm. His simple grey tunic made him look more like the devout follower of some obscure religion than a displaced Seer. "More people die on adventures than live to tell the tales."

I sat up, on edge once more. What earth-shattering news would he deliver this time? I nodded towards the book. "What's that?"

He took the book in his hands and stared at it heavily. "A journal. Written by the queen mother, Zalya. Slain King Aurel was her son." Rovaslo had ordered us to go outside after dinner, to find some peace and quiet to mull over the things he'd said. *The risk is there for your mind to find itself overwhelmed, and we haven't time for that,* he had said. "You could ask me a hundred questions and I could answer them, or I could read this to you first. It's a good place to start. As good as any, I think. I must warn you. It is frightening. Not for the faint of heart. But every word is true. I know, because I was there."

I pulled a few blades of grass from the ground and chewed on my bottom lip. Then, without thinking, I edged myself closer to Benedek, instantly comforted by his steadiness.

Benedek wiped sweat from his brow, and one corner of his mouth curved up in a smile. Rovaslo sat down.

"You will have questions as I go. Save them, if you can.

I shan't read it all, but you should let me finish. It's better that way."

I nodded.

Rovaslo opened the book. He paused, running his eyes along the page as though seeing an old friend again. "*I can feel my body and soul begin to wither from this fever. As yet, I do not believe my son knows of its gravity, and I would keep it from him a while yet. He has been blessed with a life free of heartbreak and troubles, and I should not like to be the one to shatter that. What more could a mother wish for, for her child? In a matter of days, I will step down as queen of this beautiful, wonderful land, and Aurel will take my place as its king. His wife, the lovely Tabíta, will make a fine queen, though the thought of another queen on the throne of Marcosza fills me with a kind of sadness I am not certain I was built to bear. I have loved this country since I was a child, cherished it, and I have done what I can to make it good. I suppose, in the end, that is all I can do. I hope I have used my time as wisely as may be, and left an impact that will last for ages to come. I wish to make this choice now, while I am yet well enough to do so, rather than force my son to make it for me when I am too ill to leave my bed. Already, I stay there longer every morning, and retire earlier in the evenings. It will not be long until I cease leaving it altogether.*

One of the royal Seers, Morós, has been a great comfort to me during my illness. When I am too weak to move or speak, he will be the one to push my soul from this fragile body and into this blessed castle, where I might live with my son for ever. I have found solace in our conversations, and though I am beyond the years of romance, I have found myself enchanted by his gentleness and knowledge, and we spend many hours by the fire in my chambers, speaking of souls, and his work, and the days to come for Marcosza. He tells me of Muranj, and what a place of beauty it is. I long to see it, though I never will.

Now and then, when the firelight hits him just right, or he sits just out of reach of the window, I wonder if I see a shadow in him that gives me pause. But, then again, I am ill and tired, and my mind finds trouble where it can.

We have chatted at length about my new role in the castle, and what life – or the lack thereof – will be like once I am no longer in this body. I fear it, as anyone would, but I am blessed and thankful to have the opportunity. I dare not choose the way of eternal darkness, as others have done. I have never liked the dark much, and my soul yearns for the light.

For now, I will retire. Though the sun is barely setting and it is nearly winter, I am tired in a way that cannot be revived without much sleep. But as I will have ample time – indeed, all of it – I will use this journal as a private outlet for my thoughts and feelings, and because I am afraid to forget. There are things I wish to always remember, and may they live in these pages when my mind has begun to fail me."

A bird called close by. A small insect crawled its way over my hand, a gentle tickle I barely noticed. Rovaslo's words fell silent, and no one spoke.

Souls living on in the castle. Dead monarchs pushed from their bodies to carry on with their children. A strange, frightening practice that made sense like the final piece of a puzzle.

"Muranj." I'd heard the word before, though rarely, in the sorts of tales people no longer told. I said it once more, trying to recall how Rovaslo had said it. "Muranj. I've heard of it, I think. What is it? Remind me."

Rovaslo drew in a long, slow breath. "A kingdom," he said softly, smiling a little, eyes misty. "A beautiful, wonderful kingdom, where all the magic in this world comes from. Where I came from. Where your ancestors came from. Where Morós came from." An icy cloud passed over his face. "This world, our world" – he motioned to the air around us – "Sóar, we call it, it never had magic. Everyone was magicless, just the normal kind of person. Like. . ." He began to point to Benedek, then stopped, as though worried it might cause offence. "Sóar and Muranj are as different as can be. Night to day. Earth to sky."

"Different how?" I watched a bird land on a nearby branch, beady eyes watching us for a moment before flitting away.

"In every way. The forests – and there are so, so many forests – are rich and verdant and alive, filled with zél trees. They grow these large purple flowers that bloom only at midnight, and in midsummer the people throw parties that last all night, candles illuminating the flowers. And the stars overhead..." He shook his head in awe. "The stars dance with one another and re-form themselves into different constellations to tell stories, and we watch either lying in the grass or wrapped in blankets in the snow." He stopped talking and looked down to his lap. "It's beautiful. I do hope you can visit one day."

"So do I."

"If I can tag along," Benedek put in with a sheepish grin.

"You can't," Rovaslo told him. "The magicless can't enter. It isn't possible."

Benedek's face fell. I sat up, pitying him, and turned to Rovaslo. "Why are you here? Why are any of you – of us, here?"

His face told me it was a question he'd been waiting for. "One of the oldest reasons in history, really," he said. "A trade. Marcosza sits on the gateway between this world and that world." He took two rounded stones from the ground and held them together. "That small point where two circles meet, that's Castle Vyesta. The kings and queens of Marcosza have always married someone from the kingdom of magic, to keep the peace between the two lands. So Aurel was from Marcosza. Tabíta – and myself – from Muranj."

"What does Marcosza receive from this ... trade?"

"Mages," Rovaslo said simply. "Mages who live and work among you, to soul-push, as they do in the castle, or serve as architects, if you're a Weaver, or a warlord, if you're a

193

Ruiner. Magic is terribly useful in a world where it does not otherwise exist."

"And Muranj?"

"Szinstone. The Oroszom Mountains are rich with it, as are the northern Hills of Ariu, on our side of the border. It's a reddish stone, used little here in Sóar, but invaluable in Muranj. Our houses are built with it, palaces, roads, everything. It conducts magic in a way other stone cannot and increases the potency of any spell. Weavers adore it more than most. They can change the colour of the walls in their home with just a touch, and it takes little effort. One night's sleep in a house built with szinstone, and your magic will have recovered enough for days of use. It's priceless. Truly priceless."

"So Marcosza supplies szinstone to Muranj, in exchange for mages."

Rovaslo nodded.

"But I didn't come from Muranj."

"Some mages never leave Sóar. They stay and build lives, have children, die here, and never return to their homeland. That magic passes down through the line. It can skip some generations, but it will always come back around."

"But—"

He cut me off by raising a hand. "No more questions just yet," he said. "All in good time."

"You said we have little time."

"We do, so we should read more." He opened the book again.

"My love for Morós has grown so greatly in recent weeks that sometimes I feel I might burst. I was in love before, of course, with my handsome King Jóska, but he has been dead these three years, gods bless him, and he chose the path of eternal darkness. Sometimes, I find myself wishing he had let his soul remain, that I might speak with him, or seek his counsel when our son must make a hard decision, but over time, I have learned to forget. It took time, I must admit: time to accept that he was well and truly gone, and that there was no great sin in learning to move on. He would wish for me to do so, I know it. He would not desire many years of grieving. That was never in his nature. In Morós, I have found not only companionship, but a friend and a confidant, and someone my own soul yearns to interact with. It has been a great while since I have found such friendship, and I would not lose it for anything.

But that darkness that I saw in him before has only grown stronger. Where once I could convince myself that I imagined it, it is now unmistakeable, and it haunts my thoughts throughout most of the day and night. A glint in his eyes here and there. The twist of a smile that brings shivers instead of comfort. Though his health is with him, he talks from time to time of pushing his own soul into the castle, that we may continue our life in the same way, and in the same form. It is a passionate and tender thought, but never one that I could encourage. One day, his soul may join mine and we might pick up where we left off, but until then, I can content myself with speaking through him as a Seer, and not as a fellow spirit. I feel convinced that it is the right thing to do. But if I have learned anything about him over these months, it is that he has a mind of his own, and a will of iron. I may have my say, but he will do as he pleases.

I must go. The king and queen expect me for dinner, yet I find it difficult to even hold this pen with which I write. I would like nothing more than to remain in my bed until morning light, but my days of flesh and bone draw to a close, and I must cherish each and every moment, no matter how difficult. I must compose myself before they see me."

He turned the page.

"He has done it. Despite my protests, Morós has chosen the path of eternal life far too early. His soul now resides in the castle, and what shadows I saw when he was a man have only grown stronger in him as a spirit. I shudder to think of what strength it must have taken to do such a thing to himself, upon a living, healthy person. Pushing the souls of the weak and dying has long been easy, but this. . . I fear what it means for him. I fear what it means for my country. Such powers should not exist, let alone be in the possession of one man.

I cannot look at him the same way I once did, and I know that torments him. He did it for me, yet it was against my wishes. I feel the guilt, yet it is not mine to bear. My own death came quickly and quietly, in the middle of the night *when I was meant to be asleep. He released my soul then, as my son and his wife sat by me, and once they were gone, his own soul joined mine. Even now, I only write through the aid of magic in the castle. Without it, my own pen would no longer register my touch.*

I feel sick with guilt, though I know not what I might have done to change Morós's mind, having tried everything I could. Stubborn is too calm a word for what he is. His use of such dark and treacherous powers has changed everything. When I see him, I see red eyes and the horns of a devil. Indeed, sometimes I think I see Feric himself walking in Morós's shoes.

For now, I hide away and avoid him when I can, though he works to make that difficult. When I wish to speak with the king or queen, I make use of another Seer, Rovaslo, who has been kind and understanding as I work to find normality in my new existence. Always, we work together in secret, locked away in a library, or high up in a tower where Morós would struggle to find us. I have not yet confided my concerns in my son, though I fear I must do so soon. Whatever darkness I have brought upon the castle, it would not be right for me to keep it hidden for too long.

Footsteps on the stair. I must go."

Rovaslo gently closed the book. I stared at his face for an eternity.

"Feric," I said, "is the devil."

He nodded.

"Too many questions. I have . . . too many questions." I

stood and crossed the glen to a patch of yellow wild flowers, plucking up a few and dropping them again. Everything. *Everything* I thought I understood about this world was wrong. I had been so certain that there was a simple answer to ridding us of the castle's devilry. So sure that it could be fixed. It could all be fixed, it was just a matter of time.

But all this talk of souls and devils and dark magic, things I had thought – hoped – were only bits of stories that would only ever remain stories . . . it was crushing. The weight of everything around me pressed against my chest, taking my breath away. I clenched my eyes shut until they watered and then opened them again to find the world blurred.

The market. The tavern. The street beneath my room. My lumpy, tiny bed – that I somehow yearned for. The cat who sometimes slept at my feet. Mother. Father. Alíz. Life. So simple, sometimes. So quiet and routine, if you ignored the rains. Without the castle, it was all so terribly normal. But those things would never be the same again. How could they be? Just beyond those small, normal things lay mages, secret mines, *a kingdom of magic*. That such fantastic, peculiar things could exist alongside a life as simple as mine was as hard to believe as a thing could be.

No matter how hard I tried, I couldn't force Rovaslo's words to be true in my mind. They were strange. Nonsensical. And I couldn't know if he spoke the truth.

"Béata." Rovaslo's voice came from behind me. He stood

only a yard or two away, his footsteps silent. He hugged the book before him, his face fraught with sympathy. The way he said my name rang out in the same way I'd heard it in my head since Zírany. The same voice. "I know. I know how difficult this must be. If we had more time, I would have broken this news much slower, over weeks or months. Even years. There's more to tell you, I'm afraid, but not today. We are not so pressed for time that I must tell you all at once."

"But tomorrow, maybe, you'll tell me that I imagined there was ever a town at all. Ever a forest, perhaps. Maybe we never had a king or queen, after all. That sky." I motioned above us. "Well, the sky behind this incessant fog. I suppose you'll tell me it isn't blue, or it's some sort of window to another world that we can see if we *just believe hard enough*. Right? I look forward to tomorrow, Rovaslo. I really do." I walked past him and crossed the glen.

The whole world felt wrong. And I felt wronged. I could hardly trust the ground beneath my feet, or the very air I breathed. What parts of life, of everything I knew, were exactly what they seemed? What could be trusted any more?

I wanted a dark and quiet place in which I could curl up and sleep away the pain and frustration at Rovaslo's words. I wanted home – home as I had known it before, not now. The home of my childhood.

I stormed all the way back to the small hut Rovaslo called a home.

Chapter Seventeen

Liljana

You should be terrified. You should fear for your life, as you did in Tăru.

No matter how many times I said the words to myself, I couldn't make them true. The things I had seen in the throne room, the things that man had done, they should ignite the same fear as the Ashen. Spark the need to run, to hide, to survive. But they didn't. I was alarmed, yes, without a doubt. Whatever he had done to that boy, drawing out his life force by one means or another, should have no place in this world.

But anyone with that kind of power could be nothing but useful in this . . . budding war between the mages and the magicless. Between us and them. Not a war in the traditional sense, perhaps, but it sometimes felt like one.

The Ashen hunting us down, the mages sometimes rising up in revolt. Rising up in self-defence. And the offer he had made me, of a life free from fear, hung large and beautiful before me. He could make that happen. Now, more than ever, I believed that.

Bewitched though I was by the stag's power, I found myself vaguely relieved when the forest thinned, then ended at the village of Zírany.

The town was small and unassuming. The buildings were colourful and pretty, but the air was tense and timid, people glancing about nervously, eyeing me strangely, whispering too loud. I'd given little thought to how I might not blend in as much as I always did in the city, where there were far more people to hide amongst. Here, certainly, everyone knew everyone.

A small tavern near the centre of town beckoned me inside, my magic tingling in a way I didn't understand but was too tired to explore. I transformed a few pebbles into some coins, exhausted at the effort, but with little other choice. Half the tables were occupied, small groups huddled together whispering and drinking. I found a small round table in an empty corner, and ordered water from the young girl who approached me.

Comfortable. That's what it was. What the Regina could have been, but wasn't at all. A warm hearth. Chatter. Candles lighting the dim corners. Laughter. A cat who darted between feet to lie on a cushion by the fire.

Two older men in farmer's clothing sat down close to me, deep in a conversation I couldn't hear. I watched them for a long while, until one noticed my stare and leaned over.

"You quite all right there, missy?"

I shrugged. "I suppose so. Can't find what I'm looking for." And annoyed, though I didn't say it. Who was this girl? What was she like? And why was she so bloody important?

The other man turned so they both faced me. "What's that?"

"She's here for the castle, I bet," said the other. "Be dead in a day, mark my words. Damn shame. New ones every day. The baron meant well, I'm sure, but he has blood on his hands."

"I'm not here for the castle," I cut in. Only a small lie. "I'm looking for an old friend. Her name is Béata." I hadn't directly decided to do the stag's bidding, but nor had I decided against it. Petre's words still hung large before me, but what would it hurt to ask around a bit? The more I knew, the better I could decide my course of action.

They were both quiet for a moment, exchanging a glance I couldn't read. "She's gone," said the first. "Been gone a few days now. Her mother and father are sick with worry. I expect they're waiting for her body to turn up outside Vyesta, but nothing yet."

I sighed and took a long drink of my water. "Gone," I repeated.

"Gone as gone could be. My son thought he saw her in

the forest a few days ago, headed north. But I'm sure she will have turned at some point and headed for the castle. What else is in the north but more forest?"

"Aye, the castle's got her. Sure as sure can be," said the other. "It'll get us all one of these days. Swear to the gods. Only yesterday I was out in the barn trying to find what spooked the cows so much. Something set them off, but I never found anything."

"A bird, probably. Got you all worked up for nothing."

Their conversation drifted away from me. I stood up abruptly and made for the door, passing the girl who'd served me on the way. She opened her mouth as if to say something, and I waited, unblinking. She closed her mouth and turned away. I left the tavern. *I had water*, I told myself. *I am not paying for water.*

But the moment I got outside, a weight forced my feet to stop. Perhaps it was the memory of the stag, or Petre's words – or maybe it was my magic rising up once more. With a small roar of frustration, I turned around and went back through the door, crossed the dining room, and pushed open the door of the kitchen. A man and a woman waited inside, along with the girl I'd seen a few moments ago.

"I am looking for Béata."

The woman clasped her hands together, eyes instantly glistening. "Do you know where she is?"

"No, of course I don't. That's why I'm asking you."

The man moved to stand between us, holding up a hand to stop me. "Who are you?"

"An old friend, I guess. Well, not exactly, but I need to find her. We have a common interest." They were her family, clearly. The tears in the woman's eyes seemed proof enough of that. Families confused me a bit, at least how they worked, but I felt suddenly compelled to offer some amount of solace. "I'm sure you needn't worry," I told them. "I'm sure her magic will protect her." Then I immediately wondered if they knew. They must. Surely. Why else would they worry about her well-being so much?

But they didn't. Their eyes grew wide. No one spoke.

"So, you have not seen her?" I asked, taking a step backwards. A cold hand gripped my stomach. Was that guilt?

"Magic?" the mother breathed, fresh tears rising.

"Yes," I said unsteadily. "I'm sure you've heard of it." I hated the feeling that I might have done wrong. My bitterness settled back in, an easy wall for me to hide behind.

They looked to one another. The girl clapped a hand over her mouth.

"Well, clearly you have much to discuss now. If you haven't seen her, I'll just be on my way. She can't have got far."

Their stunned silence rang out loud in my ears as I left the tavern.

I should stop and rest, sleep, find a bed to borrow somewhere in town, but I walked to the edge of Zírany and stared off into the forest. She was in there, somewhere. Something deep within me could sense it. Knew it, profoundly. This girl Béata, about whom I knew nothing. Perhaps she was kind and sweet. Perhaps she was as awful as Madam Iulia. It was better not to know. Better to stay ignorant. I'd find her. I'd do my part. I'd bring her back to the castle, and I'd escape this world for ever. Escape into what I could only imagine was a world of flowers and tea and warm baths and buildings that glistened in the sun. Gods, the thought made my heart ache.

In the distance, as though excited about the path before me, thunder rumbled.

And yes, perhaps that future meant forsaking what Petre had asked of me, but if he had been offered such a chance, would he not have taken it, too?

"Hear ye, hear ye," said a man in a tattered brown cloak. He made his way down the street behind me. I moved into the shadow of a building and watched as a few townsfolk gathered in the street. "Hear ye, as the end of the world draws nigh." He waved his arms about wildly as he spoke, hunched with age and too much walking. "Magic as dark as the midnight sky has found us. It's gripped us, strangled us, and it will see us all perish. Kiss your children. Feast on your dinner. Take in a sunset as though it will be your last. It may well be. The old gods are angry at being pushed aside.

They've sent devils and demons into our midst. Ripped open a door between us and them. Between the light and the dark. Between the good, and the very, very wicked." The bard brought a hand to his mouth and shook his head, making a show of what dark things he was forced to speak. "These days, ladies and gentlemen, are the last days. You have heard the truth; now go and live what remains of your life."

Somewhere on the street, a child cried. A mother pressed her into her skirt and marched her away. People shook their heads, and a few men took the old bard by the arm, leading him away from the village.

My face had grown hot with anger. Magic. How dare he blame all of magic for the misdeeds of a few? This was how it had all started. This was why mages in Roşesti and beyond couldn't sleep without looking over their shoulder – because of people like him. Words like the ones he'd just spoken. Words had a way of clinging to people and never leaving, being repeated over and over again until fear and hatred had bloomed into something so great no one could tear it apart.

Perhaps he spoke some truth. Perhaps he didn't. But I was determined. Soon I would leave this world for another. Somewhere beautiful. Somewhere safe. Somewhere far, far away. I had only to find a girl, somewhere in the vast forest beyond the town.

I spun away and crossed the river, delving deep into the woods without looking back.

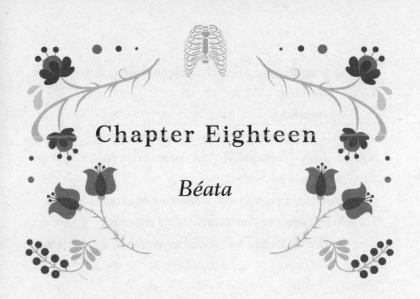

Chapter Eighteen

Béata

Rovaslo chose to begin his day before the sun. That was often the case back in the tavern, but the miles upon miles of travel had taken their toll on me, and no doubt on Benedek. I groaned at the sound of Rovaslo's never-ending humming and sat up from the pile of blankets that had served as my bed. I couldn't complain. I'd slept, and that was all that mattered to my tired, aching body.

"Ah, you're awake," Rovaslo said, motioning to the small table laid with fruits and bread.

"I'm awake," I said, sending a sorrowful glance to Benedek, who rolled over to look at me through half-closed eyes.

"Today we begin your training," Rovaslo went on,

helping himself to a slice of apple and dropping another log on to the fire.

"My training."

"Well, in a way. Your honing, really. Helping you learn how to use your magic. To accept it. To regulate it, as it were. That sort of thing."

"You haven't yet told me why we are so pressed for time," I reminded him, moving to a stool by the fire.

"Oh, I will. Today, in fact, after you've properly woken up."

My training, it turned out, was Rovaslo working to produce more of those *memories*, as he referred to them, like the one I'd had by the well. He sat before me in the glen, saying words that seemed utterly random but that he was convinced would awaken something within me.

"The bailey," he said. I shook my head. "The bailey at night. Stars overhead." Nothing. "Lady Cili. A funeral."

I shook my head again, though that one did spark curiosity.

"Sir Andor." Silence. "Midharvest supper."

"How are these things connected to me?"

"Difficult to say," he replied. "Keep going."

"Roast duck, at springtime. Tinett, the chestnut mare."

The glen faded away, the gnarled old swampland trees vanished, and in their place sprang up old fir trees and oak trees. The great, unending forest rose around me, and

before me, a horse's ears. I reached down to pat her neck –
a spectator, unable to control myself. "Good girl. There's
a good girl." Twilight was getting on. Owls called to one
another overhead. A bat darted from one tree to another.

"Not far now," came a voice. I knew it. I knew it, and
I loved it. "Just think how inviting you will find your own
bed tonight."

It had been a long journey. I didn't know where we'd
been, or where we went, but my soul was tired with travel,
and I longed for food and sleep.

"It smells like rain," I heard myself say. "I do hope it
will hold off."

And the forest slid away from me, the crooked trees
returning, the glen settling in once more. I fell forward to
my knees, unable to breathe, still feeling the horse's coarse
mane under my fingers and the joy that flooded me at the
familiar voice.

"Interesting, that that one should spark a memory,"
Rovaslo mused, patting my back. "Tinett was a good mare.
I hardly blame you."

"What was that?" I whispered.

"All in good time."

Torn. Ripped. They were the only words I could think
of. I felt like who I was had been torn away, and someone
else was thinking thoughts in my head. Someone else was
flooding my being with their memories. And when I tried to
think of the tavern, or the way the sunset made the houses

in Zírany glow like they were on fire, it all felt so distant I wasn't sure if they'd ever truly existed.

He gave me a half hour to recover. Benedek brought me water and some bread, but I barely ate, staring out at the fog without seeing it. I could sense he wished to speak, but I remained silent, and so did he.

Before I knew it, it was time for another reading.

The darkness has consumed him. I can see it writhing before him as he comes down the hall, and I can hear it slithering about as he speaks. Sometimes, I fancy it's a serpent, slinking around the castle at his feet, and yet at other times I hear what can only be the padding of hooves, hollow and distant, but desperately close. It is at those times that I imagine Feric himself roaming this place, making a home in a part of the world he should never touch.

When this castle was built, so long ago, and the practice of soul-pushing began, it had made sense to them to build it on a site where our two worlds intersect, that otherworldly powers might be easily drawn upon.

Now, though, I can only see the folly in such an idea. When a man like Morós so readily opens doors that should only ever remain shut, wicked things find their way through. And wicked things are not easily removed.

I have spoken with Aurel and Tabíta about this, although they are less certain of his devilry than I am. Perhaps it is my new state of being that enables me to see such things, but they seem blind to what I find so obvious. There is something very

wrong with Morós, and indeed Castle Vyesta. Even with a
Seer at work as kindly and good-hearted as Rovaslo, I do not
think such darkness will ever leave. Things like that, once
they have taken root, grow fast and strong. In a place such as
this, it can only flourish.

Guilt presses on me stronger every day. I have brought this
on myself, on my family, and on this country. Even the counsel
of the other spirits brings me no peace. They see the darkness,
but they avoid it like creatures of the night avoiding the sun.
Their presence here has been long, and their attempts to care
about what happens to those still living grows weaker by the
day. I can't help but feel like it defeats of purpose of remaining
here in the first place.

I do not yet know what may be done, but I have such
limited time to find out. Even now, I hear what must be scales
sliding across stone, and whispers in a language we were never
meant to hear. I would shiver, if I could feel the cold. I would
cry, if I could shed tears. I wish for nothing more than to find
a small, dark room somewhere in this castle and lock myself
away against such evil, but I cannot. I must undo what I have
done. I must save my child, if nothing else."

"Enough," I said as Rovaslo closed the book. "Enough.
I will hear no more until I have answers."

He blinked a few times, as though uncertain if he could
comply, and then asked, "What questions?"

"What is about to happen?" I asked in a whisper. "Why
so little time?"

Rovaslo closed the book with a sigh, as though finally facing the question he'd so long been putting off. "There are many facets to that answer," he started, but I interrupted him.

"Just start somewhere."

His fingers drummed on the book's cover for a long moment. Nearby, I could feel Benedek tense with anticipation. "The Eve of Saints draws near, as you know," he began. "It is a pivotal time of year for both worlds, momentous for those with magic both here and in Muranj. The Veil, whatever thing it is that separates us, that closes us off from the living and the dead, that divides the magical from the magicless, it thins on that night, and on the nights leading up to it. It is a busy time of year for Seers, as many take the opportunity to visit with their loved ones, or are reminded to visit their graves. In the castle, there is a yearly celebration of death, spirits all mingling with the living, candles and food and music drawing everyone together." He smiled, remembering. "And it is also when the door, if you will, into Muranj takes the least amount of magic to open. So it is when, traditionally, Marcosza sends its largest shipment of szinstone to Muranj. And I believe, firmly, that is when Morós will make his move."

"What move?" *Breathe, Béata, breathe.*

"Morós was once the prince of Muranj. His brother, Erazem, now sits on the Starijian Throne. Beautiful. Powerful. Coveted. When Erazem became king after his

212

father's death, and there was little left for Morós to do in Muranj, he was sent here, to our world, where his magic could be useful and he could serve the king and queen. It was a fine plan. It worked out well for many years."

Heaviness clung to the air around us as I waited for him to continue. This story, of course, did not have a happy ending.

"As we saw in Zalya's journal, Morós took a keen interest in the practice of darker magic. In the gods of the underworld. In using soul-pushing as a way to kill, rather than carry out the wishes of the dying. To bring demons here, where they do not belong." Rovaslo shivered, no doubt remembering things he had long tried to forget. "When Erazem found out, he banished Morós from Muranj and sealed off the door, hoping that by cutting off his access to the world of magic, his power would wane and it would all come to nothing. Unfortunately, that was not the case." Rovaslo cleared his throat and smoothed down his beard, sadness in every breath he took. "With Morós confined to the castle, and with the door into Muranj sealed closed, he has had all these years to cultivate his anger. I think perhaps it was why he consumed the castle the way he did. If he was confined to it, he might as well overpower it. Rule it, like the king I think he always wished he could be. All the while growing his strength to break open the door back into Muranj."

I ran a hand through my hair and looked away from

him. My veins threatened to boil over, a kettle filled too full. A roaring in my ears took a long moment to ease, and, though I fought it off with everything I had, tears burned my eyes.

Home. I wanted home. I wanted the quiet tavern on a slow night, to play cards with my sister and listen to my mother hum a tune. I wanted to sleep my way back in time and wake up with no memory of any of this. I wasn't built for it.

"Morós's last attempt to get through the door was when he killed the king and queen, trying to suck away the queen's power as he did so. He thought her magic would be enough, but he never acquired it. So he has taken to consuming everything else he can find, lesser mages, anyone with a speck of magic to offer. With the Eve of Saints approaching, I believe Morós will leap on the opportunity for the Veil to be so thin, when his power will go further. And the River of Magic that runs through all our veins has been sparking. Growing. Things are shifting and changing. There was a time when the evil was stagnant. Dangerous, but always the same. Not any more. I can feel it, sense it, smell it all around us. It has grown, and it will keep growing. Morós is nearly ready to try to open the door again, but he has not yet gained enough power. I worry that he is after the queen's power again, only this time, he will stop at nothing until it is his. And with so much magic writhing around with the Eve of Saints on our doorstep, he will use the chance to suck every ounce of magic out of Marcosza, and many, *many* will die." He shook his head and looked away, fear lighting his eyes.

"The king of magic must be stronger than Morós," Benedek said quietly. "Surely. Why can we not send for him?"

Rovaslo pursed his lips, sadness drowning any spark of life he'd once shown. "For one, we can't get through to Muranj. But I fear Morós might be stronger by now," he said with a sigh. "I have little proof, but I can *feel* the power stemming from the castle, like a bad smell grown too great. It is worse every day, thick and putrid and unavoidable. I've spoken with Sages around Marcosza and beyond, and they have all said the same thing: Morós's power is growing. With the help of whatever devils he has called forth from below, he is on the brink of greatness. Greatness in his own eyes, that is."

"Why haven't you gone to the castle?" My voice broke as I spoke, my lower lip quivering. "All the mages in Marcosza together must be stronger still than him."

"We considered it, certainly." He shook his head again, staring at the ground. One thumb ran back and forth over the cover of the book. "But with no way in or out of Muranj, we're all that's left. If Morós's power is so great that he could kill us all, where does that leave Marcosza? All of Sóar? The presence of mages might not be seen since the king and queen were killed, but their absence would be felt. Some still work in Dungléd with the baron, keeping our hungry neighbouring countries at bay. Without a little magical help, a country torn apart and left in ruin would be easy prey for Sovažska, or anywhere else. We cannot risk losing them all. Not while Muranj is closed off. Morós will consume and consume and consume until the world collapses, because he is driven by only one goal: to claw his way back into Muranj."

"I don't. . ." The words got caught in my throat, choking me. "I don't understand how you know all this. How do you know he is consuming power?"

"It has taken time to put it all together," Rovaslo replied, "but mages can survive the rains. He wants them to enter the castle. He wants them to survive."

My hands trembled, so I grabbed fistfuls of my cloak to steady them. A splinter I must have got from rowing the boat stung a bit. Benedek reached a hand out for comfort, but I twisted away. "I want an answer now," I said slowly, my voice quivering. "I want to know my part in this story. Why you called to me. Why I have so little time to do whatever I must do."

Rovaslo leaned forward and stared at me, unblinking, minutes stretching by. I met his gaze unflinching, waiting, breathing.

"Because, more than anything, Morós wants to get to you."

A shiver snaked its way up my spine. I dropped my cloak and stood, very slowly. "Why?"

A long pause. The calls of the birds vanished. The trees disappeared. There was only Rovaslo's face, and the words coming from his mouth. "Because, Béata, when the king and queen were slain, I was there. I pushed their souls from their dying bodies just before they passed on. Their time was not done yet. Pushing them felt the only way, and we hoped – I hoped, more than anything – that Queen Tabíta's power could be hidden, could be saved until she was again old enough and strong enough to use it, to come back and save us. After all, Queen Tabíta is a direct descendant of the first Seer, Vír Astar. She held more magic than King Erazem himself, and Morós will stop at nothing to take that power for himself. It was vital to stop it from falling into his hands." He paused again, fighting back the sadness that had haunted every word he spoke. "All the mages in Marcosza that Morós could get his hands on would not match her magic, her strength. If indeed he is to make another attempt at opening the door, he will need her." Rovaslo stood and walked a few steps away to collect himself, then came back, his head a bit higher. "When it became apparent that he was to kill the king and queen, I began to push their souls. To save them. I had to start with the king, only because he was closest to me at the time. It felt wrong not to do both. But in doing so, I lost precious time. As Morós approached the bodies, ready to consume the queen's power, I was forced to end her soul-push quickly, and I . . . I failed, in a way. The push was incomplete, and the queen's soul splintered, torn in two. Instead of all residing in one body, safe beyond the castle walls, it was split between the two baby girl mages born shortly before I pushed the queen's soul out of her body. One here, and one far, far away. One girl, the nearer one, got the bulk of her power, as she, too, had been born a Seer. It became my duty, then and there, to shield her from her own power until she was grown enough to face it. I was able to push aside her knowledge of it, her awareness of it, for a time, but as she has grown older, her magic has had a long time to grow. I can't keep it from her any more."

Silence.

Silence.

Silence.

"You, Béata, possess at least half of Queen Tabíta's soul. Morós tried once to kill you, and if he catches you again, no one will be able to save you."

Chapter Nineteen

Liljana

The forest had swallowed me whole, a great, jagged maw from which there was no escape. Every direction looked the same. Every tree, every rock, every patch of grass identical to the one before it. At times I was forced to dismount and lead the horse through a thicket with branches too low for me to carry on riding. And what was worse, I had no way to be certain that I even travelled in the right direction. There was a vague thread somewhere within me that I followed, but it wasn't always present, and sometimes I would wander for hours, aimless and cursing, before I felt its tug again.

I kicked the stump of a tree, the same tree I was certain I'd seen at least twice now. There was no road, no path, no houses or farms or anyone to enquire about the way north.

When the canopy above was not so dense that it blocked out anything and everything, I could use the sun to guide my way, but I'd then delve into the dense forest, so rich and old it had surely seen the world be born, and the sun would vanish.

"I hate this," I said to the mare, because the vast and wild forest bore a loneliness that even I found crushing. "I hate everything about this. I am sick to death of trees and leaves and dirt. I would wish for my city once more, if it hadn't tried to kill me."

The mare said nothing, of course.

"You're useless," I told her, but I ran a hand along her neck affectionately.

Late in the day, I pulled her to a stop and slid to the ground. Before us, in a clearing in the forest, stood several gravestones. Many of them, unevenly spaced, and so overgrown the names were nearly impossible to read. Some stood at a sharp angle, threatening to tumble over entirely. Some stood tilted to the side, as though their corner had been stuck in the earth and never righted.

The only other graves I'd ever seen were those in the yard outside the Old Church in Tăru, but even dilapidated as those were, they were more tidy than this.

I didn't like to be around death, even less so after losing Miha and Petre.

Petre. Something he had said long ago came back to me now, from a time when we were discussing why he lived in a crypt.

I find that the people who live the longest are those with a healthy respect for the dead.

I understood what he meant, that embracing life because it would one day end was one of the true ways to be happy, but it didn't make me appreciate death any more. Certainly not now, standing in a graveyard, alone.

Entering the clearing, I dropped to my knees and ran a hand over one of the stones. Most of it couldn't be read, but part of a name peeked out from under the moss and growth choking the stone.

Gilda.

"Good evening, Gilda," I said, my voice breaking the silence of the cemetery. "I thought I was lonely, but I guess you know more about that than I do." The rustling of the leaves – blood red with the approach of autumn – about me felt as a whispered response, but one I couldn't quite understand. Beneath me, something hard dug into my knee. I pulled up my legs to sit in a crouch and brushed aside dead leaves to find a bone protruding from the ground.

I should have moved away, perhaps cried out, but I didn't. I just stared at it for so long that the shadows grew longer and longer. I'd seen death before, and many times. Sometimes in Tăru, the king would behead someone for whatever crime he found particularly heinous that year, and he would hang their head somewhere in the streets. Or a funeral crowd would walk by, carrying the body of the dead on a wooden board, off to a burning somewhere else in the city. But this bone bulging up from the ground, hidden in a dense forest too far from anywhere civilized, brought about a chill I couldn't shake.

"Well, Gilda. I see they didn't bury you very well."

"They never do."

The voice was viscous and cold, miry as though the mud and dirt itself had spoken. I rose, slowly. Beside me stood a woman – if I could call her that. She was deathly pale, ethereal in a way I'd never seen. If I looked hard enough, I could see right through her to the forest behind, leaves bending in the breeze. Her white nightgown cast a glow about the clearing, and her face bore a smile so large and violent I shivered.

"They thought we had magic, you see," she told me, gesturing to the graves around me. "We didn't deserve a proper burial, they said. Just stuck us in the ground and let us rot. Family later brought the stones, but they were spoiled, marred by passers-by and time." The smile never faded.

"I'm – I'm sorry." I could think of nothing else to say. Had I fallen asleep in the clearing? Was she nothing more than a dream?

An owl called overhead, chilling and hollow.

"You are just in time," she told me as a man came up behind her. "Just in time, yes. How wonderful. How truly wonderful."

I tucked a loose piece of hair back into my braid. "Just in time for what?"

She cocked her head unnaturally to the side, as though confused. "Why, the Eve of Saints is nigh, silly girl. Or have you forgotten? No, you could not. Not when the forest has caught fire as it has, the branches alight, the trees burning." She waved two pale arms about us. "Even when I was alive, I so desperately loved this time of year. I wish more people loved it so, but they complain, don't they, Káro?" she said to the man beside her. "They complain about the approaching snow. The cold nights. The cabbage stew. How much they would wish for it when they can no longer taste!" A frantic, sharp laugh made me take a step back.

"Why can I see you now? There was no one here when I arrived."

"Nightfall," said the man. His voice resonated deep within me, a heavy boulder dragged along pebbles. "The Veil is always thinner after sunset. Everyone knows that." He shrugged, his head lolling peculiarly far to one side.

I dug a toe into the ground, annoyed. *I'm a mage*, I thought. *I should know that.* But I didn't, because everything about our existence in this world was kept under lock and key, and then both the lock and the key were burned.

"It's a very long, dark sleep down there," said the woman, stomping one foot on the ground by a gravestone. "We sleep all through the year until harvest time."

They began to frolic about, leaping and twirling until I did not know where to look, more and more of them every second.

"What are you doing?" I stood stiff, straight, turning slowly to see everyone in the clearing.

"Dancing, of course," the woman called to me. "By night, we always dance."

"Why?" I watched a young boy in a white tunic turn his head in a full circle, smiling all the while. There were perhaps twelve or thirteen of them in total, mostly older, like my mother and father would be, but a few children were mixed in here and there.

"Why what?" the woman asked as she spun close at hand.

"Why do you dance?"

The smile grew even wider. "Wouldn't you, if you had died and could only come back for a short while? No one dances enough when they are alive. Such joy it brings. Such joy. Tonight, while we may, we dance. Do join us." She reached her hands out for me, but all I felt was a wave of icy air.

I shifted from one foot to the other, a faint attempt at a dance, and tripped over an exposed bone in the ground.

"I have somewhere to be." I moved away, back towards the horse, but my legs felt laden with rocks, and my footsteps were slow. Would it be so wrong to join them?

"It cannot be so important that you haven't time for a single dance," said the woman, both imploring and menacing somehow. "Believe me. When you are dead, you will wish for nothing more."

Her words brought me to a stop. I turned back to them, the whole clearing alive with ghostly white bodies flying about, a spin, a leap, a skip through the fallen leaves. Perhaps I was dreaming. Perhaps I would awaken and find the clearing empty, the gravestones silent, the forest asleep. Perhaps.

But what harm would it do?

Slowly at first, I turned in a circle, raising my arms over my head.

"Yes," came the woman's voice, and I could hear her smile growing. "Yes, yes, yes."

I turned again, the other way, faster this time, until the dance had consumed every part of me, and I leapt about like a newborn foal, kicking up dirt and fallen leaves and tripping over bones like a madwoman.

They began to sing a song – a chant, really, begun by one voice and soon joined by all. The words came to me on the breeze as I spun and swayed in the falling twilight.

> *The gravestones stand*
> *Tall and proud*
> *The loneliness heavy*
> *The silence loud*
> *Names are carved*
> *In ancient stone*
> *Some together*
> *Most alone*

Lives gone by
I'll never know
Buried here
Where grass
Now grows
Sooner or later
Come one year
My turn will rise
And I'll be here

Night had fallen when at last my feet stopped. Every moment I lingered put more distance between me and Béata, but my soul had longed for escape. For something new and wild and beautiful. So I danced with the spirits to ease the pain, and returned to the mare breathless.

Gilda followed me, dancing all the while. "You are not the first of your kind to pass through here of late," she told me, arms dashing about. "Another travelled through only days ago. A girl with dark hair and a good heart. The kind of good you can just feel." She clasped both hands over where her own heart would be, if it still beat.

I gripped a fistful of the horse's mane, certain down to my core it was the girl I sought. "Where did she go?" I asked.

The woman stopped dancing long enough to point a long, thin finger to the north. "That way. Do come again soon. We love a warm face around here." And she spun away with that sickly wide smile never fading for a moment.

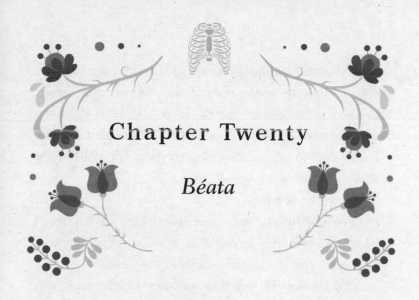

Chapter Twenty

Béata

I crept from the house before dawn. Perhaps Rovaslo heard me leave, perhaps not, but he let me go in peace. I made my way slowly through the reed grasses to the quiet glen where my world had splintered. In every leaf, every rock in the ground, every wisp of fog that reached for me, I heard Rovaslo's words once more.

You, Béata, possess half of Queen Tabíta's soul. Morós tried once to kill you, and if he catches you again, no one will be able to save you.

They were a prison, the bars of a cell to keep me in. No matter how far or how fast I ran, I was certain I could never outrun them, never escape, never again taste freedom.

And then I remembered I had never been free. Not

since the king and queen were killed so long ago, and the devil had set up house in the castle. I'd only ever known captivity. Confined to the tavern at night. To the town of Zírany, where Mother and Father had made their life. Imprisoned in a body that sometimes didn't feel like my own.

Now I knew why.

The visions, the memories that hadn't been mine. I knew now who they belonged to, and I was glad to know, but some part of me had broken at the news. The sense that I'd lost part of myself to someone I didn't know was seeping in, making my heart ache. *But I do know her*, I tried to remind myself. *You* are *her*. I wondered what it was like to be the queen, then, hiding within the body of a stranger, waiting for a chance to live again. A chance to speak. To breathe. I wasn't the only one who had lost a bit of myself. She had lost her life.

Slowly, I lowered myself to the grass and lay down, staring up at the swirling fog and treetops.

It was all too much, really. There was only so much one soul could take until life was too heavy to carry on. I wanted suddenly and desperately to leave. To take nothing but my cloak and boots and leave Marcosza behind for ever. Be someone else entirely. Take on a new name. Go to Roşesti or Sovažska and disappear from the nightmare of Castle Vyesta for ever. I could do it, this very second, and that thought kindled a joy that made me smile.

I could leave. I did not have to accept this as my life.

You cannot abandon us.

The voice was a whispered shout in my mind, as though Marcosza itself were crying out. I draped an arm over my eyes and let a sob bubble out. *Why me? Why me? Why did it have to be me?*

Something came back to me that Rovaslo had said the night before, as we were settling in for bed, though I'd been silent the rest of the day.

Magic chose you to be its bearer, Béata, and it does not make mistakes.

Magic does not make mistakes.

But I could be the exception. The first mistake. I wasn't strong enough to face it, to hone it, to practise it. What business had I to do with souls and spirits of the dead? Why didn't dead just mean dead?

And another thought found its way into my mind: who carried the other half of the queen? Was she still alive? Had I ever met her?

Too many questions. Far too many.

I lifted the book – Zalya's journal – that I'd stolen from Rovaslo's home. He must have known I'd do so, or he might have hidden it better than in a bucket by the fireplace.

At night, though I can no longer sleep in this form, I lie in bed and hear hooves on the stones beside me. I hear hisses, whispers, which I cannot understand. My own dear son came to me with the same complaint, and if I could, I would cry endlessly for having brought this upon him. Everyone now knows of Morós's dark side. It follows him everywhere, shadows I cannot remove. I work day and night with Rovaslo, studying ancient texts, consulting anyone who might possess even the vaguest of answers. There must be a way to expel Morós – if, indeed, it is even him any more – from the castle. Send him back to Muranj. I know, in this state, he cannot kill me, but he can kill my son and his wife, and anyone else in this castle for that matter, and I fear what he could then do to me. Possess me. Banish me. I am afraid to even think it, lest he can hear my thoughts and make it real.

It is twilight, and the rain beats hard against my window, yet it is still not loud enough to drown out the voices. They are everywhere, in every stone of this castle. In every room, and every hallway, and every breath. They are inescapable, and they grow louder by the day. I beg for it all to end, though I do not know what form that end will take. If it means the death of my son, then I pray for it to carry on. We are trapped. We are frightened. And if something does not soon change, we will all die.

The glen disappeared.

Around me were four stone walls, a great hearth with a fire burning low, like the life that lay wasting away in the bed. Servants stood huddled by the door, tearful and awaiting orders. Aurel held the hand of the queen as she coughed, and I put a hand on his back for comfort.

"The time has come," the queen said. "My time has

come. Please send for Morós." A servant hurried from the room.

"It will not be the same," Aurel said. I knew him well enough to know when tears were close. "The castle. It will not be the same without your presence. Your warm smile. Your dark humour." He laughed a little, but it ended in a sob.

"We may still speak," she said. "With help, perhaps, but at least we may speak. I may still watch over you, the children you will one day bear" – she winked at me – "and I will join my father and his mother and father. I will not be alone."

"I know. I know." Aurel kissed her hand as the door opened and Morós entered. With him came all the cold and wind of a winter storm – though no one else seemed aware. I shivered and hugged myself, stepping aside further than necessary to let him draw close.

"My dear Zalya," said Morós, placing a hand on her shoulder. "You have chosen the way of eternal life."

"Such as it is," she said simply. "There is little life to be had."

Morós said nothing more. Nothing in a language anyone else understood, anyway. He kept one hand on her shoulder and spoke in an ancient, dusty language that was both chilling and beautiful. The words came faster and faster, pouring from him like a springtime waterfall, filling the room, a light beginning to shine from within the queen herself. I turned away. I was a Seer, perhaps, or at least the blood of Vír Astar ran through my veins, but I could not watch this be done.

It was over soon enough. The roar of magic ceased. The queen's breathing had gone silent, and her soul now stood at the foot of the bed, looking on. There was always a period of mourning when a new soul was pushed, as it adjusted to its new state of being. To life in the in between. To the feeling of their heart going for ever silent.

I offered the queen's soul a small, bracing smile – and turned to find Morós watching me with the intensity of summer thunder. I drew back, frightened, and his lips curled into a cruel smile.

When I returned to myself, I threw the book as far away from me as I could and stood, crossing the glen in a few long strides. Rovaslo and Benedek were just emerging from the hut as I approached, Rovaslo carrying a bucket of water and Benedek still pulling on his boots.

"We wondered where you'd gone," Benedek said, smiling through tired eyes, but I marched past him into the hut and grabbed my cloak.

"I am leaving," I said, angry that tears fell fast down my face. "I am leaving. I am leaving."

"You cannot leave, Béata," Rovaslo said, dropping the water and reaching out as if to hug me.

"I can, and I am," I told him, shaking my head over and over again. "I am leaving. It is too much. I am leaving." My body ached. The very air pressed against me in a way that made it hard to breathe. Mages and magic and dead queens and souls. . . I wanted none of it. I wanted my old life back. I wanted my mother and father.

I had desired peace for Marcosza, not to uncover secrets about myself that would have been better off staying secret.

I left the hut behind with a brisk jog, wiping a hand across my face now and then to clear away the tears. I imagined I could hear glass shattering – the glass of everything I had ever known. Everything I thought I was. My childhood, shattered. Even with every step I took, things flickered in my vision. I saw the tavern and the fireplace – and I saw a great hall and a hearth. I saw my attic room and my small bed in the corner – and I saw a grand bedchamber with royal-green blankets and an ornate window. Everywhere I looked there were pieces of myself I didn't recognize, pieces of Tabíta. Things both familiar and foreign in a way that nearly made me retch.

My mother and father, shattered. Béata, shattered. In her place was a queen I never knew, someone I'd only heard of in stories about blood and boats and missing heads. That was the queen. That was the Tabíta I knew of. And that was the Tabíta vying for life inside me. She'd been hidden too long. Silenced too long. And though I, Béata, wanted nothing more than to leave her pushed aside, she would be subdued no longer.

The boat waited for me by the water's edge. I didn't stop

to think, to look back, to take in the strange and beautiful island I might never see again. I simply heaved with all my might until the boat floated atop the still waters of the lake, jumped in, and rowed with aching arms until I reached the opposite shore.

Chapter
Twenty-One

Liljana

I slept in a pile of fallen leaves. All through the night I could feel things crawling about, hear a hiss or a slither or the sound of more than two legs shuffling about around me, but then the gentle huff of the horse nearby would remind me I was not alone. The relentless birdsong when dawn was little more than a hint in the sky kept me from falling back to sleep, so I rose and pressed on, sore and in a sour mood.

By late morning I crossed a small river, but stopped to gather some rocks. Riding meant I had little energy to exhaust, so I could work a small bit of magic without paying too dearly – and I desperately required food. When I'd found two small, round rocks just the right size to turn into bread rolls, I sat down by the bank of the river to transform them.

Instantly, two warm rolls stared back at me. I smiled, my stomach rumbling at the sight, and dug into the first one with a large and unseemly bite.

When I'd eaten my fill, I eyed the cool water longingly. It had been too long since I'd had a bath, and the forest around me was as empty as I could hope. So, with little thought, I stripped myself bare and sank into the chilly, crystalline water, thankful the mare had found a patch of verdant riverside grass to keep her from running too far.

Yes, cities were nice, and I enjoyed the hustle and bustle of life, but this. . . This was nice, too. I smiled and closed my eyes, bobbing around in the water and allowing myself to dream, only for a moment, of what life would be like when I could cultivate my power and do more with it than give men I passed on the street unfortunate moustaches.

That's what I wanted. I wanted a world free of the fear of magic that had grown as a disease over the years – but after that, I wanted power. I wanted lots and lots of power that I could play with and practise with no one to tell me not to. That was the sort of power I would only get from the castle. That was the sort of power Petre would have told me not to toy with – but I wanted it. I wanted it badly.

I'd wasted enough time. With renewed vigour, I donned my clothes once more and urged the mare into a run. Wherever Béata was in this wretched world, I would find her and bring her to Morós.

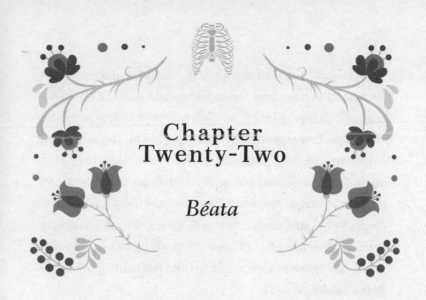

Chapter Twenty-Two

Béata

The forest watched me. Ancient as the world itself, murky as one of the grim marshes away to the south, it trained its invisible eyes on my form. The archaic, mangled trees intertwined with one another, a hundred thousand grotesque knots that could never, not in an aeon, be undone. Perhaps at one time, long ago, the bark had been that lovely amber-and-fawn colour of much younger trees, verdant and alive with the promise of a long future. But now they were ashen, sallow, like the disfigured bones of a creature long dead.

The thought sent a cold pang of loneliness through my body. I hadn't thought to ask Benedek if he wished to leave with me. I'd just left. I'd taken my cloak, hopped in the boat, and left. I hadn't even asked, I realized suddenly, how he had felt about all of Rovaslo's revelations. The swiftness with which my entire life as I had known it came crumbling down had been the only thing on my mind, the only thing I had any space for. His feelings, his thoughts, I had hardly given them a second thought. Thinking of that fact now made me sick with guilt. I was not the only one on this journey. He had come with me, joined me as I ventured into the unknown to find the voice calling to me. Benedek had been there with me when I needed him, and then I had abandoned him.

I hugged myself, feeling even smaller than before.

The forest was so much bigger when I was the only one in it. The trees seemed taller, fiercer, and the wind that bent their branches seemed to be speaking only to me. A haunting breeze played on my face and rustled the forest as it caught the hanging moss.

Everything watched.

Or perhaps it waited.

"You fool," I said to myself, startling at how loud my voice rang out in the silence. I was instantly torn between wishing to speak to ease the loneliness, and the horrific certainty that someone in these woods would hear me. Something I wished to leave alone.

With every step I took, I could feel Tabíta crying out for me to turn back. *Do not abandon us. Do not abandon your country in its time of need.*

I cannot face such darkness, I thought back, pulling my hair in frustration. *I cannot be strong when I don't even know who I am.*

You know who you are; you are simply unwilling to accept it. Tabíta's voice came strong and sharp in my mind.

I don't want to be a queen.

You are a queen, she reminded me. *A queen does not get to deny safety to her people.*

Why didn't I know of you before? Why hide for so long?

It was a safety measure during the soul-push. It was important that no one, especially Morós, knew where the queen's soul had gone. Not even the host. I think you know that.

Why tell me now? I asked.

Because it is time to undo everything Morós has built. Your magic has simmered for long enough within you, even if you didn't know it. You can face him now, even if you think you cannot. His power has grown strong enough to ruin everything. If he is given any more time, he will tear the world apart.

I shut off the voice, plugging my ears, as though it would drown out the thoughts that came from within. *I can't. I can't. I can't*, I thought.

The sky bled richer and deeper colours as the sun fell ever lower, threatening any moment to plunge the world into darkness. Here, darkness meant little, I reminded myself. This was not the forest around the castle, where the very trees themselves were nourished by the devil's blood, and the mist at your feet could take on any form in the time it took for your heart to beat once. Or so they said.

When the sun was long dead, I finally allowed myself to fully realize the aching in my feet from walking all day. It was a night when the dark seemed to have made itself a home, and dawn was nothing but a distant memory. I crashed on to a bed of moss, half-hidden behind a large rock, and let sleep find me.

By night, the call of owls and the skittering of nocturnal creatures became the hiss of a demon or the slither of a serpent, unseen but far too close. I huddled in my cloak to keep warm, listening and drifting in and out of sleep.

I'd meant to find my way south again, to retrace my steps back to Zírany. Back home. But my fright in the forest and my quick feet must have led me astray, because by mid-morning the following day, the forest gave way to a large green hill, and beyond that sat the town of Tökorona, evidenced by a crudely carved signpost. I knew little of it, only that it sat to the east of Zírany and was the birthplace of one of the old kings. A gift in disguise, I supposed. At least in a town I could gather news, perhaps find someone kind enough to ferry me back home. Loan me a horse. Gift me a seat in a cart. I hadn't the privilege of being choosy.

The cobblestone streets made me ache for Zírany. If I closed my eyes, I could see myself standing in the market square, feel the breeze from the forest so close at hand as it toyed with my hair, smell the cloud of herbs being sold in old Mar's cart. The hubbub of a tavern set my eyes to stinging. I could so very nearly see Mother sitting by the fire, knitting. Father cleaning tables. Alíz pretending to stack glasses while she played with the cat, a bit of stolen yarn tied to a stick. Home was just before me, and yet miles away. A hole broke in my chest and tears poured in, drowning me.

"Are you well?" A woman stopped walking to brush my shoulder gently, a basket of carrots tucked under one arm. Greying hair hung wildly past her shoulders; kindly brown eyes showed just enough white to make her look frantic.

"Y-yes," I said. "I'm just a bit lost. I've never been here before, and I miss home."

"Poor thing," she said, tapping my chin with a finger. "You look just as my Rósza did, when she had her fever. Are you sure you're quite well? Have you nowhere to stay? A bed to sleep in? Can't have you wandering about these parts by yourself. You've heard what things are about in this land, no doubt."

"I don't. Have anywhere to stay, I mean. I didn't intend to come here. I lost my way in the forest." I looked back towards the distant trees, hidden by the green hill.

"Come with me, then. We don't have much, but we have a roof, and that's better than nothing, poor child." And as if I truly was a child, she took my hand and set off down the road. "What's your name, little bird?" She tutted to herself more than once, as though she could not quite believe the extent of my misfortunes.

I swallowed back my tears from only moments ago, wondering if perhaps I was in a dream. "Béata," I said.

The woman stopped walking and stared at me for a long moment. I thought perhaps to ask if she knew someone by that name, or knew my mother or father, but the glint in her eye froze me to silence.

Her hand slipped from mine.

"Béata," she whispered, flashing the tiniest of smiles that didn't reach her eyes. "That's. . . That's a nice name." She glanced about in a way that made me think she might be looking for help, but that was foolish, I told myself. Help with what? My poor night's sleep in the forest and my confusion at the things Rovaslo had told me weighed heavily. I was in no condition to make judgements of people. "This way, then," said the woman, turning to walk in the opposite direction. "Silly me, taking us the wrong way. Not far now."

She moved quickly. I tried to follow, despite my body's ache, and left a healthy distance between us. Walking with someone only reminded me how much I missed Benedek – a thought that surprised me despite my exhaustion. How short a time I'd known him, to allow myself to long for his presence. But his sparkling eyes were far too easy to miss. And the way his gaze was forever darting to mine, catching my eye for a second too long before he would look away with a small smile that made me wonder what he was thinking, brought heat to my face even despite the distance between us.

You may never see him again.

I repeated the words to myself as we walked, a reminder that he would no doubt take my sudden departure as a refusal to help him any longer. To enter the castle and *bring about peace*. How foolish it sounded now, knowing what I knew. So foolish it made me smile as we walked. That I, a girl who stood barely to a man's shoulder, and a boy with nothing to go on but some visions of corridors and halls, might face down a practiser of black magic, thrown from Muranj for his deeds, and return Marcosza to a life of peace and prosperity.

You are no mere girl, said Tabíta sharply.

Perhaps it was the tiredness getting to me, but I giggled aloud. The woman spun swiftly and glanced at me, frowning, and then stopped to knock on the door of a large house.

She knocks on the door of her own home?

It was odd – beyond odd, and the small glances and change in her behaviour only began to fall together in my mind when it was too late and the door was opening. Whatever it was, she suspected me of something. I knew that now, and firmly.

"Minister Norik," the woman said. "I hope you can

spare me your help this morning. We've a stray little bird here by the name of Béata who stumbled into our midst and has nowhere to stay." The way she said it was the voice of a nightmare slipping coldly into my ears.

The man, dressed far more tidily than her and with a signet ring that bore the same seal of the town that I'd seen on the fallen sign, took a step out the door and eyed me up and down. "Béata, you say?" he mused, curiosity and fear clearly warring within him. "What are you doing here?"

"I got lost," I told him. The day was fairly warm, but I shivered. Why had I left the woods? "The trees all look the same sometimes. I was just trying to get home."

He eyed me deeply, a somewhat disingenuous look on his face as though he were making a show of trying to read me better than anyone else could. "Travelling from where, though?" he asked, with a small chuckle. "Paid a visit to Feric, have you? Had a little catch-up about what you've done to the castle? Counted up the bodies you've collected over the years? No more, missy. No more." He grabbed my arm with enough force to break it. "We know of your magic, fiend. One of your kind went looking for you in Zírany. Seemed normal enough, until she was seen in the woods turning stones into bread. She told everyone your secret while she was there. Folks all around started to remember things: how quiet you were, your insatiable interest in the castle. And what's better than that? Why, the rains over the castle starting the same year you were born. Devil's daughter, that's what you are! Devil's daughter, and what do we do with devils? We send them back to hell."

"Indeed we do, or we ought to," said the woman, beaming with triumph.

I fought to escape his grasp, cursing myself for being so tired. "I am not the only mage in the country," I nearly shouted. "How am I to blame for those events?"

"So you are a mage," he said, lowering his head yet still staring at me. The look on his face gave me a violent chill. "Mages aren't meant to be anywhere but Dunglèd, where the Weavers can manage them. So I'd say, by your own admission, you're as good as done. As good as guilty."

"I am not guilty." I swallowed back the tremble in my voice. "I wish to end the madness in the castle as much as anyone else."

"So why would anyone be looking for you?" he said, tilting his head. "Why are *you* so special?"

"Because—" But I stopped, because explaining that I was wanted by a dark prince of magic as the descendent of the world's first Seer felt like nonsense. "I can't say. I do not know. I don't know who went looking for me."

"Well, that's not enough for me," he said, pulling the door closed behind him.

A small crowd had begun to gather in the street, prying eyes watching and ears listening. They scattered to make a path as the minister of the town marched me down the street at a pace with which I struggled to keep up. My feet caught on the uneven cobblestones, but if I fell he did not stop to let me regain my feet. He simply dragged me along as my limbs flailed wildly about. All around us, word was catching fire.

"It is the mage from Zírany, the one no one knew about."

"Why is she here?"

"No one knows."

"I heard she kept snakes as pets. I'd have suspected her if I'd known her."

"Will they kill her?"

"Probably. Better off that way, all of us. Mark my words."

I turned my head as far as I could to see who'd spoken the last words. A young woman with her hair pulled back, severe and simple and anger made human. I glared at her, struggling to keep my feet, and though I shouldn't have, of course, I smiled. I smiled as if I knew something she didn't. As if I was cursing her and no one else would know. As though all the things they had said might be true.

They weren't, but I had very little power left to me. Might as well get my fill before the end.

She shrank back, disappearing into the throng of bodies.

The streets of Tökorona became a blur, one blending into another, more and more townsfolk following us, windows being flung open so the building's occupants could lean out to watch us go by. Our journey only ended when we reached an old building on the outskirts of the town, what looked like it had once been a church but was now some sort of prison. They led me in through the open gate and up to the door, where the minister told a handful of men to keep the crowd outside.

"And send word to Zírany. They'll want to know we have her," he said.

My mother and father. What would they think, so close on the heels of losing Filep? There was nothing they could do, I knew that. This fear of magic had grown too strong even in the past half hour to ever be tamed again.

We entered the dank building, along with the woman who found me in the street, and two others I didn't know. A dark and crooked set of stairs led us down to what appeared to be catacombs converted into small cells. A man hung against the bars, his head lolling about. "Sober yet, Olavi?" the minister asked as we passed.

"Not quite yet," came the slurred reply.

"Bit longer then," said Norik.

The hallway smelled of filth. Stagnant water pooled on the stones, splashing on to my boots. My weariness made all the flames from the torches blur together, a large, flaming god who waited to see me killed. I wanted to be afraid, but I couldn't convince myself this was real. The only thing I wanted above all else was to lie down in the dark corner of a cell, pull my cloak around me, and sleep for days. Why had I never cherished sleep so?

Without warning, Norik flung me into an open cell. I thundered to the floor and rolled once, cold and slimy water splashing my face.

"That was hardly necessary," I groaned, struggling to my feet.

"Disagree," Norik said. One of the men who'd come with us brought him a stool as he slammed the cell door shut. He seated himself, leaned forward, and laced his fingers together. "Who do you work for?" he asked.

I leaned against one wall. "Haven't you answered that yourself? I heard them all out there. Clearly, the devil sent me."

"She admits it," breathed the woman, bringing a hand to her mouth.

"No," I replied, yawning. "But explaining no one sent me will get me nowhere, so I needn't bother." The words came back to me strangely, not ones I might otherwise have chosen. How much of it was Tabíta, and how much Béata? "I truly need to sleep. Can we finish this after a rest?"

"Of course not," Norik spat back. "Don't be a fool."

I sighed and crossed my arms, pulling my cloak tighter around my shoulders. "What do you want to know?"

"Who was the young woman who went looking for you?"

I was quiet for a moment. Who *was* she? I knew no other mages – at least not to my knowledge. I had yet to even fully admit to myself that I bore magic, let alone think of others. Had she been sent to find me?

248

Rovaslo's voice whispered in the back of my mind. The other half of the queen, perhaps, out to find me? "I don't know. And that's the truth. Do with it what you will."

"I do not accept that. The rains are growing, you know. Spreading out to consume all of Marcosza. Perhaps even beyond. Whatever devilry began this chaos is growing stronger by the day. You are part of this, Béata. You and the rest of magekind. None of this would have happened if it weren't for magic. You owe it to us – to your family – to help us."

In some ways, he was not wrong. I tried to see things through his eyes: a frightened town, in a frightened country, with poisonous rains covering more land every day. To find a mage hiding in the midst of the town at the centre of it all, to them, that must seem like finally making headway. Finally finding answers. I knew how that felt. How many times had I sat at my window by night, longing to end the madness? To end the murders? To end the rains? I might have leapt at such a chance too, if I was being truly honest with myself. It was what Queen Tabíta wanted more than anything. What I wanted. What I had left home to do. But I was not the same person I was when I had left.

"I understand. I would give anything to help in any way I could. But I cannot. Whatever magic I have is untrained and useless." I didn't mention how much magic I truly had – Tabíta's magic. And there was little point in delving into the nature of how I could help them, that Morós was hunting me like a fox and I was stuck between two ways to die: surrender myself to him and perish by his magic, or elude him as long as may be until his power grew strong enough to blast open the door to Muranj and destroy our world in the process.

"Very well," said Norik, folding his hands together. "If you cannot or will not help us, we have but one option left to us, short of killing you here and now."

I watched his face, refusing even to breathe.

"You will go to Dungléd. Surely, Baron Izsak will pay something for your capture, and he will be better equipped to decide your fate or learn the extent of your involvement than we are."

"Dungléd." I said the word aloud. Dungléd was a great walled city tucked away in the Oroszom Mountains that separated us from Sovažska. People often said it was where Castle Vyesta should have been built. That a vast city with walls and mountains to ward off threats would be a far safer home for the kings and queens than in the forest in the middle of the country.

Now, of course, I knew why the castle had been built there: to bridge the gap between Marcosza and Muranj.

"The baron has his own mages. Why would he bother with me?"

Norik shrugged in a way that said, *Wouldn't you know that better than I would?* "We will see, won't we? He will be interested to know, I am certain, that we have found a mage in Zírany, born the year the rains began, who is being hunted by other mages whom she claims not to know. I may not know what to do with that information, but he will. I suppose it's his job."

I said nothing.

"Done. It's decided," said the minister, rising. "Pavel and Zigmund, you are with me. I thank you for your part in this, Borsca, but you may return home."

"Pardon me," replied Borsca, the woman who'd brought me to Norik, "but if there is a reward to be claimed from the baron, then that reward is owed to me."

Their discussion fell into a squabble over who would receive whatever coin the baron would offer, but I turned away to one of the far, dark corners of the cell and crouched down.

Dungléd was far. Far from home. Far from Mother and Father and Alíz. Far from Benedek – whom I was now certain I would never see again. No one would find me in the mountains, and why would they bother to look? I was a mage. An evildoer, if you asked anyone. Everything about who I was and what I loved was gone. Broken. Blown away by winds of change. Sitting here, in a dank cell, ready to depart for a distant city from which I might never leave, I saw only two options before me: accept my fate and die with grace, or allow a new Béata to be born from the ashes of everything I'd once held dear. Embrace the magic. Embrace the unknown. Fight until my hands were bloodied and my soul had given up.

Tired as I was, I rose slowly from the floor.

"When do we leave?" I asked.

Chapter
Twenty-Three

Liljana

I had begun to worry that my bum would grow into the horse's back. Every hour of the journey my hopes would rise that I would see Béata ahead, that my magic would recognize her, and my journey would be over. It felt a year since I'd left Tăru on Miloš's boat and escaped into the Hills. But each hour came and went, and there was no one else in sight. So I followed the thread of magic that guided me on, singing to myself now and then, speaking to the mare despite her silence, and daring myself into silly, sometimes foolish games to pass the time, like spinning all the way around on her back as she walked without falling off.

Eventually, we came to a town, and I almost squealed

with excitement at the prospect of seeing other people after the agonizing loneliness of the forest.

The town was alive with some sort of commotion that made it easy to get lost amongst the crowd. I led the mare down the wide main street, straining to hear the conversations swirling around us. I tapped a woman on the shoulder, who eyed me uncertainly. "Is there a holiday?" I asked, then, more hopefully, "Or a murder?"

"No murder, though we were all expecting one. Just the mage who left yesterday evening."

I stifled a sudden inhalation of joy. "Mage?" I said the word like I'd never said it before, and wasn't quite certain what it was.

"Yes, the one from Zírany. Beatrice or something, her name was. They've taken her to the baron. How have you not heard?"

"I've been away," I explained quickly, offering a small and tired smile. "My mother was unwell. We went to see a healer a day's ride away. Didn't help. I'm afraid she hasn't long." The lie tumbled out as I quietly relished the idea of being a local in a small, insignificant town such as this.

"Sorry to hear that," replied the woman, then turned back to her friends.

"One more thing," I said, again tapping her shoulder. "The baron, you say. Where is he? Why send her there?"

She frowned, as though I should have known the answer. And I should have, because anyone from Marcosza would have. I hoped my ignorance would not give her enough reason to question me too closely, or eye me too carefully.

I would leave soon enough. They were so distracted by this news they wouldn't think to come for me. "In Dungléd," she said slowly. "Where he has always been."

"Of course. I must have forgotten. No one ever talks about him."

I took the horse's mane and led her away quickly, letting the crowd swallow us up.

I sighed, frustrated. When would my journey ever end? From Tăru to the Hills, from the Hills to the castle, and now all the way to Dungléd. Before me seemed nothing but endless, winding roadway that grew longer with each step I took.

I turned back to the mare and ran a hand along her back. "Now, we go to Dungléd," I told her.

Chapter Twenty-Four

Béata

The carriage they put me in was little more than a box with bars on all sides. No seat, no proper roof, no sign of comfort at all. It was pulled by a pony who was so old she frequently had to be urged to keep walking or she would stop altogether and fall asleep. I couldn't blame her. As the sky grew darker and threatened rain, I hadn't even the energy left to complain. I crossed my arms over my chest, leaned my back against the wooden bars of the cart and dozed as we bounced down the road.

The company spoke now and again. Norik kept insisting that the baron would pay for their capture of a mage from Zírany – "The root of it all!" he kept saying – but Zigmund would remind him that Izsak had his own mages.

"There's too much about her to discount so quickly," Norik said. "Most of the mages disappeared after the killings, as they well should have. Didn't need none of their kind lurking about, playing tricks others couldn't. But she stuck around." He cast a sideways look to me. "Maybe there's nothing in it, but I'll let the baron tell me that, and pay me for my trouble."

I let their voices fall away. What did I care how much they made for me? I could embrace my new-found fire after some rest.

I awoke to rain. My neck was sore from my head having fallen to the side while I slept, and though I was cold and cramped and on the brink of tears, at least I'd slept. "Where are we?" I asked Zigmund, the one who rode closest to me.

"Twenty or so miles from Tökorona. What's it to you?"

I asked no more questions. Though the rain and fog shrouded much of our surroundings, I could tell we travelled on a wide road that wound through the forest. The land rose and fell, the pony sometimes struggling to pull the cart up a hill, and sometimes trotting as the decline gave her speed. Great evergreen trees towered away into the cloudy sky, sentries guarding the road to Dungléd. The woods smelled fresh and inviting, and in the rain it was harder to tell that everything in the world was dead and crumbling.

I didn't feel afraid, though the chill of the forest and the darkness around us was disheartening. The company waited until the last bits of sunlight – what little there was to be had through the clouds – had disappeared before stopping to set up camp. We left the road behind a ways, I guessed to hide from waylayers haunting the road by night, and Pavel built a fire over a bed of rocks. Though they left my hands tied, they released me from the cart and set me by a tree far from the fire.

The echo of their voices made for grim company as I lay on a bed of needles and stared up at the dark sky, raindrops occasionally making their way through the branches and falling on my face. Before sleep found me again, the only clear thought I could muster was, *Who was the girl who went looking for me?*

At first, I thought the shouts were in my dream. I was in a wide-open field, readying for battle with an unseen force, and the shouts came tumbling out of the mist. Then the field disappeared and the forest rose up around me, and the company were all on their feet, shouting over one another.

I sat up, blinking through my sleep, to see what had caused the alarm.

A wolf snarled from the darkness. The forest held many wolves, and though the occasional lone traveller might come across one or two, they preferred smaller prey, and kept to the more remote parts of the forest. This one was alone, fur as black as the shadows around it. The dying firelight glinted off thorn-sharp teeth, and a subtle hint of red showed in its eyes.

This was like no wolf I'd heard of. Fear reared its head, ready to swallow me whole — but something else soared above, something ready to fight and wound and resist in all the ways I never knew how.

Magic, I realized. *Tabíta's magic.*

"It's mad!" Pavel shouted. "Fetch a sword, Zigmund, you dolt, what's taking you so long?"

"I don't wish to get close enough to kill it with a sword!" Zigmund replied, though he drew it from its sheath all the same.

"No one thought to bring a bow?" Norik thundered.

"This was your idea," Pavel returned. "You should have thought it through."

The wolf entered the clearing, snarling and snapping, saliva running from its mouth. *Possessed*, I thought. *That creature is possessed.* I shouldn't know that. Béata shouldn't know that. Possessed, snarling creatures were few and far between back in my father's quiet tavern. But the queen knew. She recognized its darkness in a way that made me wonder what sort of life she had had. What sort of things she had seen.

She was right. *I* was right. Something in my veins flickered in warning. Danger tinged the air around us.

"Feed it the girl," said Pavel, taking a few steps towards me. "Give ourselves a chance for escape, at least."

"Don't you dare," Norik shot back. "If we survive I'll make sure you don't see a coin of that reward just for the very notion."

"I don't hear any better ideas," said Pavel.

I'd always been told that many wild creatures feared fire, yet the wolf skirted it as though it wasn't there, head low to the ground as if ready to pounce.

"Let me go," I called, quietly at first, and then louder. "Let me go." My hands shook against my bonds. I wanted desperately to be free, to give Pavel two black eyes for the very idea, although it wasn't something I'd ever done before. How dare he?

"Why in the hell. . .?" Norik said.

"I can help." I had little notion of what I might do, or how I might do it, but something within me was desperate for escape. My magic. Its rumbles had turned into a growl so fierce my limbs felt on fire. Perhaps if I used to it spare their lives – whatever that might look like – they would set me free. It was a small hope, but it was there.

"How?"

"I don't know, but let me try."

Pavel needed no more convincing. He rushed towards me and cut the ropes from my wrists with one swipe. His sudden movement had sprung the wolf into action. He'd leapt towards Norik, who tumbled out of the way as Zigmund raised his sword. "I don't even think he's hungry!" Zigmund cried, arms visibly shaking. "I think he just wants to see us all dead."

When my feet were freed, I ran across the clearing to where the wolf crouched, ready to jump once more. I had no weapon. No shield. Nothing.

But as its muscles rippled with the beginnings of a pounce, my mouth opened and words I didn't know poured out. The only other time I'd heard them, I realized, was in the vision when Morós pushed the queen's soul from her body.

The wolf stopped advancing, falling silent. Its reddish eyes glistened, but it remained where it stood – until a light burst from its body, disappearing into the air around us, and it fell to a heap on the ground.

Silence echoed like a drumbeat.

"What the devil was that?" Norik asked, and I heard him muttering a blessing under his breath.

"It's dead," Zigmund announced, stepping closer and feeling its neck. "Dead as dead can be."

I wasn't looking at the body. At the edge of the clearing stood the wolf's soul, pale and illuminated, looking on with a glimmer of sadness that made my heart ache. I'd killed it. *Killed it.* My heart split in two, dizziness settling in, Tabíta relieved both that my life had been saved and that her magic still worked, and me – Béata – heartbroken over what I'd done. It was possessed, I tried to remind myself. It was better off this way. But that didn't stop the sickness from taking over my body.

"I didn't mean to," I whispered, but there was nothing

to be done now. I'd soul-pushed, taken away its life force. The wolf would never breathe again.

My plan was a breathtaking failure. When the silence in the clearing was finally broken, and I'd assured myself that no one else could see the wolf's soul standing amongst the trees, Norik turned to me with his mouth open.

"It's true, then. It's all true. Put her back in the cart."

"I did what had to be done," I said quickly, shaking my head as they steered me away.

"You used magic to kill," Norik said, looking at me as though every suspicion he'd had about me had been confirmed.

"Everyone has the power to kill," I reminded him – Tabíta reminded him – as my hands were bound once more. "Just not by magic."

But my words were met with silence.

Our journey to Dungléd took two more days, and where they had been anxious around me before, now they didn't speak to me at all. I took to humming at first to ease the loneliness and quiet, but the sudden crash of a sword being knocked against the bars of the cage turned me silent. I'd spent a long time trying to silence the queen each time she attempted to speak, but now, lonely as I was and confined to a small space, I grudgingly began to listen to her.

My sister, she said, *you will need a bit more verve if you are to get through this life with magic. People in Sóar do not trust your kind. You must be watchful and careful and strong.*

Perhaps my counterpart got all the verve, I replied sourly.

She did, but she revels in loneliness. She has my magic, but none of me. It's strange for me, a bit like looking through a foggy window. I'm aware that she's out there, but little more.

I shifted in the cart. *How long have you been aware of me? Or is it like sleeping until Rovaslo woke you up?*

I was always aware, but I couldn't speak or interact with you. Not until you knew I was there. There was so much for you to process over the years: the murders, the magic hiding within you, your brother's death. I couldn't simply pop out and add to that. Sometimes, though, I would start to remember something by accident. Something you would do or say would remind me of a time gone by, and I'd get swept away.

The visions.

Yes.

I closed my eyes, suddenly wanting to cry. I should be thankful that everything made sense now. That I had explanations for the things that had plagued me for so long. But it was so heavy. So much.

I don't want to talk any more.

So we rattled along the road for two days, the mountains eventually looming over us like the overgrown tombs of ancient gods, and by the time the walled city of Dungléd sprawled out below us, I couldn't think of a word to say even if any of us had been speaking.

"About damn time," Norik muttered with a sigh.

"Never been here," Pavel said. "It's a fine-looking city.

I could use a drink."

"We could all use a drink," Norik told him, urging their horses on. The narrow road towards the city was steep and winding, a treed slope on one side and a sharp drop on the other. I gripped both hands around a single bar of the cart, tied together as they were, hoping against all hope that the old pony wouldn't misstep and send us both tumbling to our deaths in a rocky ravine.

"Frightened?" Norik asked me suddenly. I started. No one had spoken to me in days.

"Yes. It's a long fall."

"Not about the fall," he said, then jutted his chin towards the city. "About what awaits you down there."

I eyed the bone-white walls that harboured a sea of red roofs, all the buildings in uneven sizes and four great towers rising up along the walls. *Four sharp teeth*, I thought, *ready to devour me*.

"No," I lied.

"You should be."

I shivered, but dug deep for enough of the queen's arrogance to give him pause. "Perhaps Dungléd should be frightened," I said in a low, deep voice.

It's good to keep wicked men a little bit afraid of you.

Norik didn't speak to me again.

The gates were tall and wide, guards standing sentry on either side, and more watching from the towers. In a sense, we blended in with the others coming and going from the city, carts and horses and carriages all filtering in and out. But in another sense, we stood out enough to draw the attention of everyone around: a girl in a cart with bars and a lock. I made it a point to smile at everyone who looked at me.

No one smiled back.

One of the guards moved to stand in our way, a spear in one hand that stood taller than him. "Who have you got there?" he asked, nodding to me.

"A prisoner for the baron," Norik explained. "She's a mage from Zírany. She is linked to the castle and the rains. It's a bit of a long story. Is the baron in?"

The guard drew back in surprise, then made a signal to the guards in the tower. A moment later, four of them had surrounded my cart, and a messenger was dispatched on horseback to carry word to the baron before our arrival. I smiled at the guards around me, half hoping it appeared as a kind gesture, and half hoping it unnerved them.

We trundled along the streets, my knees pulled up to my chest. I'd never been to a proper city before. Zírany wasn't small, but it was far from the size and grandeur of Dungléd. The buildings were tall and full of windows, separated in places by closes so narrow I thought I might have to turn sideways to traverse them. Near the centre of the city we passed a great cathedral, and I wondered which gods they worshipped within. Its colourful windows depicted a starry sky, with trees below it, and fire below that. I stared at it until we rolled out of sight.

How can people live amongst so much stone? I wondered as the imposing walls of Szaliri House drew closer. The green of the forested mountains just beyond the city must be a torment to always see and never enjoy. Here, everything was white, and red, and noisy. My soul longed for the freedom of an open space. For the flicker of a fire in the hearth of our small home. For a sign of anything familiar.

The gates of the castle were hauled up as we approached. One of the guards who walked with us shouted something I couldn't quite make out to one of the guards by the gate, and they waved us through. Inside, the courtyard was a swarm of activity; guards and servants and people whose role I didn't know all milled about, peering over one another for a glimpse of me.

High above, on a balcony from which hung the flag of Marcosza, stood a man clothed in green. He watched us enter the courtyard, and I stared up at him until he was blocked from view by the crowd. When I again peered between heads and craning necks to see the balcony, he was gone.

"Out you go," barked one of the guards, his spear pointed at me.

Norik unlocked the cart and I stumbled out, my body groaning with the sudden stretching.

Inside waited a busy and colourful great hall, the walls lined with Marcoszan flags and tapestries, the floor lined with a rich green rug. A wide and winding staircase led up and disappeared far above, the banisters ornately carved with griffs and dragons. Windows that stretched from a distant ceiling to the floor looked out on an enclosed, grassy garden. It was difficult to believe, taking it all in, that this castle belonged to a country in such disarray. Things here were still beautiful. Still alive.

"Aren't you going to show me to my room?" I said to the guard nearest me.

He grunted his disapproval at my joke and nudged me along the hallway. Norik, Pavel and Zigmund were all ushered away, and I didn't bother looking back at them as I followed my new companions. The beautiful parts of the castle, I soon learned, were not meant for me. We entered through one door after another, descended stair after stair, the world growing ever darker and the torches brighter, until, when I was almost certain we had walked to the centre of the earth, a masked guard turned a very loud key and we were ushered into the dungeon.

If I had thought the cells beneath the church in Norik's town were bad, this was desperately worse. Ill-kept, dark cells glowered out on either side, as old as the land on which this castle sat, I was very nearly certain. Webs caught the light of the torches between most of the bars, and in one cell, though I glimpsed it only briefly as we walked by, I was sure I saw bones.

"Here's your room," said the guard, pushing me into an open cell. "I trust you'll find it comfortable."

"Bit small," I quipped to cover my fear. "But I'll make do."

He slammed the door shut, and another guard turned the lock.

"Now what do I do?" I asked, taking a seat on a wobbly stool, the only piece of furniture in the cell.

"Now you stop asking questions," he replied through the bars of the door.

Everyone left me, and the dungeon fell into darkness.

Chapter
Twenty-Five

Liljana

Dungléd felt so like Tăru in countless ways, and so unlike it in countless more. It was cleaner, for one, with less dishwater pooled in the streets, and only a few of the smaller streets had laundry hanging above. With no harbour, the air didn't always carry a hint of fish and seaweed, replaced by the occasional waft of evergreen trees and fresh mountain air. Familiar yet unfamiliar. So close yet so far.

I wondered what the world of magic smelled like. Flowers, I imagined, or freedom, if that had a scent.

Having left my horse and few belongings at an inn, I adjusted my boots, pulled up my hood, and wandered down the noisy main street of the city, head turning slowly this way and that, listening and watching and feeling very much at home. I liked a city, I realized. Not Tăru, perhaps, but I preferred the towering of buildings and the throng of people I could so easily get lost in to the towering trees and endless silence of the forest. It left me feeling exposed, like prey that would be hunted at any moment. Here, I could just be. Hide away as a face in the crowd and disappear for ever if I wished to.

Sometimes in Tăru, I would sneak into a shady place for a few rounds of cards with men twice my age and twice as drunk. The drink kept them from seeing the magic I used to win every time, and I would leave laughing at how dumb they'd all been, with a pocket full of coins I would use to buy food for Miha.

Her name was a punch to my stomach. I stopped walking for a moment to breathe away the ache and collect myself.

Dungléd felt very much the same, and if I wasn't so pressed for time, I might seek out a card game just for the sake of nostalgia.

I took a smaller street that branched off to the right, then stopped. Ahead, perhaps halfway down the street, I saw two young men walking side by side. They spoke aggressively, harsh whispers passing back and forth. In the hand of one, fire danced for a brief second.

My feet stumbled, halting briefly. Who could be so foolish as to display their magic in so public a place? The very idea put a tightness in my chest.

Still, I smiled.

The two young men carried on their argument. Who better to help me hunt down a mage in a city unfamiliar to me than two mages themselves? Perhaps it would lead me nowhere, but it was a start.

I followed them at a safe distance as they wound through the streets, the quarters growing cramped and less clean the further we went. At one point, we descended a few stone steps to a lower level of the city, which hung like a vast balcony over a cliff that looked out over the fiercely green mountains. I lingered a second longer to take it in, the sweeping views, the trees as small as ants far below. I hated to admit it to myself, but this city really *was* better than Tăru. If I wasn't intent on leaving altogether, I might set up a life here.

But Miha wasn't here, and no amount of drink or card games would ever make me forget that. How would anywhere ever feel like home again?

I nearly lost sight of the young men as I hurried to catch up. They had split up to walk single-file down a narrow close so dark I used my fingertips to brush along the walls for support. On and on and on until … their footsteps stopped. So I stopped.

A second later, a door opened to my right, a hand gripped my shoulder with unnecessary strength, and I was pulled violently inside.

A wide room with a low roof greeted me, lit by a

handful of candles but still dim. Stools and straw littered the floor, and perhaps eight or nine people sat conversing, falling silent when I entered. The one who'd pulled me in, I soon realized, was one of the two young men I'd been trailing.

"I suppose I wasn't as stealthy as I thought," I said, adjusting my cloak and smoothing down my shirt. "How long did you know I was following you?"

"Who are you?" he asked.

"I'm Liljana," I answered, and then, taking on a quiet and mournful voice, "and I'm far from home. This city is so very large and frightening."

He furrowed his brow, messy fair hair falling almost into his eyes. "Why were you following us? What do you want?"

"I saw your companion here" – I pointed to the quiet boy with the dark hair who stood in the shadows behind him – "make fire from nothing. You're a Ruiner, aren't you?"

Silence. Wide eyes watched me uncertainly.

"Calm yourselves," I said, pulling up a stool and seating myself. I'd rather they feared me than pushed me out. "I have little patience. If you can't run with the wolves, get out of the forest." I crossed my ankles and made myself comfortable. "I am not out to kill you. At least not yet. I'm in the city looking for someone."

"Is this about the mage they brought to the castle?" the fair-haired boy asked.

Aha. "It is. What do you know about her?"

"Very little. She was brought here yesterday. Made a big show of parading her through the city in a cart to the House, and that's all we know. She hasn't come back out."

"Are they going to kill her?"

"I said that's all we know."

I huffed and sat up to look around. "Who are you all? Why are you hiding out in this awful place?"

"Why would we tell you that?"

"Because I am a mage, which I'd thought you'd have realized by now. I'm an Alterer."

"How do we know that?"

I had hoped they wouldn't need a demonstration to prove it, but I couldn't blame them, and I needed their help. So I demonstrated by turning my stick into a knife for the briefest of instants. "Now, once more, why are you all here?"

The boy leaned one shoulder against the door and crossed his arms. "Marcosza is not kind to mages. Well, other than the ones who serve the baron. They all came here after the murders, and just stayed. No one minds so much if you're a mage here, or at least they don't kill you if you are. I think having us in a border city makes them feel a little safer." He shrugged. "To us, the city feels safer than the wilds beyond, where we can hide amongst so many people and look and act just like them. Safety in numbers, I suppose, in case they change their minds about how they feel about us. We wait for freedom, or a chance to act. For anything to change, I guess."

"Stop." I held up a hand. "Who serves the baron?"

"The Order of Weavers," the boy said. "They are based in Szaliri House. They serve Marcosza and use magic to help when they can."

I snorted. "Why haven't they just used their power to end the nonsense in the castle?"

"Not enough magic, I suppose. It would take a lot. And if anything happened to them, they wouldn't be here."

"So some magic is considered good, but not all of it." It was meant to be a question, but snapped out as a statement.

"It is good if you are trained as a member of an Order and use it to serve Marcosza."

"Why are they so terribly interested in the mage from Zírany?"

"Because she's *from Zírany*, I suppose. There hasn't been a mage from Zírany since the murders of the king and queen in the castle. She must be involved, at least that's what they say. Or if she isn't involved, she must know something. I heard she was born the year the rains began."

"That isn't how it works."

"I am just telling you what I heard."

I thought for a long moment. "Sometimes I think I should have just stayed in Roșesti," I mused. "I could have built a house high up in a tree where no one would find me, or at the bottom of a river. Anywhere but here."

"Roșesti?" the boy said. "How did you get all the way

here?"

"It's a very long story," I said languidly. "I walked. Well, not that long a story, I suppose. More of a long journey."

He said nothing.

"Right." I stood. "I have things to attend to. I'm sure I'll be paying you another visit. And" – to the boy with the dark hair – "do not play with fire in plain sight. The wrong person might notice." I sent him half a smile and left the building.

Chapter
Twenty-Six

Béata

All sense of time had left me. I sat huddled in the corner
for what could have been an hour or a year. I slept in fits
and starts, which only worked to further confuse my senses.
My stomach rumbled with hunger, and my body still ached
from its time cooped up in that cart. Zírany felt further
away than ever, a memory, a dream I had once, very long
ago.

If I closed my eyes, I could take myself back to the
hearth in the dining room, back to cold winter mornings
trying to regain feeling in my feet after a night spent in my
cold attic room. I could taste the cabbage stew Mother liked
to make on cold nights, and I could hear Father telling us the
stories of forest elves who slept on beds of moss and drank

dew from flower petals. Sometimes, when Mother wasn't around, he would tell us of the babaka, the tiny witches who lived in the shadows cast by the moon, who made friends of spiders and ants and rode on the backs of bats.

Home was just within reach, if I closed my eyes. My heart ached for it; my head longed for my own pillow. I could almost hear the gentle purr of the cat, sleeping by the fire. I envied Alíz, safe and warm at home, far away from me and the troubles growing in my wake.

A distant light began to grow down the hall, and the clanking of doors being opened and closed rang sharp and loud in my ears. I watched from my corner as a procession of men and women made their way towards me – the man in the green clothing at their head. He stopped before the door to my cell, a torch in one hand, silent, while the others chatted amongst themselves.

"Béata," he said, his head tilted a bit. Silvery hair was combed neatly back, and high cheekbones descended to a mouth that looked thoughtful.

"Izsak," I replied. Perhaps baron would have been more respectful, but some of Tabíta's cheek was rubbing off on me.

He handed the torch off to someone else and motioned for the cell to be unlocked. When he entered, he took the stool and sat facing me, resting his elbows on his knees.

"This is a very interesting predicament," he said after a long moment.

"Is it?"

"Indeed. I have little idea of what to do with you, but they all" – he swept an arm to his entourage – "expect me to do *something*."

"I've had some time to give that some thought," I said, still curled up in the corner. "I say you forget I was ever here, let me go about my life, and spend your time finding the person who is actually responsible for what happened in the castle."

He laughed softly. "Which isn't you, I presume?"

"Which isn't me."

"Then who *is* responsible?"

I faltered for a moment. I knew so much more than I could say. His presence was strangely warm in a way that made me think I could trust him, but a chill wafted through the bars of the cell from those standing without. The baron followed my gaze and eyed his companions for a moment, then turned back to me and asked a different question. "How much magic do you have?"

"Mmm. I don't know. How do you measure magic?"

"It's possible."

"Between one and ten," I said, making a show of thinking long and hard, "I'd say I'm a three."

"I doubt that."

"Why?"

"These folks seem to think it's more than that," he said, gesturing to his entourage.

"Ah, and who are these fine folks?" Many of them wore the same white robes stitched with a symbol I was too far away to see clearly.

"Of course, introductions are so important. I forget myself. I, as you know, am Izsak Sebestyen, Baron of Dungléd and Protector of this fine and chaotic country. And the people you see out there in the white are from the Order of Weavers. They work here with me, helping to control our borders. It's helpful to have some ... *power* ... when dealing with foreign affairs."

"Are they meant to be a threat?"

"No, not at all. But also yes."

"What do you need magic for?"

He smiled and darted his eyes to the mages. "Dungléd is the first stronghold within Marcosza. No one would bother attacking a city filled with Weavers who can create weapons from nothing and rebuild damage faster than they can cause it."

"What if they have stronger mages?"

"Ah, but our neighbours in Sovažska do not allow magic. Too much uncertainty and fear around it. In fact, I've heard some of the mages harboured within the very walls of this city have come from over the border. That's nice, you know. Makes us seem terribly charitable."

I sighed, ready to move on. "How long will we drag this out before you learn that I had nothing to do with the castle?"

"As long as necessary."

"Then you will be wasting valuable time. The rains are already growing, you know. And they won't stop until they've consumed everything. Even you."

"Another instance when it's helpful to have mages working with you."

"If they're so great and powerful, why don't you send them to the castle?"

"Now *that* is an interesting problem. We did send a number of mages to Castle Vyesta a year or two ago. It took a long while to find the right ones, to train them up and detail what they would do. Send them in quietly when your town wouldn't notice, so as not to cause a stir. And – would you believe it? – not one of them came back. Haven't heard a word from them since. Our fearless leader of the Weavers, Csáno here" – he motioned to a man, clad in white like his companions – "sent a hawk to the castle, seeing through it eyes for only a few moments, but he could see nothing but blood."

I shivered.

He said nothing for a moment.

"Why do you suspect me, and not other mages? If a mage is a mage and we are all to be feared, why am I more guilty than they are?"

"A fair question. But these particular mages have worked with me a long time. They were here when the murders happened."

"I was a baby when they happened, so surely that *must*

exonerate me."

"Let me be clear," the baron said. "We do not think you killed the king and queen." *I am the queen*, I wanted to scream. "But we do believe whatever is working in the castle has reach. Is using mages to further its power. To feed it. To grow it. That's why the ones we sent in never came back. That's why we haven't sent more after them."

He let a silence ease by, watching me.

"I think perhaps you can help us."

I sat up slowly. "Help you how?"

"By going into the castle."

A shiver crawled up my spine. Morós wanted me. He wanted me – Tabíta – more than anything. If I went into the castle, I would be delivering him exactly what he desired, and delivering myself to my death.

"My colleagues here seem to think you are full of magic. Brimming with it, practically. Whatever sensory network you all share has come alive the closer you've come to our city. And perhaps that is why that girl went looking for you back in Zírany. Everyone wants your magic. And sending one single, solitary little girl into the castle might cause less of a stir than the group we sent last time. It may be just what we need, someone to slip in and do what needs to be done. Someone with enough magic to survive." There was a fire in his eyes as he spoke. He wanted to fix this, and desperately. It was written in every line of his face.

"Sending me to the castle will do little good." I said it

slowly, heavily, imbuing my words with as much layered meaning as I could. I glanced at the Weavers again. I could feel them listening intently, and it sent spiders crawling along my skin.

Izsak looked thoughtfully around the cell. There was something about him I couldn't quite place – almost as if he was asking the questions given to him, but not the ones he truly wanted to ask. He tapped two fingers on his temple in quick succession, deep in thought, and then said, "We can pick this up again later. The Weavers would like a few moments alone with you. They have ways to see how deep your magic runs. To see if sending you to the castle will be worth our time."

I stiffened. "I would – I would rather not, please. I'm sure they will only be disappointed." He shrugged, and his eyes rolled subtly in a way that said, *I am doing my best*. He rose and left the cell. "And do feed her," he said to the others. "We need her alive."

They did feed me, and better than I'd expected. I had bread with real butter, and an apple, and a glass of deliciously cold water. A glimmer of hope sparked within me, but was soon crushed when the Weavers returned and my cell was unlocked. They said nothing to me as two guards beckoned me out into the hallway, and I followed them through the underbelly of the castle.

The pathways were uneven, perhaps due to the castle

having been built into the side of a mountain. Sometimes, a curved bit of what looked like tree root would protrude from the wall or the roof, and sometimes the floor itself seemed like nothing more than earth. Everything about it felt ancient, unkempt, an echo of centuries past, when this castle was new and grand and magnificent.

"Where are we off to?" I asked, but there was no answer. "You should have more light down here," I went on. "It's good for the soul, you know. No one likes the darkness."

The hallways wound on and on. Eventually, we were no longer in the dungeon, or at least there were no more cells. But the air still felt heavy and close, so we were still somewhere far underground. We took a few stairs up, then traversed a hall so low the tallest member of our company had to lower his head to pass through. At long last, we exited into a wide, round room – and far, far above, I saw the sky. The walls were a smooth stone I'd never seen before, and in the middle of the room was a dais with a handful of stone seats.

Szinstone. I'd never seen it before, but I knew it instantly, as if my magic had shouted it into my ears.

"Sit," said the man who walked at the head of the group – Izsak had called him Csáno. His robe bore an extra sign that the others did not have. He pointed to the seat at the centre of the room.

I swallowed, and obeyed. The others, two men and three women – the guards had stopped just short of entering the room – all took seats around me.

"What a charming space," I said, by way of masking the fear burning hotter every second.

"Humour has no place here," Csáno gravely. "It is your human side, trying to find magic in things you do not understand. Leave it for another day."

I said nothing.

"Do not move or speak while we test your magic," he said. "The only way out of this room is through the door you came through, and the guards are waiting just beyond it."

"Not unless I can fly," I said quietly, eyeing the sky so far above us. I wondered darkly if perhaps I could. If I had as much magic as they claimed, perhaps I could soar out of this room and fly home. Anything to be home.

Csáno heaved a deep, warning breath.

At once, they all assumed the same position, sitting stock straight with their palms resting on their knees, eyes closed. Csáno said a few words in that grating but beautiful language, and the others joined in. It was a chant, spoken in the same tone, in the same way, without fluctuation or emphasis. As instructed, I kept my head perfectly still, but moved my eyes around as much as I could to watch the mages before me. They looked like anyone else I might meet in Marcosza, varying hair colour and height, but all clothed in the same white robes with those signets stitched on to the chest, and all with their hair pulled back.

I should have been afraid, I thought. And part of me

was, a little bit, but I also felt strangely protected by my magic. If I did harbour so much of it, they wouldn't be likely to kill me or harm me. They needed me too much. Whether to use me, sell me, or teach me, one way or another, I was valuable to them.

The chant wound on and on, rhythmic and resounding in the round room so that the words echoed back to me and I was no longer sure which were the new ones and which were the echoes. My veins tingled, magic simmering and responding to the call, and my skin flushed red hot the longer they spoke. I began to itch and burned to scratch, but worried if I moved it would break the spell and they would have to start again.

Then the room began to rumble. The stone shook, dust falling to our heads from high above. With a thunderous snap that frightened me so much I couldn't see for a moment, a crack appeared in the rounded wall of the room, running from high overhead down to the floor. I worried for a horrifying moment that we would be crushed, buried alive by falling stone and magic.

In unison, the mages opened their eyes.

Silence fell, and I knew whatever they had learned was not what they had expected. The itching subsided in my skin, cooling me down, and I sat very still.

"It's her," one of the women breathed.

The others stayed silent for a few minutes more. *It's who?* What had they learned about me? Rovaslo's words all came flooding back in a jumbled, jarring mess. *You, Béata, possess at least half of Queen Tabíta's soul.* Had they seen her magic? I had run away from Rovaslo, yes, but I knew with iron certainty that no matter what befell me, I should keep the things he'd told me a secret. Anything I said aloud could find its way back to Morós, and that could spark the beginning of the end.

"That was terribly uncomfortable," I said finally. "I'd enjoy a rest now, please."

One of the mages let out a short, sharp whistle, and the guards raised the door. "Take her back to her cell. Do not leave her alone."

I rose and curtsied, as though thanking them for the chance to perform, and hurried from the strange, dusty room.

The guards walked close by my shoulders as we wound back through the labyrinthine depths of the castle. My arms and legs shook after the test, and I felt profoundly tired in a way I hadn't before I'd gone in. I was just wondering what the Weavers would do with whatever information they'd garnered from me when the guards abruptly stopped walking and pulled me into a small room with an ancient wooden desk covered in cobwebs. One motioned to the other, who waited outside and closed the door, and the other took off his helmet.

Izsak stared back at me.

"Oh," I said, because I could think of nothing else.

"I don't trust the Weavers," he said quietly, taking a seat at the desk. The chair creaked as though it might crumble into dust.

"I'm glad we can agree."

"I do not understand their games or what their goal is, but I know I am not a part of it. I am only playing the role they wish for me to play."

I said nothing.

"I trust they learned something in the Hall of Ïden."

"Isn't Ïden one of the old gods?"

"He is," Izsak replied. "Little known today, but he was the first Weaver."

"Ah." I now understood why the room felt more like a temple than anything. "Yes, but they said nothing to me before I left. I – I am not certain it went according to plan."

"I thought it wouldn't." He drummed his fingers on the desk for a moment. "I hope you can see my dilemma," he said. "Entrusted with this corpse of a country while keeping a horde of mages from seizing power for themselves – which I have long suspected but haven't voiced. I find it's easier if I seem dim, malleable. I've learned that strong people in a position of power often have a target on their back."

I nodded, understanding.

"I doubt very much that you had anything to do with the killings," he went on. "And I further doubt that sending you to the castle will bring about any real change, but if I do nothing, I'll appear weak. Weaker than I intend to, anyway.

It's a fine line I walk, sometimes as thin as a spiderweb stretched over a sea of fire. Too strong, and they will kill me. Too weak, and they will unseat me. If I lose my place of power, I fear what will happen to this country. I refused the title of king, naturally. It didn't suit me, and I never fancied myself a king. But heavens, did that not sit well with them." A humourless chuckle escaped. "I do not distrust magic, only some of the people who use it." He studied my face. "I wish I had more time to learn your story. The Weavers clearly think there's something about you worth knowing. But I have few options before me, and the best thing I can think of to do is to send you back to the castle."

I froze. I'd begun to hope that whatever the Weavers had learned about me might keep them from sending me away. That they couldn't risk losing me. Now that hope began to vanish, and the fear I'd pushed aside seeped back in.

"It's what everyone expects," Izsak continued. "If you die, then what will be will be, as awful as that sounds. But if you live – which I suspect you might – then you can do what no one else has managed to do and, for the sake of the gods, stop the rains. Stop everything. Just end it all."

"Why do you suspect I might live?"

His lips twitched as he decided how best to respond. "Because no one has ever made the Hall of Íden rumble before."

Chapter
Twenty-Seven

Liljana

It took an age to find my way back to the Witch's Eye – the inn I'd chosen as a resting place – after following the two mages down four hundred different streets. I could have stopped and asked around, but common sense told me to lie low, to not make any sort of impression on anyone in the city, if I could help it. Mages belonging to an Order so close at hand changed how I had come to think of Marcosza. They feared magic so much that anyone who carried it kept it as a close secret – and yet mages worked in the castle in this very city. If there was magic here, then the streets might be crawling with feelers looking for other mages, especially now that Béata was here. They would be on alert. Curious. Searching. And I had better things to do than get caught. Every day wasted was a day I could have spent in the kingdom of magic.

My feet were sore as I climbed the stairs to the room. Time away from walking hard city streets had made me soft. I hoped there were cities where I was going, sweeping, beautiful cities filled with nothing but mages. I could build my own home, my own life, have something to call my own. I imagined a library in a lofty tower with mornings spent reading ancient texts on magic. Restoring all the books' covers to their former glory, gold and red and blue, as though they'd just been created by the first mages. The daydream brought a smile to my lips as I ascended the stairs.

I spun the key in the lock, but froze. The lock did not click, and the door swung open without effort. The bed was mussed up and the room was untidy, as though someone had been looking for me in it.

I thundered back down the stairs. "Has anyone been in my room?" I said to the owner, then reined myself in and took a breath.

He thought for a moment, head tilted. "I've been busy. Just got in some fresh flour. The sacks are heavy, you know, and it's just me here. I used to have more help, but not so much any more." I shot him a quick look of warning. "But I might have seen a boy. Your brother, perhaps?"

A boy. Had one of the mages I'd met got here before me? Had they sent guards or the baron's men after me? To capture me like they had captured Béata? I had to find out. I spun towards the door.

"Will you be coming back?" the owner called. "Someone else might want your room."

I didn't reply. The street was a blur of movement. I stood in the middle and turned slowly, people on horseback and pushing carts cursing as they were forced to skirt around me.

The boy could have left ten minutes ago or an hour ago, and either way, this city would have long swallowed him up by now. I may as well find a single drop of ink in the sea.

At the end of the street, a peddler stood by a small stall selling bunches of herbs and flowers tied together with string. I approached her quickly, as she shouted over the din of the city.

"Keep the spirits out!" she called, waving a bunch of her dead plants around. "Spirits, magic, devilry, keep your home free of it! Hang it above your door, your bed, your child's bed! Keep the spirits out!"

She finally noticed me staring.

"Have you a need for fending off the spirits?" she asked, white hair wild and long. She stood far shorter than me, a frantic air about her that felt almost charming. "I've got just the thing for you."

"No," I said shortly. I looked around the street again, feeling whatever boy had come looking for me moving further and further away. "I'm in search of my brother.

Perhaps you saw him leave the inn? It would have been only a short time ago."

"Sorry, no. I see a lot of people. Keep the spirits away!"

I rolled my eyes. "Shame. I would have left you with another plant that I've heard is *instrumental* in warding away spirits."

Her eyes darted to me again, and she stopped waving a smudge around. "What plant?"

I held a bunch of herbs I'd swiped from her cart and transformed them into a brookside weed common in Roșesti, but less so here. I held it up to her. "It's called the bură plant. Spirits can't stand the stuff."

Her eyes glimmered. "I saw *a* boy leave the inn, perhaps a half hour ago. He went that way." She pointed up a street across the main road. "I only remember because he smiled at me, and I liked his smile."

I spun away, tossing her the bunch of useless plants. "You've been truly a delight. I wish you many visits from spirits during this blessed month, and hope you see many smiling faces peeping in your window." I made a nonsense gesture as though I were blessing her in some mysterious way, and left her with eyes wide in horror.

I darted across the main road, narrowly missing horses and carriages as they rushed about their day, and up the street the woman had indicated.

When the bodies thinned out, I began to run. A brisk trot up the street, darting around people and doors that opened without warning, until the road forked and I was forced to a sudden stop. In one direction the street was almost entirely empty, and ended at a tall building that looked a bit like a church. The other was full of people but in between two men walking side by side and lost in earnest conversation, I swore I caught a glimpse of a young man in a blue coat, walking with a step quicker than those around him.

I pushed a girl out of the way and ran with furious steps. A crowd of people all tumbling with raucous laughter out of a tavern forced me to stop, and I roared with frustration so loud one of them turned to me.

"You quite well, dear?"

I said each word deadly slow. "Get out of my way."

His face blanched, and he stepped aside, tapping the shoulders of his friends to do the same.

I darted forward again, brushing shoulders, tripping over feet, watching the road before me for another glimpse of his coat. This time when I saw it, he was turning down a narrow close. His hair was tied atop his head, though messily and wild.

Definitely not one of the mages I'd met earlier, then. I'd never met him before in my life. Why was he looking for me? *Was* he the one looking for me?

I slowed to a stop and peered around the corner down the close. He had stopped walking about halfway along, leaning against a wall to catch his breath and consult a map in his hands.

I rounded the corner and slipped down the close with quiet steps, stopping only when I was a few yards away. I cleared my throat. The boy turned to me, and our eyes met for a long moment before either of us spoke. Had I, in fact, met him before? Something whispered I had, but I could not recall when.

He was no mage, or if he was, my magic didn't recognize it. His face, though handsome and friendly, was dirty, dark circles beneath his eyes giving away a lack of sleep. His hair was in desperate need of a wash.

"You're Liljana, aren't you?" he said, a knowing half-smile twisting his lips.

I tilted my head. "It's Miss Liljana Vahani, actually. How did you know?"

He shrugged. "I've been looking for you. A friend named Rovaslo called on mages all around the country to find rumours of you, traces, breadcrumbs. Asking around until I had enough to go on. He told me you would burn like a beacon. He said I'd know what that meant when I met you." He reached out to shake my hand. "I'm Benedek. *Mister Benedek Csekeny.* It's nice to meet you."

His words so far had meant nothing to me, but he had a nice face, dirty as it was, and I admired his confidence, so I shook his hand. "I don't know who you are, Benedek Csekeny, and I don't know who Rovaslo is, and I don't know what you mean, and to be honest, I'm a little worried about you. You aren't making an awful lot of sense. Can I get you some water?"

He sighed, a quick sigh that was almost a laugh. "I know. There's a lot to talk about, but we don't have a lot of time."

I held up a hand. "I noticed you're using the word *we*, but this is still very much a *you* and a *me* situation. And, why, exactly, were in you my room looking for me to begin with?"

He blinked at me a few times, eyebrows knitted, then said, "That was the last place anyone had seen you go. Rovaslo's mages, I mean. You probably haven't seen them. They're a bit cagey. And also, why are you in Dungléd?"

"I'm looking for someone."

"For who?"

"A mage."

"What mage?"

"She's called Béata."

He stiffened, and a dark glint entered his eyes that came very close to frightening me. "Why?"

"I have my reasons. She can help me achieve something I badly want. I've been following her for days, she's just so bloody godsdamned difficult to find." I shifted from one foot to the other, impatiently. Sometimes I felt like my imaginings of Muranj were growing weaker and more distant by the second.

"I think perhaps you ought to tell me why you want her." His voice had taken on the sharp edge of a knife.

I drew my head back a little. "Oh, you think that, do

295

you? I'm sorry, and who exactly are you to tell me what to do, stranger boy who needs a bath so desperately I'm pretty sure the undergods can smell you in hell?"

He stiffened, hurt. "I. . ." He looked around, eyes falling on all the windows and open doorways lining the close. "I can't tell you out here. Come on." He touched my hand as if to pull me, but let go immediately at a look from me. Instead, I followed a few steps behind him as he entered through the doorway of a small but busy tavern – exactly the kind of establishment I might have played cards in, or used magic to swindle a few free drinks for me and Miha.

Gods, I missed Miha. Being in a city brought it all back.

When we were settled in the only free seats left, a tiny table shoved up in a corner, and he seemed satisfied that no one would hear us over the din of chatter, he spoke. "You asked who I am to tell you what to do. I have an answer for that, although it's one I'm still trying to face myself." He rubbed one finger back and forth on the table, absentmindedly, and stared at me without really seeing me. I studied the flecks of colour in his eyes, the sweet lines of worry between his eyebrows. "I know Béata," he went on presently, though I wasn't sure if he realized he hadn't finished his previous thought. "I know she has power, and I know that you have power. I think you can help us. I've been sent to ask you to help us." He cleared his throat, and then spoke even quieter. "We want to enter the castle. She can survive the rains, and I know the way around the castle. We can work together, and we can end this nightmare."

I smiled half-heartedly. "Funny, that. I also plan to take Béata to the castle, but for different reasons."

"What reasons?"

"My reasons."

"Liljana..." He ran a finger thoughtfully along the tabletop. I kept my face bold and hard, but inwardly I *needed* to know what he was about to say. What secret had been weighing him down since we'd first spoken. "Rovaslo—"

"I'm going to stop you right there. Who is Rovaslo?"

"A Seer. Formerly a royal Seer in Castle Vyesta, before the murders. He sent me to find you."

I said nothing, torn between shock and pride that someone from any royal court would know who I was.

"I don't quite know how to tell you this, Liljana, but he told me you would need to know. And I suppose you deserve to know."

Frustration made my body tremble. *"Know what?"* I snapped, far too loudly.

He jumped and looked around, waiting to speak until all eyes had left us after my outburst. "The king and queen were murdered, but Rovaslo... He pushed their souls from their bodies before they died, into other hosts who could harbour them until they'd grown up. But the push was stopped too soon, and the soul of Queen Tabíta was fractured in two. Béata has one half of it, and . . ."

I knew what he was about to say, somehow, yet it still felt as jarring as a wave of icy water when he said the words aloud.

". . . and you have the other."

The tavern was still loud. Nothing around us had changed, but everything fell weirdly silent in my head. I could see nothing but Benedek. Hear nothing but the words he'd just spoken echoing around. The world felt tilted suddenly. Off in the most peculiar way.

"The evil in the castle wants the queen back," he explained gently. "It wants her power. Your power. Béata's power. It's hungry for it."

I slumped over until my forehead rested on the table.

The black stag in the woods. The errand he'd sent me on – to fetch him Béata, but also myself. I would not just be delivering him her, but me. Both of us together. What a simple plan it had seemed, once upon a time. *Why is nothing ever simple?* How could I not have seen through his lies? I should have known better, that was certain, and I kicked my toes against the table legs over and over again in frustration. I should have known that the man inside the stag with the dark power and a trail of murders behind him might not be telling the truth, but I *wanted* it to be true. I *needed* it to be true.

I had been blinded by my dreams of Muranj, and everything else had vanished.

But I had come this far. I had so very nearly reached Béata. I could not stop now. One way or another, either with her help or by trading her to the man in the castle, I might still be able to find my way into the kingdom of magic, dangerous though that now seemed. She might still be the key, and if I didn't finish this task I had set myself, and I didn't finish the task Petre had set me, what was I good for?

But I didn't want Benedek to know any of these thoughts. He was still a stranger. Still someone I couldn't trust.

So instead, I said, "You were explaining to me why you spoke with such authority earlier."

"Ah." His eyes darted around, more nervous than I would have believed possible. "Béata doesn't know this part yet. Rovaslo only told me after she had left." He brought his hands up to support his chin, then, presumably finding that uncomfortable, rubbed his palms on his trousers instead. "The queen's soul was split in two, like I said. But the king wasn't. He never had any magic, so he could be pushed into anyone. In the few seconds Rovaslo had to decide, he went with the magicless baby boy born the most recently in the country. And that was me."

I laughed a little, to cover my surprise. "So, you're a king?"

"I *was* a king."

Tears were pressing behind my eyes at everything he had said, but being so light-hearted was a welcome distraction. "I'm so embarrassed," I said, smoothing down my clothes. "I would have worn something better if I'd known."

Benedek sighed and gave me a dead-in-the-eyes kind of look that silenced me.

"So anyway, I'm currently trying to work through that," he said, bringing the discussion back to what a heavy piece of news that must have been for a boy like him. "I'm telling you this because I want you to know that I understand how you feel."

"Do you? There's a lot about me you don't know, so I find that hard to believe." A sob began to rise up.

"I mean about the soul-push, and the queen. I know how overwhelming that is. I really do."

"I've—" I stopped quickly, choking on the sob and looking away to collect myself. "I've spent years working for a godsawful woman in a godsawful tavern in Tăru just to get by. Just for a roof over my head for me and my best friend. And sometimes we didn't even get that. I talked about running away for years, and I never did it, and now my best friend has been murdered, and I'm out here, wandering about like a lost child just trying to find something or somewhere that feels like home, hoping I could get into Mur—" I stopped myself again, and stared at the floor. "I have had a long and difficult life, Benedek," I whispered. "And you're sitting here now, telling me all this time I have been a queen."

"It's ... difficult, yes," he said. "I know. I grew up poor after my father left. Life was hard. I would never have known I had once been a king."

I rested my face in my palms for several long, winding minutes. My mind was in turmoil. The world had grown dark. I hated everything. I hated this weight on my chest.

"Have we met before?" I asked suddenly, desperate to think of something else.

He started at my sudden subject change. "You mean apart from when we lived in the castle? No. Not since then."

"Are you sure?" I smiled a bit through tears, fighting off the crushing weight of everything. "Have you ever been to Roșesti? Found yourself in Tăru to try out our wine? It's very mediocre. I bet you'd love it."

"Roșesti," he whispered. "No. Never."

"Hmm. You're very handsome. A memorable face, you know. Familiar. I was hoping maybe we had passed each other before, somewhere, by chance." I clapped my hands on the table a few times, shaking with apprehension. It all boiled up, and I slipped the stick from my belt. "Either way, I think you'll be helping me find Béata."

"Why?"

I shrugged, as though it was obvious, and held up the stick I had transformed under the table. "Because I'm the one with the knife."

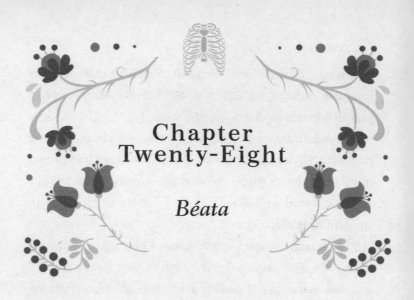

Chapter Twenty-Eight

Béata

I should have fought harder. It was the only thing I could think as I sat withering in my cell. Why had I not tried harder to get away from Norik and his men? To run away when we were in the forest, when the black wolf attacked us? It had seemed impossible, but not as impossible as it did now. Locked in a cell, in a dungeon deep beneath the city, crawling with guards and mages, awaiting shipment back to Castle Vyesta, where Morós would finally do what he'd tried to do so long ago: destroy me.

At least Benedek would make it out of this alive. The castle wasn't after him. How lucky, to be born with no magic. To not have to face these terrible things. But what would he do? Forget about me, and return home? Or had he already forgotten about me? Our friendship had grown furiously quickly, but I had given little thought to what would happen after all of this ended, even if we were successful. Rid the castle of evil. Stop the deadly rains. And then what? And then I would go back to my quiet life in the tavern, and he would go back to his mother in Kupesno, and that would be that.

The longing to see his wry, sideways smile weighed down my heart suddenly, and I closed my eyes, picturing it.

Izsak had told me we would leave today. The longer he waited, the less decided he would appear. He had to move swiftly. Strongly. I tried my best to understand that, as he'd made it sound so clear and honest, but as I sat in my cell, awaiting what could only be a death sentence, it felt nothing but unfair. What good would my death do for Marcosza? The only thing that would come out of this unscathed would be the baron's reputation.

I shifted where I sat on the hard floor. At the very least, he could have come up with a reason to store me somewhere more comfortable than this.

A distant scraping startled me. I'd grown used to the heavy silence, my ears ringing, broken only by the occasional falling drop of water.

All was silent again for a moment, until the sound returned, this time closer.

I stood slowly, waiting. Something was coming.

The Weavers, perhaps, back to test me again before my departure. Or the baron, ready to send me off to Vyesta to die. Whatever awful thing made its way towards me down the hallway, I braced myself, standing as tall as I could.

A single guard approached my cell. Wordlessly, he turned the lock and carefully swung open the door, then said gruffly, "It's time."

I swallowed. Breathed deeply. Ran a hand over my hair. "Very well," I said. I could fight. Attack the guard, despite his armour. Run through the dungeon as far as I could before I was caught. At least I'd be able to say I tried. But to no end. I'd exhaust myself and crush my soul to no avail.

So I stepped calmly out of the cell and walked with my head held high down the hallway, following the guard into oblivion.

It took several minutes of walking to realize we had come the opposite way I'd gone before, to the right of my cell this time, instead of the left, where I'd first come in. More cells lined the way, these even more run-down than the others. No torches were lit here; the only light came from the single guard who walked just before me, turning now and then to ensure I still followed. The light glinted off dark eyes through his helmet, and in the gloomy silence all around, I thought of asking questions.

"Have you served the baron long?" I asked, dodging a chain that hung precariously from above.

"No."

"Do you have family in Dungléd?"

"No."

"Are you allowed to speak to the prisoners?"

"No."

"Fine. I'll just talk to myself. I can't stand the quiet down here. It's too much, too heavy. I can't imagine how you can work down here without dying a little bit. But I suppose the silence wouldn't be so awful if there was just some light in the cells. I know this isn't an inn, but even one candle would be an improvement, or an extra blanket for some comfort. I know it's hard to think about these things until you're the one staying in the cell, but I have some thoughts—"

Without warning, the guard darted into a room that looked more like one of the cells but without bars, only stone walls and a narrow door. I looked up and down the hallway, then followed him inside. On the far side of the room stood an open door, and behind that, a dark and cramped staircase leading up.

The guard pulled off his helmet, and Benedek smiled at me.

A thousand thoughts boiled to the surface, but all I could say was, "Huh." A warmth tumbled over me, lifting my heart, my spirits, my very soul in a way that made me feel as though I could fly.

He hugged me gingerly, the armour pressing into my

skin, and didn't let go for a whole minute. "I'm glad you're well."

"I have questions," I said matter-of-factly, but I couldn't hide a smile. It pulled at my face until my cheeks tingled.

"I know. I can explain it all later, but we have to go. It's a long climb, so ready yourself, but I bet you'll be happy to see daylight." He winked at me.

I instantly wanted to cry. "Yes. Yes, very happy."

I soon learned why he had warned me. The stairs were small, barely big enough for my foot unless I stood on tiptoe. Our progress was slow, and at length I started to hope with each step we climbed we would soon see a light ahead. But always the stairs wound on. My legs ached. More than ached. They throbbed down to the bones, and I kept having to stop just to give them a moment's rest. Benedek had left the torch behind to make the climb easier, and in the blackness, the sounds of movements seemed dreadfully loud.

"You said it ends," I said softly, at long last.

"It does." He said it quickly and firmly, as though reminding himself of the same thing.

And end it did. Finally, the bluish-grey glow of moonlight shone ahead. I let out a cry of relief as I followed Benedek up the last few steps, and on to a patch of grass surrounded by shrubs. We were still in the city. I couldn't see much from where we sat, but the sounds of voices and hooves and life echoed around us.

The cell was gone. The baron, the Weavers, the guards, they were all gone, too. There was only me and Benedek, the hum of the city, and the scintillating stars far above me.

"How did you find the stairs?" I asked after what felt like an hour. My breath slowly returned, along with the feeling in my legs.

"I had help," Benedek breathed, sitting up once more after lying still for so long. "I'll explain later." He swallowed in a way that struck me as nervous. "There's someone I need you to meet."

"Who?"

"You'll see. It isn't far from here. Can you walk?"

"If I must."

"I recommend it. It's not safe to stay here."

"Where are we?" I asked.

"Just outside the walls of Szaliri House."

As I watched, Benedek's amour disappeared, leaving behind only his old clothes. I stared, then tried to speak.

"Again, I had help," he said quickly. "It's a long story."

The walk was slow, winding through city streets that were thankfully largely empty for the night. I didn't speak, on edge with questions and uncertainties after my unexpected freeing. And I wanted food. I wanted food more than anything else. My insides ached with an emptiness that grew more pronounced with every second.

I followed Benedek down a small street and into an inn that reminded me of home. Of my father's tavern. Dining tables. A hearth. The scents of drink and food and sweat. I turned my eyes to the floor as we walked, and climbed a few stairs to a small attic room.

Inside, a girl was asleep in the bed, but she sat up when we entered.

"Béata," Benedek said with a shaking voice, "this is Liljana."

Chapter Twenty-Nine

Liljana

I had just gone from a deep, black slumber to a dream where I was being served a feast of roasted goose, rabbit stew, plum wine and fresh berries when the door opened and I was ripped away from the table. I could still very nearly smell the stew as I opened my eyes to find Benedek entering the room at the inn, followed by a girl who something within me instantly recognized as Béata. I sat up and stared at her. She stared back. Benedek was quiet.

An unease settled over me the longer I looked at her – less like I was looking at a girl I just met, and more like I was looking in a mirror to find someone who looked nothing like me. I hated it. I wanted to claw every bit of the queen's soul out of my body and give it back to Béata. What did I want with it?

"You're shorter than I imagined," I told her, because I didn't want her to hear any of my thoughts. Could she hear my thoughts?

She tilted her head. "You're the one who went looking for me in Zírany, aren't you? The one who blabbed my secret like a child who doesn't know any better."

"Ouch. That stings."

"Liljana is—" Benedek began, but Béata held up a hand to silence him, anger simmering in her soft features. He wrung his hands, nervous like a mouse who'd just seen a cat.

"Why would you do something so ludicrous? The only reason I'm even here is because of you." Her words crackled like kindling just catching fire.

I placed a hand on my chest, offended. "Excuse me. I didn't know that no one else knew."

"You should have known that most people with magic don't like others to know they have magic," she shot back, her voice growing louder with each word.

"Your own family, though? You never thought to tell them?"

Hurt cut at her face. "*I* didn't even know," she said in a whisper.

"Well, now you do," I replied. "We all do, and we all know about the. . ." I stumbled over my words, and stopped to clear my throat, still overwhelmed by the thought. "The soul split. All hail the queen, I guess." I dropped into a mock

310

curtsy, but despite my flippancy, my lower lip trembled. I hoped she didn't notice.

"Please," Benedek said nervously. "We haven't time for this. Béata, I told her. I told her everything. Well, everything I could remember. Rovaslo said a lot, and I think he lost me in places." He ran a hand over the back of his neck. "I think if we put our minds together, we can do what needs to be done."

"That wasn't your news to spread," Béata shot to Benedek.

He looked away, his eyes darting around the room. "I know, but we need help, and it was Liljana's magic that got you out of Szaliri House. She turned my clothes into the armour. And some mages she found showed us the way in. And anyway, Rovaslo told me to find her, and to tell her. You left, so what was I supposed to do?"

Béata's fiery eyes fell on me. "Why would you help Benedek if you don't know him? Or me?" she asked.

I winked. "I love a good gentleman in need. And you..." The opportunity for a lie sprang to life before me. "My magic, I guess. It pulled me to Zírany. I think it wanted me to find you. Now I know why, us being the same person and all."

"We are *not* the same person."

I heaved a breath and looked around. "Whatever we decide to do," I said, "we should get out of the city. I do enjoy a city, but there is too much chance for capture and misstep."

"*That*, I agree with," Béata said, as if it would be the only good idea I would ever have in my life.

"See? Now we're getting somewhere." I smiled wider than necessary.

Voices rose up from below. I glanced to the window, then back to the others.

"We should leave soon," I said. "I've – we've all come too far for anything to go wrong now."

"Yes," Béata said, turning towards the door, "we have. But you will not do any talking until we are out of the city and out of earshot of anyone but frogs and rabbits, because your mouth has got me into enough trouble."

Now my own anger simmered. "Pipe down, princess," I said softly, but my words were heavy with menace. "If it wasn't for me, you would still be in that dungeon, and I'm beginning to think I should have left you there."

She crossed the room in two great strides, her face only inches from mine. Benedek rushed forward and held a hand between us.

"I will never forgive you for telling my family what you told them before I could," she whispered to my face. "I want to get this over with, fix the castle, and send you back to whatever pit you crawled out of."

I leaned in even closer, and whispered even quieter, "I don't need forgiveness, and nor do I forgive. Now kindly get out of my face before I give you two black eyes, and not by magic."

We left the inn with Benedek walking in between us, jumpy as a moth in a spiderweb. Having slept, I had enough energy to change our hair colour for long enough to get us out of the city Béata's I turned to grey, because I felt a bit vindictive and she could do nothing about it, and mine I turned the colour of sand in the sunlight. Benedek's didn't need changing, since it would take more energy and no one was truly after him. At least not that we knew of.

We were in a hurry, but I let my feet slow now and then, savouring the stones beneath my feet, worn smooth over time, the buildings sweeping up around us, the gentle hubbub of life that made my soul happy. Soon enough there would be nothing but trees and dirt trails – and now Béata's voice snapping at my ears for the remainder of our journey back to the castle.

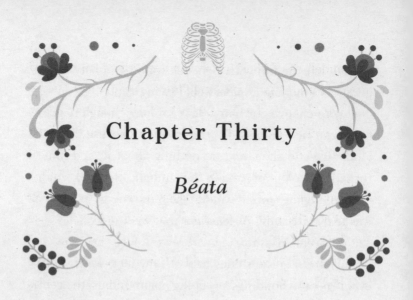

Chapter Thirty

Béata

Benedek kept staring at Liljana as we made our way through the streets and to the gates, eyebrows knitted, worried. I looked away from him and to the ground as we walked, my heart heavy.

It was so easy to forget how silent the forest was after our time in the city. Like the dungeon. I hated being able to hear myself think.

"We need to discuss what will happen when we get to the castle," Benedek said finally. "Without a plan in place, we are all going to die."

"It doesn't matter any more," I said with my eyes down. "We'll probably all die anyway."

"I can see you dying, oh queenliest of queens," Liljana

said snidely. "But I have no reason to be killed, and frankly neither does this all-too-human boy."

"We are the same person," I hissed. "Whatever magic I have, you have. Believe me: Mórós desires you dead just as much as me."

"I'm not a Seer," she said softly.

"No, but you could be a very powerful Alterer, if you tried. Or so I'm told. Magic doesn't make mistakes. It chose you. Live with it."

Liljana fell silent. She stared at me, unflinching, but her face had lost its colour. There was something else at work there, something else consuming her mind.

"Why is it that you wanted to find me so badly?" I asked, my voice heavy with the threat of what might happen if she didn't tell the truth. "Why go through all this trouble? Why journey so far?"

Another long silence while she stared at the road ahead. "Why didn't he just kill me, then?" she whispered, ignoring my question.

I stood straighter. "Who?"

She looked away from the road, eyes darting to mine for a moment. "I don't know who to trust any more. All I wanted was to find somewhere safe. Somewhere I could practise magic in peace."

"Who could have killed you?" I felt I knew the answer, even before she sighed and began to speak.

"I met a man in the woods outside the castle. Well, he

wasn't a man, but he had the voice of a man. It was a stag, flanked by two shadows who never spoke. He asked me to find you and bring you back to the castle, as though he'd been trying and failing for a long time. He promised me entry into the kingdom of magic if I did it, and of course I agreed."

"*Of course?*"

"Oh, don't be so righteous. If someone promised you your life's dream in exchange for someone you didn't know, wouldn't you take it?"

"No."

"You would; you just don't like how it makes you sound. There's a difference. My closest friend died, and I have no one left here. You can't begrudge me the hope of a life of safety and quiet, free from fear and hiding. I've never had that pleasure."

"I can begrudge you offering me up so you could get what you want!" I nearly screamed. Benedek shushed me, gesturing to the forest around us. The baron's men, and the Weavers, would certainly be after us by now. I moved further into the underbrush, away from the more open part of the forest, and the others followed. "So you were to bring me back to the castle, deliver me to my death, and then cross into Muranj without a second thought? Did any part of you think for a second that the man in the possessed stag asking for the life of a girl might not, in fact, hold true to his word? Because I promise you, Liljana, he knew what

316

you were. He knew you carried part of the queen in you, and he'd found a way to lure both of us back to the castle."

She crossed her arms. "As far as I can tell, your plan with Benedek was to enter the castle to heroically stop the poisonous rains anyway. How is my plan so different?"

"If you can't see the difference between putting yourself in harm's way for the greater good and delivering someone's life knowing they'll be killed, then there's little point in carrying on this discussion." My skin burned with rage. I wasn't used to being so angry at anything other than the castle, but there it was, alive and fiery. What sort of person could think to do such a thing? What sort of person was she?

A few long minutes passed. Benedek fidgeted with his cloak, clearly out of place, his face giving away his roiling mind. "You both seem to forget my place in this," he said. "One way or another, you've both known there was something different about you for a long time, Liljana with her magic, and Béata with her immunity to the rains. I, on the other hand, am just a normal, magicless boy, and I . . ." He trailed off and looked me in the eyes. I stopped walking, meeting his gaze without wavering. "You left before Rovaslo explained this part," he whispered, then found his voice. "I was the boy he pushed the king's soul into. I was King Aurel, years ago. It's why I have such distinct knowledge of the castle. I feel better knowing that. Better having an answer. But I still have to face the fact that I was once a king, which is a lot to stomach for a boy who grew up penniless. So why don't you both take a quiet moment to think about someone other than yourselves to put everything into perspective?"

I stared at him, those rich eyes glistening with worry, hope, affection – I thought – and fear. He was right, though my cheeks burned with shame: I hadn't given a thought to how Benedek had fit into all of this. What had happened to the king's soul. Why he did, in fact, have knowledge of the castle. I'd run away to feel better and to escape Rovaslo's seemingly never-ending bits of news, but my only thoughts of Benedek had been about how I missed him. Not about what things he might be learning in my absence.

"I'm – I'm sorry." I brushed his shoulder gently. He leaned his cheek against my hand for a brief moment, before coughing and looking away. I could still feel the tingle where his skin had touched mine.

"Thank you. There is much to think about, for all of us. Bickering will do no good." His voice was stronger then, like a leader's, and he was right. Without each other, we had nothing, and frustrating though I found Liljana, if she had power, we could use it to stop Morós.

Liljana looked thoughtful for a moment. "It makes you think, doesn't it?"

I sent her a questioning look.

She pointed to Benedek. "So you were the king, and

we" – gesturing to both me and her – "were your queen. Oh. How *delicious*." She smiled wryly.

"Don't be a child," I told her, but the thought had crossed my mind, too. Not about how *delicious* it was, but about what it meant. How we were supposed to behave.

Liljana ran a hand over her hair, which had already returned to its normal colour. "Look, all I want out of life is somewhere peaceful and free from people trying to take off my head. I know that is a lot to ask in this world, which is why I wanted so desperately to go to Muranj. I don't care how I get there, I just want to get there. If I have to work with you lot, I'll work with you. Just get me out of this godsforsaken country. Get me out of this world."

"This country is our home," I told her sharply.

"Well, it isn't *my* home."

No one spoke for a long time. Benedek led the way, pushing aside vines and shrubs so we could more easily pass by.

The mist of the Oroszom Mountains was thick, the air heavy and fresh and clean after the scents of the city. It reminded me sickeningly of home, of the forest around Zírany, of everything I missed and loved. None of us spoke.

The second day of our journey was sunny and bright, but cold like the days of early winter. The chill wind bit into my body as we traversed the mountain ways, calming only when we descended into a valley or passed trees whose trunks were large enough to break up the wind.

The silent journey left too much time to think. What would the townsfolk make of our arrival? Would I see my family again? What would happen when we entered the castle? The tiniest part of me still harboured some hope that we might stand a chance against Morós and bring an end to the cursed place, but with only my and Liljana's magic, it was a very small hope. Mostly, I wondered what the world would look like when Morós's power grew strong enough. When he'd finally gained enough to break through to Muranj, sucking the life out of Marcosza. Everything beautiful would die away. Everything good and right and normal would vanish. The magic would consume and consume and consume until there was nothing left, and like vultures who'd picked too long at a dead animal, there would be nothing left but bones.

My thoughts were all too dark. I began to hum an old child's song to take them away, but in every silence and every breath, they were waiting.

It was on the second night, when the mountains had slipped away behind us and we were setting up camp amongst some large rocks off the road, that my skin began to tingle. Something in the air was changing, and I was not the only one to notice. Liljana stared off through the trees, listening, on edge. When Benedek noticed our stillness, he stopped moving and watched us.

Four white-robed figures melted out of the night.

A feeling like a knife poisoned with hopelessness and dread sank into my heart, and I closed my eyes for a brief moment.

No.

Csáno and the other Weavers stopped walking with a few yards between us, their hands clasped before them. The picture of elegance, with nothing to fear.

"I admire your effort," Csáno said, his voice deep and resounding, as if the trees themselves were speaking. "We should have known magic might set you free, strong as you are. But what's done is done."

"Forgive me," Liljana said with what was clearly feigned shock, "but are you *angels*?"

"Charming," Csáno said, casting her a brief look. "And my, my, aren't you magical." He ran a hand through the air before her face, until she swiped it away. "Morós was right. If we harness the power of the two of you, the possibilities are endless."

The air around us grew icy cold. I took a step back, then stopped, fear rendering me still.

"Well," Csáno said, "there's no use carrying on like this. We brought horses. It makes travel so much easier." He clapped, and a handful of mages came from the forest, leading horses saddled and ready. "Come. Let us take you home, oh queen. Morós is waiting."

My blood had turned cold, setting my body to

shivering. I'd felt an uneasiness in the presence of the Weavers back in the city, and the baron had only strengthened that unease. I hadn't for a moment suspected them of working with Morós. "No," I said quietly, and then Tabíta's fire sparked stronger. "No, you cannot take us to him."

Csáno moved closer with deathly slow steps. The air around him was singed with magic, a smell like smoke filling my senses. "We can," he said under his breath. "We will. And we are." With a snap of his fingers, my wrists were bound with a rope so heavy and finely woven I didn't think even a freshly sharpened knife could cut it loose.

"How, if I may be so bold as to ask, did he get his claws into you lot?" Liljana ventured. Despite her impertinence, I could see her fingers trembling.

"Power of his strength calls out for aid," Csáno replied. "And the sort of power he wields – I think you would call it *dark magic* – comes with its own ways of communicating. We know everything that goes on within those castle walls. And he knows you are on your way. He knows we managed to find you. And" – he spun to Liljana – "he knows you failed to bring her to him."

Liljana took a small step backwards.

"Mount up," one of the other Weavers called, motioning to the horses. "We will ride through the night."

But then a whispering began softly through the trees. My eyes met with Liljana's. She could no doubt sense it, too. Something was changing. The air around us moved, yet there was no wind.

A voice came from the darkness, rich and strong and speaking the language of magic without pausing for breath. The Weavers turned to face it, hands up as though ready to create death from thin air. And perhaps they could.

I turned slowly, watching the darkness and waiting. I knew that voice. I knew it very well.

Rovaslo entered from the trees, his simple grey tunic smartened by the addition of a red cloak with a gold chain, and black boots that rose to his knees. Somehow, he was no longer the grandfatherly figure I'd known on the island, but someone powerful to be followed and revered – if not feared. His hands were raised at his sides, palms up, and his eyes never left the Weavers.

I watched him, enthralled, confused, relieved, but then movement behind him drew my attention away. Rovaslo wasn't alone. More mages followed him, five or six, all in red cloaks and chanting the same words as him, melting out of the forest like droplets of blood.

My heart picked up speed. There was fear, of course: these were dark times, and a fight between powerful mages must necessarily end poorly for one side. *But we weren't alone.* I could think of nothing else. We weren't alone, and hope began to flicker once more.

"Who is this?" Liljana asked. "He reminds me of a Sage I used to know."

"He's a Seer," I told her. "Like me."

"Right. And he *doesn't* like the Weavers? This is all frightfully confusing, do forgive me."

"Yes," I said with a small smile. "I think he's here to help us."

I could feel the tiredness in the waning day. The Weavers had travelled long and hard to find us, and Rovaslo had clearly been trailing us. Trained as they were, even these mages were not built to practise such strong magic on so little sleep. I searched within me for what bits I could find, but what could I do? Was it even possible to soul-push another mage? Was I strong enough to kill a Weaver?

Was I capable of *killing* someone?

From the air before the Weavers grouped hands came a snapping, roaring sound. A winged serpent, jade green and the size of a small wolf, beat its wings in the air and screamed, fire roaring from its mouth. Rovaslo stopped his advance a few yards from the beast – though he never stopped chanting. What words did he speak? They made no sense to me, and I was furious with myself for not allowing myself more training with him. How different things would be now if I hadn't been so hasty.

"End this now," said Csáno. "You may outnumber us, but our strength is far greater. This needn't end in bloodshed."

"My magic never causes bloodshed," Rovaslo replied, ceasing in his chant temporarily. "Pushing a soul leaves very little mess."

"Then it needn't end with loss of life. One way or another, we will take this girl to the castle. If you stop us, there will be someone else in our place. This is a fight you cannot win."

"My favourite words," Liljana said. "There's nothing like the impossible to light a fire under your feet." Her eyes burned hungrily.

"What do you get for serving Morós?" Rovaslo asked. The other mages stood behind him, two on either side, still chanting softly. Still keeping the magic strong and ready. "Why align yourselves with such darkness?"

"We are mages," Csáno replied. "Magic is everything. Everywhere. Sense should tell you to follow where it is the strongest. In this age, it is strongest with him."

"He is a summer storm," Rovaslo told them with a small laugh. "He is strong and loud and fascinating, but it will pass as soon as it began. He will be nothing but a memory in a few years' time, and you'll have sold your souls for nothing."

"He has designs," Csáno said, almost wistfully. "For the blurring of lines between worlds. For mages roaming as freely here as they do in Muranj. For opening the doors and leaving them open. No more division. No more walls."

Rovaslo laughed again, as though he had never heard something quite so full of folly in his life. "That is absurd," he exclaimed, flailing his arms up in the air. "Marcosza – Sóar itself was never meant to house so much magic. It will wither and die away and you'll be left with a husk. Our worlds were designed by the Creators exactly as they should be. Muranj was meant for magic; Sóar was not. You cannot blend the two together and expect beauty when oil and water will always be enemies. You can see that, Csáno, certainly."

"You are a Seer, not a Sage," Csáno shot back, the winged serpent dancing about his head. "Your knowledge has limits, even if you refuse to accept that."

"I am a Seer," Rovaslo agreed, "but I know Morós more than any of you. I know the extent of his power, and more importantly, his pride. His designs will crash and burn the world with it." "If so, then we will always have Muranj. Sóar can burn, but when Morós finally breaks open the door between us again, we will have the freedom to return to Muranj and live amongst our own kind. Look at these children you have around you, Rovaslo. A Seer, a revered magical skill, and she knew nothing of it. An Alterer who can turn a stick into a knife. These are a child's games. Magic is wasted on them."

"They haven't been trained," Rovaslo said defensively.

"But I would love to try turning you into a worm and then feeding you to a bird, if you would perhaps find that to be more impressive," Liljana offered in her most genuine tone.

Csáno ignored her. "Think of what great things could come to be with such power as Morós's on the Starijian

Throne. Erazem's day has come and gone. With the door between us closed for so long and no szinstone going through, he will be weaker than ever before. Whatever you say of Morós's designs, he has carefully thought them through. The door must be opened, and magic and life must be drawn from Marcosza and beyond like water wrung from a cloth. It is the only way to open the door. The only way for us to get our kingdom back."

I stepped forward, terrified, but bound by a sense of duty I didn't quite understand. "What do you mean by *magic and life?*" I asked quietly, afraid to hear the answer.

Csáno sighed, as though bored with the question. "I mean magic and life. I mean that Morós's power is finally great enough that he can call upon ancient forms of magic to blow open the door using all the magic and life forces bound up in Marcosza. I mean people. Animals. Trees. *Worms.*" He cut his eyes to Liljana. "Every living thing. It takes a lot of life to counteract the kind of magic Erazem used to seal that door shut. It must be done somehow."

"No, it mustn't," Rovaslo breathed. "You monster. How could you even think such a thing?"

Csáno gently brushed a fly from his shoulder. "Because Marcosza bores me, Rovaslo. All of Sóar bores me. There is little magic here. Nothing but people living all-too-ordinary lives. Kings and queens wishing for more power than they're worth. Storms that bring only rain and thunder. Do you remember Muranj, Rovaslo? Do you remember the storms of magic that singed your very skin? That made you feel *alive*? When was the last time you felt alive? Living here, working here, it was all made to sound like such an honour. Such a great opportunity. But it was a prison sentence, and I have served my time. Now I wish to go home."

A strange, sharp silence settled in. Night creatures called all around us. The leaves brushed together overhead, unsettling. Words had abandoned me, so I stayed silent, hugging myself, feeling hope slip further and further away.

"Then your mind is clearly made up," Rovaslo said with a sigh. "I have done what I can to save you." He began to chant again, palms up, and my skin felt singed with the sudden draw of magic so close at hand.

Csáno waved an arm in the air, and the serpent swept forward with a fiery shriek, diving through the air towards Rovaslo. With a shout and a flick of the hand, palm out, a light flashed, and the serpent fell on to the bed of pine needles, lifeless.

"You may conjure more creatures and I will push their souls until we are both shells of beings too drained to speak," Rovaslo whispered, visibly exhausted from the effort.

Csáno sighed. "You are not taking the prisoners," he said, raising his hands again to Weave something new. "And you've burned yourself out on the serpent, so what have you left? Had you thoughts of pushing *my* soul? It would take an army's worth of power, Rovaslo, and you haven't a fraction of that."

"I haven't any army," Rovaslo agreed, "but I have something you don't." For the first time since his arrival, he turned to me. "I have the soul of Queen Tabíta. With her, I could push every one of you and still have power left for Morós."

Csáno glanced at me, and I fancied I saw a spark of worry in his eyes. "She hasn't been trained. She's a pup, useless."

"She's done it once. By accident, perhaps, but she's done it. That's all it takes. You have seen how much magic she carries in her veins. It is desperate for escape with the right coaxing."

I had little by way of a plan. My heart told me Rovaslo wasn't right, that though I may harbour magic, it was wild and unruly and I had no way to tame it. But I *wanted* to use it. It reared its head and bellowed and clawed at my skin for escape. I took a few steps forward, towards the Weavers, and as though pulled along by that hungry magic, Liljana followed on my heels, reaching her hand out to grab mine.

I was only a handful of yards from Csáno when I realized I was speaking. The words were quiet, low, but my soul ate them up as though starving. The Weavers behind Csáno began to move, arms spinning and fingers weaving in the air, trying to beat me to whatever I was about to do, but I was faster. I felt a tunnel open up inside me, and I pulled at Liljana's magic like drinking water from a pipe. I could apologize to her later – maybe.

And when it all boiled to the surface and I thought I might explode, I shouted and thrust my palm out in the air towards Csáno. His body crumpled to the ground and didn't move again.

Chapter
Thirty-One

Liljana

Our journey from the encampment where Béata had killed the Weaver was a silent one. We rode swiftly with Rovaslo, who'd explained how the rains over the castle had spread so far they had nearly consumed the town. Those who had been displaced were finding their way to other towns, but were being turned away and refused help, people saying they'd been tainted by the devil.

I wanted to be angry at Béata for using my magic without warning me. She didn't seem like the type to kill, but Csáno was fast becoming a thorn the world didn't need. She'd done the right thing – I just wished I had been the one to do it. Presently, she voiced my very thoughts.

"I killed someone," she said, though I wasn't sure

her words were directed at me. She just spoke staring at nothing, slumped over.

My frustration at her use of my magic dwindled. "It's not so bad," I assured her. We weren't exactly friends, or really anything that resembled friends, but I knew the feelings that came with having just killed someone, and my thoughts took me back to the courtyard outside King Costel's castle.

Béata looked at me, her eyes somehow both empty and brimming with tears. "How is killing someone not so bad?"

"You did what you had to do." I shrugged. "Csáno was a rotten egg, and you want to do good things. Save your country. You couldn't do that with him around."

"But did he have to *die*?"

"Well, he's dead, Béata, so you might as well accept it. I've had to kill before. Both directly and indirectly." Marek's screams sounded in my mind, and I shook my head. "I killed a captain back in Roşesti. If I didn't, I wouldn't be here today. I try not to make a habit of it, though. I mean, I'm not *that* sort of person."

She looked unconvinced.

"Frankly, I'm surprised you did it as well, but it's done. You can't bring him back to life. You don't have that kind of magic, so there's no use tormenting yourself. There's enough to think about as it is."

"I can't think about anything else. I keep feeling that moment over and over again, like I can't escape it. I keep seeing him fall. I feel sick." She wiped a hand across her face. Nearby, Benedek watched her sorrowfully.

"Béata," I said

"What?"

"Look at me."

She did, slowly.

"You know your father, and mother, and your sister, and all the other people you used to see every day back in your town? You know Rovaslo, and Benedek, and me?"

She nodded.

"Csáno's death might be the only reason they live to see tomorrow. He was out to destroy their world. Our world. Keep that in your heart, and don't forget it. All right?"

I looked her square in the eyes as I awaited her response. She nodded, sniffing, then sat up straighter.

More than once, I dozed off in my saddle. Whatever magic Béata had pulled from me left me empty and faint, more so than any transformation I'd ever accomplished. We let Rovaslo set the pace, and I slumped forward over the horse's neck and drifted in and out for hours or days. There was no way to know.

It was finally the Eve of Saints when we at last entered the part of the forest that I recognized as being near the castle. The afternoon light was orange and gold, the forest alight with colour. Rovaslo slowed our pace, closing his eyes on occasion to mutter things to himself I couldn't hear. The mages who'd arrived with him had followed us, silent but close.

Here and there amongst the trees, I saw pale forms dancing about, vanishing and reappearing. I was not a Seer, and though everyone could see the dead on the Eve of Saints, now I couldn't help but wonder if I'd been able to see Gilda and the others because of the queen's magic. Because of her Seer soul fighting to come out.

Benedek had gone very quiet on the journey. I watched him, sitting straight in his saddle and staring forward into the forest. What thoughts roiled away in his mind? He'd said his life had been a lie. I didn't feel quite the same. It was jarring, certainly, to learn that part of me harboured someone I didn't know, but it also answered questions. Why I always felt as though I had more magic than other mages. Why I'd never felt at home, never felt settled.

I was stunned a bit, but the more I probed, the more I found myself not bothered so much by the news. At any rate, what could be done about it?

I eyed the trees around us, wanting to climb inside one of the great trunks and disappear. I might bear some of the queen's power, and whatever parts of her soul that had fought to stay, but I didn't really want any of it. Béata did, or if she didn't, she was at least the right person to have it. And where did that leave me? As a crumb fallen by the wayside? An extra part no one needed? I didn't belong here. I didn't belong in Roşesti, or Marcosza, or anywhere in Sóar. At least that's how it felt. I wanted to leave. I wanted to set this world to my back and never return. Reinvent.

Rediscover myself. Hell, maybe I'd even change my name. I always fancied myself as an Ecaterina, or something dramatic and lovely.

We weren't far from the castle now, and a distinct gloom had settled over the group. No one spoke. Even the horses moved more slowly. Ahead, the incessant sound of rainfall made my hair stand on end. I needed a distraction. I let my horse fall back until I was riding beside one of the mages who'd come with Rovaslo, a handsome young man with long blond hair tied behind him.

"What's your story?" I asked with a delightful smile. "They're all so glum up there. I could use some conversation."

"What do you mean?"

"Well, I suppose we could start with your name."

"Leonar."

"Leonar. I like it. It fits your face. Where are you from?"

"Dungléd."

"Lucky. I rather liked that city. Shame about the Weaver business. I feel I could have made a life there."

He glanced sideways at me, eyebrows knitted. "You can always go back if this ends well."

"It probably won't, and even if it does, I've decided to leave."

"Where?"

"Muranj." I said it with an air of mystique that made even me shiver. Admitting it aloud somehow made it seem more real. I *needed* this to end well. I *needed* to get there.

"All right."

He fell quiet, staring ahead of us. I thought of what else to say, deciding to ask him about his age and perhaps what sort of magic training he'd had, but Benedek spoke up, his horse stopping. "I know another way," he announced, his voice solid and level. "Another way in."

"To the castle?" Rovaslo asked, holding up a hand to stop the company.

Benedek nodded. "One Morós does not know about. Only the kings and queens knew about it, in years past, but it fell out of use centuries ago."

"He speaks the truth," Béata said. "He has memories of the castle, even if he's never been there as Benedek. I've seen the drawings."

Rovaslo pondered this, staring into the trees, then at Benedek's face. He studied it long and hard, as though confused by something. "Is it close?" he asked.

"Yes, but we cannot bring the horses. The way is narrow and long."

The night was settling in, the sun creeping lower and lower and sending shadows stretching long and unwieldy between the trees.

"Then show us the way, and be quick," Rovaslo said at last. Benedek urged his horse on to a trot and turned us towards the right, moving faster now through the forest.

At a large clump of boulders protruding from the

ground, he swung off his horse and motioned for us to do the same.

We tied the horses to the trees and followed Benedek to where thick moss nearly shrouded a hole in one of the rocks. When he pulled it away, it was wide enough for us to crawl into on our hands and knees, one at a time. Benedek went first, then Béata, then Rovaslo. I followed him, grumbling quietly but just loud enough to be heard. My body was sore after so long on horseback. The last thing I wished to do was crawl through a stone tunnel of indeterminate length and into a cursed castle without at least a refreshing nap and a full meal first.

"Why didn't you tell me of this before?" I heard Béata whisper to Benedek after a few minutes of creeping along. "Before we left Zírany. We could have gone in ourselves."

He stumbled over his words. "I – we – I didn't know of it back then. I can't control when the memories come."

She didn't reply. It was a strange friendship between the two of them. Sometimes I wasn't sure if they were two seconds from kissing or killing one another.

My knees throbbed. They were surely bleeding by now, which would only be one more thing to ruin my entrance into Muranj. Torn trousers? Bleeding knees? Hair that hadn't been washed in weeks? If I had any strength left after whatever chaos was about to ensue, I could make a few small changes here and there, but not enough to make myself presentable. What an awful first impression I'd leave.

After what felt like four years of crawling, light shone ahead. A series of relieved sighs and murmurs passed down the line of our company.

I hurried my pace, despite my stinging knees, and tumbled out of the end of the tunnel just as a shout rang out from Rovaslo.

When I shuffled to my feet and looked around, I froze. Before me stood Morós, and filling the dungeon into which we'd crawled was row upon row of writhing, screaming shadows.

Chapter
Thirty-Two

Béata

I couldn't look away from Benedek as we stood before
Morós. Not even when Rovaslo exited the tunnel and
shouted in surprise, or when Liljana tumbled out and
found her footing with a start. Nothing could draw my eyes
away from where Benedek stood smiling at us. Something
gleamed out from within his eyes, something that wasn't
him. Hungry and dark and wicked, not unlike the gleam in
the eye of that wolf I soul-pushed and killed back outside
of Dungléd. How could I not have seen it? How could such
a possession, right before my eyes, have gone unnoticed? I
shivered, tears building. I should have known that Morós
would get to him, too. He'd get to everyone who mattered
to me, eventually.

"Welcome home," Morós said, holding up his hands. "At long last." He looked from me, to Liljana, to Benedek.

Rovaslo sighed, his shoulders sinking. "I had hoped we would never meet again."

"You have been little more than a thorn in my side, Rovaslo," Morós said uninterestedly. "You will be the first to go."

My skin crawled like a thousand spiders newly hatched. His power thickened the air, singed my nose, sent out heat like a too-warm fire.

"Surprise," Liljana said, throwing her hands up as though this were a party. "I see you were expecting us, which ruins the effect."

Rovaslo sent her a look.

"What did you do to him?" I asked, still looking at Benedek, who grinned back without wavering.

"Oh, he's just a human," Morós said as though it were nothing. "An easy possession for one of my shadows; he doesn't have the same defences a mage does, even an untrained one, like you." He gestured to the demons lurking all about, wriggling, waiting to feast at a motion from their master. I swallowed. "Get it out of him."

Morós turned to me, eyes like pools of midnight that consumed me whole. "Excuse me?"

"Get your demon out of him."

"On whose authority? Darling, you are in my castle now. I give the orders here."

"Darling," I said, my hands beginning to tremble. Perhaps I imagined it, but I was almost certain the walls began to quiver, too. "*Get your demon out of him*, or I will send your soul to hell." Tabíta's fire flared to life once more.

It was she who spoke, and her voice and anger shook the very foundations of the castle. The castle that had once been hers. The castle she had called home. And the castle where her blood had been spilled.

"Ah, my dear queen. What a delight to see you again, and under better circumstances." He bowed a little, his black fur cloak swishing against the dusty floor. The way his long hair clung to his head made it seem as though it had never been washed, sweat and grime all gathering on his skin like a swamp creature playing at finery.

"You look poorly," Liljana said, as though reading my thoughts. "Power doesn't suit you well. I can imagine you more as a blacksmith, or a pig farmer. Something where people don't often have to see you."

He turned to her very slowly, casting her a look that might have slain a human where they stood. "You have played your part in this, you fool," he breathed. "You were to bring me the girl, and deliver both parts of the queen to me. Nothing more. You will serve no other purpose than to feed me and my power and get me through that door."

She took on a look of true offence. "But you promised me safe passage into Muranj."

He cocked his head ever so slightly. "Sorry."

She turned to me, and I couldn't help but admire the spark of fire in her eyes. Maybe this was the first wicked mage bent on ruining our world, but this was not the first wicked man Liljana had met, and she was enjoying tearing him down word by word. "You were right, Béata. He's a miserable old lout, and I do so wish to see him suffer."

He raised a hand towards her, but in a movement so quick it made my own magic startle, she drew a stick from her belt, transformed it to a knife, and severed two of his fingers from his hand. They thudded to the floor and rolled over, collecting dust.

The brief moment of stunned silence was so delicious, I couldn't help but smile, but Rovaslo tensed beside me. Morós had taken enough provoking. The storm clouds that had been gathering in the room began to erupt. The walls shook, the torches danced as though blown by wind. Dirt fell from above, stinging my eyes. A roar began to thunder up from deep within him, darkness swirling about his feet and growing stronger by the minute.

Until it all fell silent.

"Morós."

A woman's voice came from behind him.

The trembling ceased. The torches went still. Slowly, Morós turned. Rovaslo's breath grew shallow.

She stood in the centre of the dungeon's hallway, her hands folded before her. Her dark green dress shimmered in an unnatural way, and now and then she flickered like a candle flame being teased by a breeze.

A spirit. A soul. And one I recognized.

"Zalya," Morós breathed.

She studied him for a long moment, dark hair braided away from her face, her neck long and graceful, standing straight. Everything about her spoke to the queen she had once been.

Then her eyes fell on Benedek – her son, once upon a time. She lowered her chin ever so slowly, a subtle but defined anger building in her ethereal eyes. Every word from her journal came roaring back to me, and I felt the rage along with her.

Suddenly, her eyes flicked to Rovaslo, and whatever wordless conversation passed between them filled the room with a thick fog of disquiet.

"Morós," she said sternly, then worked to soften her features. "I am here only to say goodbye. I hope you'll join me. I'd rather it happen above ground, closer to the light. I never liked the darkness."

Morós said nothing, staring at her with furrowed brows, confused.

"Come," she said, and held a hand out to him. He twitched, reaching out to take it but letting his hand fall.

A game. Zalya was playing a game with him that I didn't fully understand, but she knew he was weak enough to listen. That love he had once felt for her could be his undoing.

He turned back to us, thinking, then looked back at Zalya.

She is taking him upstairs, away from the confines of the dungeon, Tabíta said with a touch of awe. *She is giving you the space and time you need to build your strength. To undo him, and at great cost.*

What cost?

The only thing she has left to sacrifice.

I still wasn't sure I understood, but Morós had begun to follow Zalya with slow, uncertain steps down the hall, led on by whatever love he still harboured for her. Perhaps with each step he was taken back to a different time, a time when he still had hope that they might be something great. That she might be his, and he might be hers. Before his love for dark magic grew stronger and consumed him. As one, the shadows all went with him, leaping and bounding off the walls, a thunder of nothingness that filled the room with a chill.

The moment Morós was out of sight, Benedek fell to the ground. I forgot Morós, forgot Zalya, forgot about everything but him as I fell to my knees.

"Benedek?" I said, lifting his head to cradle it in my lap. "Benedek, can you hear me?" Liljana moved to stand close by, silent, watching.

His body stayed limp for a long, long while, and my heart began to ache as though it might break in two, but at long last, his eyes flickered open. The smile was gone.

That awful glimmer was gone. All that remained was the real, true Benedek.

He looked up at me uncertainly, then around at the room. At Liljana. At Rovaslo. "Where are we?" he whispered.

I glanced at Rovaslo. "We're in the castle," I told him gently. "That's all we have time to explain for now." I wanted to stay with him, to hold him and help him and assure him that I knew it was not his fault for leading us here. He'd been forced by something inside him, something that was gone now.

But we were inside Castle Vyesta. We had only been gifted a few moments' respite by Zalya. So we helped him to a dungeon cell with a straw bed and laid him down despite his protests. "We will come back for you," I promised him, his eyes wide and wild. My heart pounded at the thought of leaving him behind, of losing sight of him again, but there was no other way. "We will, Benedek. I swear it. But we must go to face Morós. We cannot wait." The words were meant as much for myself as they were for Benedek.

"Come," Rovaslo said quickly. He grabbed my elbow and pulled, leading me down the darkened, narrow halls of the dungeon. Here and there, some stones had tumbled from the walls and lay in a heap on the floor, a sign of age and disuse that reminded me how long it had been since this castle was lived in. Without missing a step, Rovaslo grabbed a lit torch from the wall and held it before us, the light falling on closed wooden doors, cell bars, and the occasional sword or bow leaning against a wall. Here and there, empty suits of armour stood at attention, too lifelike in the dim light to keep me from checking over my shoulder that they had not begun to follow us. I still knew little of the castle's layout, but I felt, deep in my bones, as though we were far beneath the surface of the earth, the air thick and close, a weight pressing on my chest.

It was all far too much like my time in Baron Izsak's dungeon.

I could feel Liljana and the other mages following behind us – and something else, a weight along my skin like my magic was sensing something. As we walked, Rovaslo carried on muttering to himself like he had been for days, strange words in the language of magic that I didn't understand.

At length, the tunnel ended at a winding stairwell that took us steeply upwards.

On and on. We wound ever skyward, at last ending at a long hallway with a window to the world outside. It had been days, it felt like, since I had seen sunlight, though it was thick and golden, the sun soon setting.

Voices came from far along the hallway. Without hesitation, Rovaslo strode towards them, ascended the three steps, and stopped just outside the throne room door.

"Béata," Rovaslo said. "And Liljana. I do not know how this will end, but I know one thing with certainty: it must end with Morós leaving Marcosza for ever. He cannot stay here if he fails to open the door to Muranj. His presence will rot the world. Save your magic until I tell you it's time. We will need all of it. Every ounce. I fear even with all of us, it will not be enough. Let us hope the others get here in time."

"What others?" I asked, but he ignored me, turning to face the throne room.

"If we wait for his move, we will die. The queen has pulled him away to the only place in the castle where our magic will be stronger. Queen Tabíta's throne is made of szinstone. You can draw more power from it. It will be as if you've just had a full night's rest."

And suddenly I understood. Only a little, but enough. Why the queen had lured him away. Why she had brought him here. Without her, this was a battle we might have had to face deep below ground, in the dark and confined space where Morós was sure to win.

Rovaslo pulled open the door.

The room was large and drab, lifeless in every way. Unlit candles. Bones. Rain beating against the windows. Zalya and Morós stood deep in the room, at the foot of the dais, where my eyes fell and stayed.

Something dreadful caught my eye, and my stomach began to turn, my breath quickening. Dark stains ran from the cushions of the thrones themselves, down to the carpets beneath. They were dried and faded, but unmistakable.

Blood had been poured here, and much of it. The stories of their bodies, headless and lying limp in the boats, came back, and I let out a small shriek.

This was where they had been killed. Where I had been killed. A thousand fears and screams and nightmares came rushing at me in a wind of horror and shadow, and I fell to my knees.

"I'm so sorry," I whispered. I reached out towards the thrones, but dropped my hands. As if seeing the blood had brought the past back to life, I could hear screams, cries, the thud of bodies as they fell to the floor. My stomach lurched as if to retch, but I was too frozen with fear to move. The room had come alive with sound. Before me, the dark blood stains grew brighter, redder, and the sickening drip, drip of thick blood became louder. For a terrifying moment, I thought the blood ran from my face, but they were only tears, falling hard and fast.

"Béata." Rovaslo's voice came from far away, shattering the sounds around me. The room fell quiet again, the blood settling darker once more. And from the dais, Morós watched me.

"I have long wondered how you might feel returning here," he said. "I can feel your anger like a knife, but have you thought for even a moment, Tabíta, of the things you could have been with my help? Rovaslo can make you a Seer, but I could have helped you become so much more." He opened his arms wide, proudly displaying the darkness that swirled about him.

"I have no need for shadows and wicked playthings to make me feel whole again, you small, sad man. I would not follow in your footsteps for all the world." It was me – Béata – who spoke the words, but I knew they belonged to Tabíta. "You will never again know a beating heart, the warmth of sunshine, the taste of plum wine in summer." My eyes darted to Zalya for the briefest of seconds. "Or the warmth of a lover. You are something to be reviled, and little more."

"She is a queen," Zalya said. Morós turned his eyes slowly to her, a dark and heavy pain pulling at his face. He saw in her what could have been. What he had given up. A life that might so easily have been his. "And she will reign in this castle long after it has been rid of your devilry. I think often, Morós, of what you could have been, and what I saw in you. Once upon a time I was able to remember, but now all I see is the weakness that made you succumb so easily to corruption. No true man would have fallen so swiftly, as if throwing himself off a cliff. If I could claw back every moment I spent in your presence, pining for a man so small, I would do so, and I would give almost anything in return."

The pain in his eyes deepened, and his mouth fell open as if to say something rash, but he closed it again. The brief glimpse of humanity passed as quickly as a dead leaf falling from a branch, and he was once again himself. The man cloaked in darkness, eyes shimmering with a kind of malice I thought lived only in dark stories.

"You are a spirit," he whispered, his voice the hiss of a snake. "You bear no weight on this world, yet you cling to the castle like an insect. Do not speak to me of weakness, when you were too weak to let go of this world when your time of rotting in bed came to an end. The practice of soul-pushing is founded on fragility, of a desire to clutch on to a life that is no longer yours. It is human to be weak, and you more than others."

"I chose the path that would keep me close to my son," Zalya replied. "My actions were born of love, not hunger. And that will always separate us."

"My actions were born of love, Zalya," Morós whispered. "I tried to stay with you, but you would not have me."

"No," she replied. "I would not have the devil."

The shadows around Morós seethed more, growing darker by the second, taking on shapes and forms. A hoofed creature danced about from foot to foot, the clanking sound sharp and harsh on the floor.

"Zalya," he said, and his voice had taken on the weight of stone. "Your usefulness has run its course. I'll spend no more time wishing for a life with you that is never to be. You have served only to make me weak, and I am fed up with weakness. I hope you find Jóska in the way of eternal darkness, and I hope you tell him of me. Tell him how I loved you more than he could ever think possible. But if you don't find him, I hope you learn how it truly feels to be alone." He raised his arms, a vile language emanating from his mouth, but Zalya turned away from him to face Rovaslo.

"My time here *is* finished," she said, folding her hands together and squaring her shoulders. "I have long known that." She offered a small smile to each of us in turn, Morós momentarily confused by her words. "I wish you only goodness in the future, and I know all the kings and queens of old will smile on you as you return their castle to its former glory. As you rid the world of darkness. And do not worry that love made Morós weak. Do not let it sour your hopes and dreams."

Morós lowered his arms for a moment, as though trying to guess her plans, then raised them quickly.

Zalya nodded at Rovaslo.

Instantly, that language of magic came tumbling from his mouth. He rushed forward, placing a hand gently on her shoulder, and in the same way I'd seen her soul pushed from her body in Tabíta's memory, her soul left the castle in a flash of light.

"Tell Benedek I love him," came a distant, hollow voice as the light began to disappear.

The room fell eerily silent. Morós stared at the spot where she had just stood, his body trembling.

"Zalya?" he whispered, moving forward and reaching out to swipe the air as though she had only gone invisible. "Zalya."

But Zalya's soul was gone. Gone from the castle. Gone from the world.

Gone.

A roar of fury so great it pushed me back a step rose up from Morós as he spun to face us again. "Monsters," he breathed. "Monsters!"

"You were only going to do it yourself," Rovaslo told him, though his voice was heavy with sadness.

"I could have stopped. I could have chosen not to. I could have saved her, and she would have loved me all the more," he said. He clawed at the air again, then at his cloak with an inhuman shriek.

"She never loved you, Morós," I told him – Béata's words, not the queen's. "And she never will."

He turned slowly to face me, horror and pain twisting his features. His glare was an icy wind, a ton of falling rocks, a fog of poison. I had to fight to stand firm, to not fall back and put more distance between us.

"I will destroy everything in this horrid land. Everything. Every living, breathing, growing thing. I will open that door, I will return to my kingdom, and I will make sure that nothing remains of Marcosza, all of Sóar, but a story. I will not leave a single blade of grass standing. So help me gods."

He raised his arms again, and a flock of screeching crows flew at reckless speed from the sleeves of his cloak, diving around us and cawing relentlessly. I covered my head and ducked to the floor, but caught sight of Rovaslo still standing. They looked real. They sounded real. They *were* real. But as they touched his skin, they disappeared in a puff of black smoke, as dangerous as the soot given off by a candle.

"I hope you brought more than a goat and some birds," Rovaslo chided, as though disappointed.

"This goat you see has far more power in a single hoof than you could taste in a lifetime, you child," Morós spat back. "Don't pick a fight with the devil unless you're ready for a war."

"Don't pick a fight with the world unless you're ready to watch it burn," Liljana returned. "And that includes Muranj." I would have smiled at the poison in her words if fear hadn't stopped me.

Morós scowled at her, then looked back at Rovaslo. "What did you bring? Children? Some nameless magical riff-raff you dug up in Dungléd? I looked forward to seeing how strong you'd grown over the years, Rovaslo, but you have truly let me down."

My eyes met with those of the ram. Its lips parted to reveal a smile lined with teeth like the thorns of a rosebush. Though the blackbirds could have been made of smoke, he was not.

"Excuse me," Liljana said sharply, and I tensed beside her. "I know I look young and fair, but I killed the Roşestian captain of the guard, left a young mage to die so I could be free, and journeyed from Tăru to Dungléd and back to Zírany with hardly a scratch. I wouldn't quite call myself a child, and last I checked, you had to requisition my help to catch Béata after years of failing to do so yourself."

Morós sighed. "Yes, you were difficult quarry, weren't you?" he said to me, thoughtfully. "I'd hoped the pull of the castle would eventually deliver you to my doorstep, but you managed to elude me for years. I thought for sure when your brother died that would do it, but then you disappeared."

"I—" I started, then stopped, clarity smacking me in the face. "The rains. The deaths. You were trying to catch *me*?"

"It seemed like a good plan. My brother bound me to the castle, so I had to find some way to capture you. Then I realized if I put my Seer magic to good use and consumed the souls of mages, I could grow my power faster. The baron putting out a reward was exactly what I needed. I've nearly had my fill of mages by now. I feel full, as though after a good feast, but I haven't quite had enough dessert."

Something clicked into place. "And so, this was why you tried so desperately to find me and Liljana. To consume our magic."

Morós looked wistful. "Imagine Erazem's face when I blow open that door, at long last, and return to Muranj with the power of Vír Astar running through my veins. Imagine what he will think. He will wither and die the moment he sees me. How delightful."

"I thought Tabíta was a royal from Muranj, just like you. Do you not all possess Vír Astar's power?" Liljana asked plainly, as though a child asking something of a parent.

"Muranj is a world as rich and wide as this one, you

354

imbecile," Morós told her with furrowed brows. "Richer, even. Are all of your kings and queens the same? No. Do not waste my time."

"Morós," Rovaslo said, nearly a shout that sliced through the room. "We played enough cards together in the days before your undoing to know you never show your hand at the start."

Morós cocked his head, listening.

"You have done enough harm in the name of magic. Made mages all around Sóar suffer. Caused deaths and suffering where it was not deserved. Liljana here can speak to that, but I have a few people who would like to meet you. Who deserve to face the man who has brought them so much destruction. They deserve to bear witness to your downfall."

I turned, along with Liljana and the other mages who'd journeyed with us, to face the throne room door at the sound of feet approaching. The great doors were thrust open, and a thousand bodies poured in, a thousand different ages, heights, clothing styles. People from Marcosza and beyond – a man with a tunic stitched with the symbol of Roșesti's castle, mages in cloaks the rich shade of Sovažska's royal purple. Young and old. Men and women and children. They poured into the throne room until the cavernous room felt small. Cramped. Mages lining every wall. Surrounding us in every direction.

"How did they know?" I whispered to Rovaslo, my magic

dancing at the presence of so many like me. Liljana stood with her mouth open, staring, turning in a slow circle to take them all in.

"I have been calling to them for weeks," he said quietly, sighing in a way that made me think he was proud of himself. "Just as I called to you. I knew we couldn't do this alone."

I remembered the way he'd been speaking to himself, muttering things I couldn't hear.

Then, louder, Rovaslo said, "They have come from far and wide. All with a story. All with a history. All with a desire to see this finished. Mages from every skill, every Order. You, boy, what are you?"

"I am a Seer, sir," the boy replied, his jaw set tight, eyes fixed on Morós.

Rovaslo pointed to the girl beside him.

"A Ruiner."

"Weaver."

"Seer."

"Alterer."

"Ruiner."

"Seer."

"They would all rather risk their own lives here than suffer in a life where your evil has made others hate them."

At a chuckle, we all turned back to Morós.

"You have had some foolish ideas in your day, Rovaslo," he said, shaking his head. "But this might be your worst."

Even as he spoke, his eyes darted around the room. I wanted to think he was nervous. Nervous in the face of so much magic ready to see his undoing. "No, forgive me. I meant your best idea."

We stared, waiting.

"I have had to tire myself out with waiting while I lure one at a time through these gates, each of them hungry for recognition, or for the baron's reward. But you, my dear friend, you have brought me everything I could ever need. Everything I could ever hope for." He turned and ran the remaining fingers of his left hand over the cheek of a mage girl who stood close by him. She didn't move. Didn't flinch. Just stared at him with hatred so heavy it could crack the stone floor beneath her. "And on the Eve of Saints," he whispered to himself, musing. "When all of your power is so rich and alive."

"You cannot consume the soul of every mage in this room, you damned fool," Rovaslo said. "They'll rip you apart limb from limb before you've made it through your first."

"You are right," Morós said, tilting his head thoughtfully. "I could never do it all myself. Luckily" – he clapped his hands together and turned, black cloak whispering along the floor – "I have something for just this occasion. I've been so looking forward to using it, and now I have just the reason. Rovaslo, you dear old fool, you are too kind. We could be mere *minutes* away from the door being open once more. Do not tell me you aren't a little bit excited." He shivered in a way that spoke of mock excitement.

Morós's eyes remained open, but unfocused, as though seeing something in a realm entirely apart from our own. Slowly, they began to roll upwards in his head, his mouth chanting in the same way Rovaslo had done – but this time the sound was cold and wicked, like a nightmare had made itself real and whispered dark things in my ear between sharp teeth.

And a deep, heavy sound rose up from the bowels of the castle. The stones around us groaned as something began to move towards us, slithering its way up from the deep halls we had traversed earlier. An ice-cold darkness snaked its way into the room, the candles flickering and going out altogether. For a long, dreadful moment, the only sound in the vast room was the dancing of the ram's feet on the stones as it waited with a distinct eagerness for whatever dark thing approached.

I could wait no longer. I crossed the room slowly, then faster and faster, until I'd passed through the doors and into the grand hallway to see.

It came from the shadows with the slow speed of coagulated blood. Large and heavy and lazy, but pulled on by the call of the devil and the scent of death. It filled the hallway from ceiling to roof, four powerful arms brushing against the walls as it moved. I saw no eyes, but one large mouth that, when opened, seemed to sever its head in two. Three rows of teeth, each as sharp as the tip of a freshly wrought sword, lined its jaws, wide enough to swallow my body whole. Feathered horns rose up from its head, and it moved along the ground on a mass of ropelike limbs that swarmed about the floor of the hallway. A red glow lit up its mouth each time it opened, as though it had swallowed a great fire that burned hot within.

I had never felt fear as present and deep as now, my heart too frightened to beat, my eyes too frightened to move.

Behind me, a murmur swept through the mages. They were torn between staying and going. Fighting and dying. Facing a sorcerer was different than facing a creature from hell.

"What have you done?" It was Rovaslo's voice.

"I have spoken myth to life," Morós breathed, awe tinging his voice. "There are creatures from your tales that are nothing but fable, and creatures as real as this stone. Some have long been lost to myth, but the sárkul, the soul-eater, is as real as you or I. It speaks to those with the Sight, but such souls are often too fearful to call upon it."

"Or," Liljana countered, "they have no use for such a monster. I'm sure I've never found it necessary in my life."

It was close enough now that I could feel the rush of warm air each time it breathed out. I could not tell where its eyes sat, but I felt them, keenly.

"A monster to join the monster in the castle," Rovaslo breathed, moving to stand close to me. "Fitting."

Morós bristled.

Liljana, standing close by my shoulder, said, "Perhaps it's my Roşestian ignorance, but I don't know what in the devil a sárkul is."

"I hardly remember," I whispered, drawing back at a hot breath from the creature. "A beast that sends the wicked to hell. That's what my grandfather told me."

"Your grandfather was right," Morós said with a contented sigh. "It resides in the shadow world, consuming the souls of those who are sent below, and ferrying them away. But here, in this world, it can do my work for me. Consume each and every soul in this castle and send the power to me. It has no use for such things."

"How?" Liljana asked, as though she desperately wanted to know.

He winked at her without a smile. "Magic. But even better, with the sorts of magic I enjoy . . . dabbling in, it can do far more than consume souls, if I ask it to." He rubbed his hands together, as though hungry. "It can consume everything. Eat all the life in Marcosza and feed that power, that strength, that *vitality* directly to me. If the door to Muranj is locked, the sárkul is the key."

I stared at the beast, seeing it all unfold before me. Seeing Zírany empty and lifeless, bodies lying about the streets. Seeing the great, lush forest wither and die, all vibrancy gone. The trees shrivelled and dead. Seeing dust where the river once ran, all voices and birdsong silenced.

And something within me died at the thought.

Something whizzed through the air and landed with a thud in Morós's shoulder. Slowly, deliberately, he reached up and pulled the arrow from his skin, the blood instantly ceasing its flow and the wound vanishing. With an air of deadly calm that froze the room, he turned to face the mage standing on the dais with a bow.

The boy dropped it, but stood tall with his shoulders squared and his eyes alight.

"Did you truly think an arrow would be my undoing?" Morós said gently. He held up his hands invitingly. "A single human arrow, shot by a sapling mage with poor aim. Do go on. Tell everyone present what you thought."

The boy's courage visibly faltered, but he stood tall. "I did not think it would kill you. I hoped it would weaken you. Nothing more."

The drop of a feather would have rung out loud in the silent room, until Morós chuckled, shook his head, and said, "Morgöl."

The word echoed off my bones. *Morgöl.* I knew little of the language of magic, but I knew in my heart this meant death.

The beast let out a roar that sent dust falling from the ceiling, and a black, ropey limb shot out from beneath it and swept across the great throne room. It wrapped around the boy's throat, yanked him from his feet with a snap that sent everyone in the room stumbling back, and he had disappeared down the sárkul's throat a heartbeat later.

A faint light shone around Morós's person for a fleeting moment, and then all was still.

"I suppose that was as good a start as any," he said with a sigh, and turned to face the rest of the mages. Fear haunted the room, a shadow gathered in the faces of all who looked back with blatant terror. "Morgöl," he said again, and another limb launched across the room and devoured an older man.

Screams erupted, mages running in every direction as the doors all along the hallway began to close.

"Béata, Liljana," Rovaslo whispered as we shrank back against one wall. "Stay close." Then, over the din, he shouted, "Insenj!"

The word burned searing hot through my veins, and all around the hall, the doors Morós had closed by magic began to burn. Dotted amongst the crowd were mages with their hands raised, mages chanting, fixed on the doors. *Ruiners.* They had to be. No one else could make fire so quickly. When Morós conjured yet another flock of shrieking blackbirds, the Alterers amongst us turned them into butterflies. Black, smoke-like butterflies, but silent and harmless all the same.

And all the while, Morós's monster continued plucking mages from the floor, and they would disappear with a scream down the sárkul's throat.

My soul ached. I wanted to cry, I wanted to scream, I

wanted to laugh at the horror of it all. I stared at Morós, my hands rising as I imagined tearing him apart piece by piece. For what he was doing to the mages. For what he had done to the king and queen all those years ago. For what he had done to the castle, and still did.

For what he had done to Filep.

All the anger I had ever felt came thundering back until my body shook so much I could hardly stay standing.

"Béata," Rovaslo whispered. All around us mages were scattering, disappearing into burned rooms, finding dark corners of the throne room where the sárkul couldn't reach them. "We have to try now. We have to try to soul-push him. It's the only way to stop it. The only thing we can do. It will take every bit of strength we have, and we will need Liljana's magic – where has she gone?" We looked around the room of chaos, and found her moving with slow steps towards the beast. "What is she going to do?" His voice rose with sudden terror. "She'll die!"

"I—" I was about to say I didn't know, but when she stood tall and held a hand out before her, palm facing the beast, a rush of cold air embraced me. "She's going to try to change it."

"No!" Rovaslo shrieked, starting forward but stopping when the beast turned to face her. "Liljana, we need you!"

A light began to gather in Liljana's palm as the beast turned. Its mouth opened wide and hot, orange fire burning deep within. She stumbled backwards at the heat, but stayed standing, the light in her hand growing stronger. Morós, confused as to why his pet had ceased to feed him souls, turned to see what had happened. He waved a hand in the air, and as though half a room didn't separate them, Liljana flew backwards through the air and landed on the ground.

I darted forward, but Rovaslo gripped my elbow. "You cannot help her," he said sharply, looking straight into my eyes. I looked back to where she lay still on the floor. "If you do not help me soul-push, then *everyone* in this castle will die, and everyone in Zírany will die, and everyone in Marcosza will die. Do you understand that?"

I tried to run again, but couldn't escape his grasp. "Without her help," I said with deadly calm, "we will all die anyway."

The terror all around us grew louder as the beast began to move forward, reaching behind pillars where mages had sought safety, its tentacle limbs flying through burned-out doorways to pull forth a screaming form.

Rovaslo studied my face for a handful of seconds, and then sighed, releasing my hand. "Hurry."

I crashed to my knees at her side, cradling her head. A red mark had appeared on her face as though Morós had slapped her from across the room. I couldn't focus on both her and the dangers in the room. I had to trust that the others would protect me.

"Liljana," I whispered, brushing her hair from her face.

"Liljana, we need you. Please. Get up."

Close at hand, I heard Rovaslo call my name with a sense of urgency that set my hands to trembling.

"Please, Liljana."

She stirred, blinking up at me a few times. "Miha?" she whispered. There was a light, a glimmer of hope in her eyes I didn't understand, but it melted away almost immediately. "Where—"

"I need your help," I told her hastily, pulling her to her feet. She swayed this way and that, holding her head as though it might fall off. "We have to push Morós's soul. There's no other way, and I cannot do it myself. We need all of Tabíta's magic. All of it. Can you do that?" I held her by the shoulders and looked into her face, though she said nothing. The queen's impatience flared to life. "For gods' sake, will you or won't you help us?"

Something twitched in Liljana's face, as though she recognized that voice. She looked around at the destruction in the room, and nodded.

"Come with me." I took her hand, and made to move towards Morós – but he had gone.

I turned to take in the throne room, but he wasn't there. Rovaslo caught on to my gaze, and rushed out into the hallway.

"Morós!" I heard him scream, but there was no answer.

Only a hollow, sickening laugh that rose up from somewhere in the castle.

Dread burst forth from my heart, filling my veins. I kept hold of Liljana's hand, and walked at her careful, slow pace out into the hall. Even the beast left the room, devouring as it went, off to follow Morós to wherever he had gone.

And I suspected I knew where that was.

"The door," I said, turning to face Rovaslo, terror momentarily blinding me. "He's going to open the door."

Rovaslo started to say something several times, then stopped himself. "I – I don't know how to stop him," he said at last. "I don't know what to do."

I didn't know what to do, either, but I knew it wouldn't involve standing in the hallway while Marcosza was robbed of every bit of life it had to offer. So I passed Liljana's hand to Rovaslo, and I ran down the hallway after Morós.

Following him was like following a bad smell. I could feel it, sense it, the closer I got. Now and then all I could follow was the sound of distant slithering, the footsteps of the goat that followed him, or the whispering of the devils that shadowed his every step. I wound down a wide, shallow staircase that seemed to spiral into the very centre of the earth, then down a hallway lit only by infrequent candles attached to pillars, and so large that the roof and walls were hidden distantly in the darkness. My footsteps echoed around, haunting me. But I carried on.

And finally, more candlelight shone ahead, and I

again heard the sound of the great beast moving about, its tentacle legs dragging it along the floor. All the shadows and devils and ravens made of smoke had gathered around Morós, who stood before a door so large he seemed as a child before it. It was tall, sweeping up and away and disappearing into the darkness beyond the reaches of the candlelight, and carved to appear like great tree roots from the forest overhead. It blended into the earth and stone surroundings, unless directly illuminated as it was.

I let out an involuntary breath, awed in the face of something so great. Beyond that door stood a kingdom, a world entirely apart from our own, brimming with magic and beauty and light.

It was hard to believe in light – true light – so far below the surface of the earth.

Morós, either hearing my breath or sensing my magic, spoke to me without turning to face me. "It is beautiful, isn't it? Made long, long ago, and just as perfect as it was on the first day." A chuckle. "Even despite all my efforts to destroy it." He ran a hand along the carved roots. "This door holds more magic than you or I put together, Tabíta. Than you or Erazem. It is a thing of beauty, truly, and it will be a shame to destroy it."

"Then don't," I said. My voice cracked as I spoke.

Morós laughed again. "I must, I'm afraid. Erazem will never free me, and your world holds limits to magic that will never allow me to be what I could be. What will all of these years and all of this work have been for, if I don't? All those unfortunate mages will have died for nothing. Do you think that would be right?" He turned to face me now, his cloak brushing the dusty floor.

"Their blood is on your hands," I told him quietly. "Being wicked once does not require you to be wicked again."

"Ah, such a saint," Morós said, shaking his head. "Good people are easily forgotten, my dear. It's the wicked ones you can't forget."

"I'd sooner be forgotten, then."

"And so you will be. Soon enough." His eyes moved past me, then, to take in something behind me. I turned to find dozens of forms melting out of the darkness: Rovaslo, Liljana, the mages who had survived the sárkul. I rushed to grab Liljana's hands, and she offered me a small, reassuring smile. "I see you've all served yourselves up to die," Morós said through a smile. "How very brave of you."

"Is that it?" Liljana breathed, staring up at the door. "Is that the way into Muranj?"

I nodded. The way she eyed it, as though it was the end of a long journey I might never fully understand, made me happy for her. Perhaps she wasn't wholly good, but she had nearly sacrificed her own life to do a good thing, and I would never forget that.

"It is time," Morós announced, bringing his hands together and turning to face the door. "This door has been closed for long enough."

I turned suddenly to stare into the darkness, certain I'd heard a noise coming from the shadows, but the candlelight didn't reach that far.

That vile language began to tumble from Morós's mouth as he placed his hands on the door. I needed to move, to act, to do *something*, but my body ached with exhaustion, and he had consumed so many mages and so much power I didn't know if even Tabíta's power could stop him. I looked to Rovaslo, who only stared, defeated.

Then the door began to rumble. I thought for a terrible second that Morós had succeeded, and that in a moment's time we would all crumble away as everything that gave us life vanished to push open the door – but even Morós stopped chanting. He let go of the door and took a step back, suddenly on edge.

A handful of deadly silent seconds ticked by, and then a brilliant, blazing white light filled the room, pouring in from the edges of the door. It opened – just a crack, but it opened – and a man stepped through.

Morós cursed and took another step backwards.

The sárkul stood still, awaiting its bidding.

From the shadows where I had heard a sound, Benedek came forward uncertainly, staring at the door.

I tried to speak, but words failed me.

Without warning, Rovaslo shouted, "Línc!"

Two Weavers thrust their hands towards Morós, and a heavy black chain wound itself around him and sealed his arms to his sides. His eyes grew wide, and he struggled to break free, but the chains held fast. He was stunned to silence for a moment. Then he smiled. "I do not need my arms to work magic, Rovaslo," he said. "What a dreadful waste of time."

"Oh, Morós," said the man who had come through the door. Everyone turned to face him again.

I had never seen him before in my life, but my magic recognized him with a kind of joy that forced a smile on to my face. He stood tall, taller than Benedek by a head, clad in white leather armour with the pale blue insignia of a tree on the chest. In lieu of a crown, his rich brown hair was braided across his head, and eyes as dark and blue as the depths of a lake took in the room.

"Erazem," Morós breathed. All arrogance and nerve had slipped from his voice, leaving the shaky rasps of an unwell child.

"My dear brother," Erazem said. His voice was stone and ice, rich like the forests at winter and heavy as the mountains. "I see your banishment has not had the intended effect."

A cauldron of rage and fury bubbled up from my core, and I stepped forward until only a yard separated me from the king of magic.

"You left him here with us," I whispered, before finding my voice. "You left him here, locked on our side of the door, that we might be killed and ruined by his magic. This is your fault, and yours alone." Tears flooded down my face, running into my mouth and making everything taste of salt. I waved a hand. "My brother died just outside these walls. Drawn in by your brother's dark magic until the poisonous rains murdered him. I saw his body, just lying there, and I couldn't bring him back. He would still be here if it wasn't for you." Benedek put a gentle hand on my elbow, but it did nothing.

The king stared at me, his gaze unyielding and alive. I didn't look away. It was only right that he see the pain he had caused. That he see what his own brother had done.

Then, without warning, he fell gracefully to the floor and knelt on one knee, taking both of my hands in his. "Words cannot be apology enough, I am sure," he said. Was that a tear glistening in his eye? "I could not have known what might happen if I banished him to your world. The sorts of magic with which he plays are not a part of my world. I had hoped that he would lose his strength over the years, but he has not, and for that, I will never forgive myself."

I wiped the tears from my eyes, though more appeared. "You left us all to die," I whispered. "You left us to die."

"I have wished only to go home," Morós snarled, struggling against the chains. At long last, the Weavers who'd constructed it tumbled in a breathless heap to the floor, and the chains vanished. Morós thundered closer, his hands pulled tightly into fists. Where I'd once found him imposing, even frightening, he now stood far shorter than the king of magic. Weak and insignificant before him. "I have worked long and hard to gain this power, to open the door that should never have been closed to me, and if I can't use it to open it, I will use it to destroy you. You banished me and left me to rot in a world where no mage should ever have to go, but I did not rot. I used the chance to become something you could never be."

Erazem sighed, shaking his head once. Every movement bore the grace of a deer. "Something I would never wish to be. I'd have thought you stronger. More resilient to the wiles of dark magic. But the plague you've brought upon these people has gone on long enough. Some would say you should face the Magical Court, and take whatever wicked punishment they set you." He thought for a moment. "But I am not so sure. I think that might be far too easy."

Colour drained away from Morós's face. "How did you get in?" he snapped. "I tried for months, years, even, to open that door. I tried everything. *Everything.*"

"For one," Erazem said, "it helps to be the king of magic, and the one who sealed the door. If you're the one to lock it, you usually have a key. And secondly. . ." Erazem swept a hand to Benedek. "This young man found the door."

Rovaslo tilted his head thoughtfully. "How did you know to come through today, after all these years? I know no messages could go through. Believe me. I would have found a way."

"There was no message," Erazem replied, smiling proudly at Benedek. "But there was a bell, if you knew where to look. Only a former king or queen would know that, though. Only someone who knew about the castle. I heard the call for help, and I came as quickly as I could."

I smiled at Benedek. After all those years of castle knowledge tumbling around in his head, tormenting him with no explanation, he had found a use for it. I could only imagine the relief he must be feeling in this moment.

But my pride was quickly dampened at the realization of how easy it might have been to call for help, if only Morós had let anyone into the castle.

"I told you I knew the castle," Benedek whispered, moving closer to me. I reached for his hand, squeezing it tight.

"So, what now?" Morós asked, wiping sweat from his forehead with the back of his hand. "You take me back with you to stand trial? It will take years and a thousand mages to clear the power I've imbued into this castle, Erazem. Even you cannot undo it all."

"No," the king of magic replied, "you are not welcome in Muranj. Such troubles do not belong there, and I will not have my kingdom tainted with it." He sighed. "But nor do they belong here. And if these shadows and devils are tied to your soul, then I believe your soul deserves some time spent in the shadow world to think about what you've done."

Morós said nothing.

I knew a little of the shadow world, through my grandfather's stories. It wasn't hell, but it might as well have been, a dark and twisted place where undergods and demons spent years tormenting those who went there. Sometimes they were rescued by higher gods, and sometimes they were sent on to hell.

"Now," the king said, moving to stand between me and Rovaslo. "Do let us rid this castle of sickness and death, shall we? I feel the time for healing has come."

I wasn't trained. I knew little of how to work the magic that waited just beneath my skin, but I knew he meant for me – for us – to push Morós's soul from the castle. To push it into the shadow world. The push I'd done on the wolf had been an accident, a way to survive even if I hadn't meant to do it. But this was harder. The hardest thing I would ever have to do, and the weight of it all, the weight of everyone's survival now resting on me alone, nearly made me sink to the floor.

But I wasn't alone. Two hands slipped into mine, and Liljana stood before me. Her face was still red and inflamed from when Morós had knocked her off her feet upstairs, and her eyes bore an exhaustion I wasn't sure I would ever truly understand, but there was fire there, too.

"Béata," she said, her voice resonant. "You were born to do this. Born to face evil. Born to be queen. I am here. You are not alone." Then her eyes twinkled some. "So let's send this devil back to hell, shall we? I've grown tired of him already."

I nodded, some semblance of strength creeping up from the floor, flooding my legs my arms, my head. I raised my hand, tired as I was, and let my heart speak the words of magic. I didn't know the language, but it was there somewhere, waiting for release. And with every word I spoke, the fire in my body grew stronger.

"You haven't the strength to push me even with the aid of every Seer in this castle," Morós spat. "I am made of a thousand souls, and it would take a thousand and one to undo me."

His words began to fade away. Liljana's hand never left mine, and something like a new fire sparked between us, magic flowing and writhing and growing, two parts of the same magical soul finally meeting again.

I spoke louder, stronger, the noise in the room growing softer until my voice and Rovaslo's voice – somehow stronger in the presence of the king of magic – were all I could hear. There was no sárkul, no castle, no chaos. There was only Morós's form, my hand out before me, and the chant Rovaslo and I shared that filled the air around us with so much magic I could smell it, hot like an extinguished candle.

Our words built to a crest, the push close at hand, and I opened my eyes to take in Morós one last time. To watch as he was destroyed after every wicked thing he had done. Though I hadn't known what form it would take, or who I would be facing, I had spent years dreaming of this moment.

I wanted to savour it.

Hand in hand, Liljana, Rovaslo and I carried on the soul-push, and though all of our magic came together as we neared the end, it was only Liljana and I who spoke the final words. Only the queen who could truly finish this.

And finish it we did. Morós's soul left screaming and snarling like the wolf I'd met in the woods. The moment it left and his body collapsed to the floor, a noise rose like thunder, louder and louder, and from the castle above us and the hall around us, blackbirds and shadows came tumbling forth, shrieking and howling as they went. They were pulled down the hallway by some invisible force, like a strong wind from whose grasp they couldn't escape. They disappeared down the mouth of the sárkul, and once it had devoured the very last one, a great, rumbling roar bellowed up from its chest, and it devoured itself, vanishing with a thunderclap that shook the room.

When the river of shadows had passed and dried up, the air around us grew lighter. I could breathe again.

Slowly, we returned to the upper parts of the castle, each step harder than the one before it.

"Look," Benedek said. He stared out one of the great hall windows, where the rains had ceased to fall and the clouds were parting above to reveal a sea of stars.

A moment of delicious silence slipped away, all eyes fixed on the window. The cursed castle. The deadly rains.

The pile of bodies outside. This was finally the end of it all. The beginning of for ever. The point at which it would all become a memory, and no longer a waking nightmare.

I moved slowly to stand beside Benedek, who stared up at the sky without expression.

"How did you find him?" I whispered, darting my eyes to Erazem.

He smiled a little, then tapped his temple. "All that useless knowledge finally paid off," he said. "I could see a doorway, but I didn't know where it led. So I found it."

"We would all be dead if you hadn't," I told him. "All of us. You saved every life in here today."

He turned to me, taking both hands in his. "You did what no one else could, Béata," he said, so gently and so close to my face my breath caught. "You freed this castle. I will take no credit for what only you did."

"I had help."

He placed a finger over my lips to silence me. "*You.*"

Chapter
Thirty-Three

Liljana

I hurt in a way I hadn't before, as though my soul itself had been bruised. I hated to show it, but every step and every breath was agony. If the floor of the castle were softer, I would lie down and close my eyes and let sleep or death come find me.

"Your era of rebuilding begins now," Erazem said to Béata and Benedek. I wondered if he knew that I, too, harboured part of Tabíta's soul. That I was as much a queen as Béata. But something within me wished to keep that quiet. I didn't love Marcosza, not in the way she did. And I certainly didn't wish to be its queen. "I cannot tell you with words how sorry I am for what I have inadvertently done, but in time, I hope you will accept my magical help in building Marcosza to be stronger and better than ever. For now, I will leave you to find what new life can arise from the darkness. In the years to come, I hope our lands may once again be friends. I will return on the next Eve of Saints." He shook Benedek's hand.

"Wait," Béata said, and she looked directly at me. "There is one among us who has dreamed of Muranj from the moment she heard about it. If you can take someone with you, would you please take Liljana? She has journeyed far to find somewhere peaceful. Somewhere she can find safety and friendship. It has not been an easy life."

Erazem turned to me and thought for a moment. "Muranj is not heaven," he told me. "It is not perfect. We have trials and troubles and illnesses, like anywhere else."

"But you have magic," I said, my voice breaking. "I want magic, and I want to not be killed for it." I reached my hands out towards him, as though begging. I could not have come this far to be turned away now. I was tired. Tired. Tired. *Tired.* "*Please.*"

"Your friends are all here," he said. "Your family. Your life."

I smiled wryly, but only briefly, too tired to keep it up for long. "I have no friends," I said. "And I have no family. I left what life I had behind in Roşesti, and I have no wish to go back." That wasn't fully the truth. I'd thought many times about returning to take vengeance on Madame Iulia, the king, all of Tăru. Make them suffer for what they'd done. But I was tired. Vengeance could wait for another day, and my visions of Muranj, of beauty and safety and rest, were far too strong to push aside.

"The choice is yours," the king replied. "But Sóar must take some time to heal. The doors between here and Muranj will not open again until next year."

I nodded, swallowing. "I understand."

"Very well." He stood aside and swept his arm to Béata and Benedek, a silent instruction to say my goodbyes.

Ugh. When had I allowed myself to grow attached to anyone? Miha was my family, my friend, all I had needed. After she'd died, I had promised myself that I would never care for anyone else again. Yet here we were, with a boy who walked the line between infuriating and charming, and a girl who had somehow become a sister over the course of a few days.

Tears lit Béata's eyes as she embraced me. "I wish we'd had more time," she said into my shoulder. "I wish we could have been friends. I wish you could have taught me how to be a little bit dangerous." She winked through tears.

I smiled. "It can't be taught, I'm afraid. It's something you're born with."

"I hope you find some peace," she said, taking a step back. "And get some rest."

"Yes, I fancy I'll find myself a bed and I won't leave it for a week. That's the dream, anyway. But I'll see what awaits me." I cocked my head, thinking. "Perhaps I'll find someone to settle down with. I've always wanted to break a heart."

"Let us go," Erazem said, motioning gracefully towards the hallway. "Murani awaits."

Excitement danced, momentarily making me dizzy.

Benedek embraced me firmly, rocking me back and forth as he did so. "You *do* have friends," he said. "Like it or not, you will always have friends here."

"If they were all as handsome as you, perhaps I would stay." I winked at him, mostly to fight off the tears. "But I'm thankful for friends. Just don't tell anyone, or they'll think I've gone soft." He chuckled and stepped back to stand beside Béata. They looked so well together, companions, friends, lovers. Young, but worn with age beyond their years. Their eyes on fire with the hope of things to come. The weight of their country resting on their shoulders, but still strong enough to hold it up. Cracked, but too resilient to break.

As every king and queen should be.

Erazem stepped through the door first, his body bathed in light before he vanished into the sunshine. I hesitated, suddenly terrified. When this door closed, it would not open again for a year. Not until the next Eve of Saints. Who would I be in a year? Would I ever want to come back? Would I want to come back immediately? It was a bit like when I'd crossed over from Roșesti, the border between countries giving me pause, the uncertainty of what was to come so sharp it frightened me.

But my soul ached for something new. To find a life where I could be a better person. To learn what it meant to be Liljana the mage, not Liljana the outlaw. Just like Marcosza, I wanted to heal.

So without another thought, I stepped through the door into Muranj, leaving Tăru, Roşesti, and every wicked thing so far behind it could never find me again.

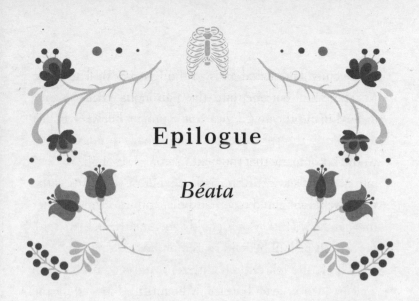

Epilogue

Béata

I stood in the doorway to the courtyard as the sun slowly dropped behind a marmalade sky. The mud had begun to clear, the grass was greener now than I ever thought it could be, and living bodies moved about the grounds, where in years before, there had been nothing but ghosts and bones.

A handful of townsfolk were gathering the last of the bodies from the grass, leaving a marker where each of them had fallen so we could plant a tree in their wake, let a forest of new life rise up from death. I watched as the last cart of their remains was pulled away, off towards the village to be buried and remembered – like they should have been long ago. Finally. They would finally be honoured, after so many years of hopelessness.

I remembered my words to the first body I had come to when I'd ventured into the poisonous rains so long ago. *Maybe one day I'll give you a proper burial.* I hadn't anticipated the sense of joy – and heavy finality – that would accompany that moment.

I had never seen the castle devoid of the rains – the rains whose only purpose had been to lure in mage after mage in hopes that Morós could consume the queen's soul, *my* soul. It had all been in search of *me.*

The castle felt entirely different, unrecognizable with a clear sky overhead, but deeply beautiful. I longed for the days to come, when Mother and Father and Alíz could live here with me, when again we could be a family.

Baron Izsak had been sent for, that we might work together to see what we should do going forward. To see what Marcosza truly needed, and what his part in it might be.

"Look." Benedek's voice came from beside me. I turned to look where he pointed, and a sudden sob rose up from deep within me.

High in one of the towers, a man and a woman were hanging the flag of Marcosza, freshly sewn and washed, the green glistening in the last remnants of the sun. It was such a small thing, a bit of cloth hung amongst stone, but it symbolized everything. A beginning, instead of an end. A birth, instead of a death. Hope, instead of anguish and sorrow. All the little broken pieces of my heart I'd lost along the way began to heal, and a wide smile spread across my face.

"I will not let that flag fall again under my watch," I said, and I no longer knew where the line was between Béata and Tabíta. Sometime over the course of the past few weeks, we'd melted together, like wax that had been made into something new.

"I will help you catch it if it does," Benedek said softly, sighing. I glanced at him, that same sense of quiet shyness burning my cheeks, just like the first time we'd ever spoken in my father's tavern. His hand reached slowly for mine, but uncertainly, and only our two smallest fingers gently intertwined.

His breath was warm so close at hand, and as our arms touched, I ceased fighting the impulse and rested my head on his shoulder. I felt him startle a little, then relax, leaning his own head against mine. Everything was quiet. Perfect. Whole. And I savoured every second of it.

I turned back to face the castle grounds. Two women were sweeping mud and stones off the bridge, and their children played in the treeline just beyond. The same treeline where I had first seen Benedek so many years ago, watching as I danced about in the deadly rains.

It had taken longer than I'd hoped, but it was done. Done.

Morós was gone. His evil was gone. The sickness he'd brought to the castle had been healed.

Everything that had long felt old and dead had become new again, glistening with the hope of the future. Things ended could begin anew.

And hopefully, that healing would creep out from here, reach everywhere in Sóar that had been tainted by his evil. Reach into Roșesti and undo what darkness it had brought there, if Liljana's stories were to be believed.

Liljana. Frustrating as she could be, I wished her well where she had gone. I hoped she had found peace, and beauty, and friends.

I sighed.

A new world opened up before us, and like a long-lost sunrise, a new life. As if coming out of one never-ending night, filled with bad dreams and horrors that would forever leave scars, before me stood a world of death and darkness that had finally seen the light.

Thank you to:

My husband, Thomas, for your unending support. To Atlas, for being the greatest son I could have hoped for. And to the doctors and nurses who cared for me during my pregnancy and the time I was working on this book. You are all actual heroes.

Thank you to my family, near and far, for absolutely everything. I am thankful every single day for you.

Thank you to my friends, especially fellow writers who are an endless stream of support and kindness. I am grateful to have you in my life.

Thank you to my agent, Silvia, my editors, Sophie and Lauren, and to the wider team at Scholastic who have made this book possible.

And thank you to everyone who has read my books. You make me want to keep writing.

© Thomas Catterall

Lisa Lueddecke was born in California and has since lived in four countries and six states. She now resides in New England. If she isn't writing, she is likely gardening with her son, playing board games with her husband, tending to their two cats, or buying candles.

Follow her on Twitter @Lisalueddecke